W9-AZI-130

Richard Lloyd Dewey

THE
PORTER ROCKWELL
CHRONICLES

Vol. 4

STRATFORD
BOOKS

The Porter Rockwell Chronicles
Vol. 4

Book Cover Painting by Clark Kelley Price

ISBN: 0-9616024-9-X
The Porter Rockwell Chronicles, Vol. 4

Copyright © 2002 by Richard Lloyd Dewey

All international rights reserved.

No part of this book may be reproduced or transmitted in any form or by any means, electronic or mechanical, including photocopying, recording, or by any information storage and retrieval system, without permission in writing from the publisher.
For information address:

Stratford Books, Inc.
Eastern States Office
4308 37th Road North
Arlington, Virginia 22207

Stratford Books, Inc.
Western States Office
P.O. Box 1371
Provo, UT 84603-1371

First Printing: December, 2002

This book is printed on acid-free paper.

Printed in the United States of America

To a group of friends who inspired me in England years ago:
John M. Madsen, the leader
Don Parker Jr.
Roger Evans
Glen Hunter
Jerald Lindley
Clyde Williams
Galyn Proctor
Gerald Livezey
William Blackwell
Kingsford
John Cook
William Murdock
Robert Lillian

Salisbury Crew:
Glen Christensen
Daniel Aubrey
Jerry Tryon
Tuttle, Thorpe, Lowry

Plymouth Crew:
Dan Lewis
Forsythe
Gary McFadyen
Steven Bastian
Roger Neeley
David Price
Mark Sumsion
Greg Kjar

A few others:
Dale Gardiner
Brent Meikle
Kelly Johnson
Collin Sorhus
Rod Davies
Steven Miner
Kevin Dewitt
Mel Bennett
Richard Rowe
Val King
Misters Bradshaw, Scott, Brenchley, Turner, Fisher

And still others I'll probably remember
the day after this book is published

OTHER BOOKS BY THE AUTHOR:
Porter Rockwell: A Biography (1986)
Rockwell: U.S. Marshal, A Novel (1987)
The Porter Rockwell Chronicles, Vol. 1 (1999)
The Porter Rockwell Chronicles, Vol. 2 (2000)
The Porter Rockwell Chronicles, Vol. 3 (2001)

Richard Lloyd Dewey

THE
PORTER ROCKWELL
CHRONICLES

Vol. 4

STRATFORD
BOOKS

PROLOGUE

Journey

Upon Rockwell's departure from his former wife Luana, her new husband Alpheas Cutler, and his own four children in Iowa, he rode westward. On December 29, 1846 he joined a meeting at the main Mormon camp at Winter Quarters, Nebraska. There he met with 15 leading Council members and was chosen as a scout and chief hunter to lead the 147 member advance party to the Rocky Mountains. The main body of Mormons would wait in Iowa and Nebraska to leave shortly after the advance party.

In March 1847 a copy of the *Warsaw Signal* was brought to camp. When William Clayton read it aloud, Porter listened intently. Editor Thomas Sharp's epitaph to the church included a final statement that "Porter Rockwell just married a prostitute."

At the campfire Porter kept the camp up till late, laughing. As always, he stood out among the group with his long, shoulder-length hair and bushy beard. But each day, thoughts of his family tore at him.

On April 14, 1847, the advance party of 147 moved out with Porter in the forefront. The first two weeks across the plains kept his mind busy as he searched for a lost horse — that of Willard Richards, a friend of Joseph Smith's wounded at Carthage Jail when Joseph was killed. Porter also delivered mail back to the main camp at Nebraska, then returned to the expedition. All such activities helped him deal with his thoughts and fears for his family.

At times his mind would lapse into depression, usually when horseback as he had too many hours to think. Nevertheless, he had to arise each morning to myriads of problems to solve — helping wagons cross streams, finding enough food for the expedition, and responding to every other conceivable challenge itinerant to a major journey. He realized quickly the anguish in his mind could never be so severe as to keep him from filling his assignments. Their commander Brigham Young, in his ever-astute manner, discerned the depression and kept him as meaningfully occupied as possible.

On April 26th Porter was awakened by gunfire. Indians were seen crawling into camp and were chased off by guards.

Soon afterwards, he and three others chased down Willard Richard's willful horse, when they were confronted by 15 Indians springing to their feet with bows and arrows aimed. The white men threatened the Indians, and all 15 backed away.

Two weeks later his party faced a buffalo herd. He felt hot blood racing through his veins and dashed ahead of the other hunters. He then focused on the most feared of all western wildlife — the lead bull buffalo.

"He can't be dropped with only a ball shot in his head," shouted fellow scout John Matthews. "Don't go for him."

"Why not?" yelled Porter, who galloped after the beast with merely his pistol. He rode 20 feet ahead of the bull, turned half way around to aim at him, and fired.

The bull wagged its head, stunned, and stopped. It then shook its body, caught sight of Porter, and took after him.

"Wait a minute!" shouted Porter, laughing to Matthews. "It's supposed to drop over dead!"

The buffalo chased him five solid minutes, zigzagging with his horse until Porter finally escaped. Matthews and the others, seeing his difficulty, chuckled heartily.

As Porter returned to them he noticed their laughter, and glowered at them. They quickly silenced, intimidated. Suddenly he burst out laughing.

They joined in loud and long.

Over the next several days Porter became more adept at killing buffaloes, learning what did and did not work.

By May 25th he had shot four more bulls before the herds finally vanished on the horizon. He also hunted antelope and helped keep the party alive shooting other big game.

The next morning, Brigham Young studied him riding ahead of the group, and consciously caught himself thinking that Porter would blend in naturally with the freedom of the wild West.

Brigham and several others had recently begun calling him "Port," and the appellation would stick till his dying day. In his earlier years he had been known simply as Porter, and to a few as "O.P.," "O.P.R." and "Orrin Porter." Most however would usually call him "Porter."

His mother, meanwhile, was back in Nebraska with the main body of Mormons waiting to go West. His brothers and unmarried sisters still looked after her. Until the trek, Porter had visited her weekly, and now missed her. They still held a strong concern for one another though each had pursued different lifestyles: His mother had become known, ironically, as one of the prime peacemakers of Brigham's community.

Meanwhile, Porter thought of Emily incessantly, wondering if he had made the right decision to essentially dessert her. Hopefully, Luana would raise her right and live up to her claim that she'd do a better job at it than he.

On June 1st, 1847 the advance expedition arrived at Fort Laramie. There, Porter traded personally with James Bordeaux, the proprietor. Afterwards, he resumed leading his party west-

ward. Brigham then announced exactly where they were going: Joseph had seen it in vision, and from scouts' reports the
place was known as the "Great Basin."

Porter presently rounded up four mountain men returning from the Great Basin, and Brigham invited them to dine
with him. These seasoned scouts gave conflicting reports of
"Great Salt Lake Valley," as they called it. Jim Bridger was the
only one positive: "If ever there was a promised land, that must
be it." The others scoffed, claiming they were about to settle a
worthless desert.

Soon, Sam Brannan came on the scene. To Porter, Brannan
was a harmless, colorful chap, who thought rather highly of
himself; he was of medium build and had small eyes, green in
color, and because they were too close they gave him somewhat the look of a shrew. He had led 250 Mormons on the ship
Brooklyn from England to San Francisco, had launched a newspaper there, and then had set out eastward to find Brigham and
convince him of where the Promised Land really was: California.

Brigham listened to him but, not being the most tactful of
sorts, told him he was, simply, dead wrong. Brannan felt squelched
and went back to his paradise alone, where his 250 settlers were
awaiting his return. (Later, Brannan would admit collecting tithes
from his band of 250, keeping the money for himself, and building
a huge mansion in San Francisco, where he was summarily ex-
communicated by Salt Lake City headquarters.)

By June 11th many on Brigham's overland journey were overtly discouraged. Porter's optimism, however, remained irrepressible.

The next day he was chosen to lead a small band of eight men. They faced rock slides, steep ravines and rattlesnakes, until they found the Donner-Reed trail. Porter rode back to Brigham with the news, then rejoined his small patrol in order to find the valley of the Great Basin.

While Orson Pratt and Erastus Snow were the first and second Mormons to ever enter and see Salt Lake Valley, Porter was third. Upon sighting it, Pratt threw his hat in the air and shouted with Snow, "Hosannah!"

Porter heard them ahead and galloped forward, gazed through the canyon entrance with them, and beheld a vista that took his breath away . . .

At that moment, staring at the awe-inspiring scene, Porter decided that whatever his conflicting feelings were for Emily, he would wait for her letters to see if there were any indication that she was unhappy. And if so, he would somehow get her West with him — at all odds. As he gazed at the view, he knew he had only one goal: to build a home in the New Land in anticipation for the day she would arrive. He also felt exhilarated to start a new life in a land of peace. At long last.

PART I

Settlement

CHAPTER 1

At dawn Porter sat on a boulder beside the Great Salt Lake.

The wind caused small waves to blow onto the rocks, and the sun's emerging light shot brilliant colors onto the clouds directly above.

Porter and three other scouts were exploring the lake on assignment from Brigham and had stopped to build a fire on which to warm their coffee.

Another scout rode up, bringing their mail which had just arrived from Iowa and Nebraska. The other scouts received two letters each and Porter received one. It was from Emily. He gazed at the letter a moment, his heart beating, then handed it to another scout beside him.

That fellow stared at it and said, "Why don't you open it?"

Porter was embarrassed and said nothing.

Another scout set down his letter and said, "What's the matter, Port, why don't you open it?"

Porter cleared his throat and finally answered:

"Still don't read."

The others chuckled and Porter's face reddened. Hearing that, and not participating in the laughter, the scout holding the letter opened it and began reading aloud in order to help Porter save face.

Emily declared without reservation her love for her father and how much she missed him.

Porter listened and lowered his face. The others glanced at him and noticed his lower lip trembling. They looked away respectfully.

The scout reading the letter paused, and Porter mumbled: "I shouldn't have left her." He could not shake from his mind the scene of her in Iowa weeping when he had ridden away.

The scout continued reading, "Mama's new husband is a good father to the younger children. But I don't get along with him, and I'll be coming West to join you in the next handcart company after this one that brings you the mail." Porter stood and shook his fist in the air.

"My turn to yell, 'Hosannah!'"

Porter arrived at the mouth of Emigration Canyon. Several months had passed and he had written — actually dictated to others to write — numerous letters to her — with no response. He was fighting a tendency he had developed, since leaving Iowa, of getting down — so far down that he was tempted to not even work, but had fought it with such success that he had over the same time period built his cabin — as well as his mother's and siblings' cabins several miles south. Porter lived north of the city at "Porter's Spring," choosing to live away from the crowds. In so doing he turned down free land offered him by Brigham in the city proper.

The mountainous cathedrals of nature mesmerized Porter each time he looked in any direction. In Salt Lake Valley itself, across the glistening Salt Lake, lay lower mountains which framed the valley artistically.

"We'll turn the few trees here into tens of thousands," proclaimed Brigham. "We'll irrigate the land. Crops and fruit trees will grow abundantly and we'll become an agricultural people."

"All I see is a desert," mumbled Porter to himself, "so that's a pretty tall order in the way of prophecies."

The more he thought about it however, the better it felt. It would be a miracle to turn this barren desert into something green, but he was finally able to admit to himself one morning, while laying fence posts on his ranch, "So what're prophets for? To predict the unexpected."

Years earlier Joseph had prophesied of a future civil war over the slave question, but since it had not yet come to pass, his detractors had claimed all these years that Joseph was a fraud — not a prophet.

"So just give it time," Porter had told Luana and others all these years. The prophecy had still not come to pass, but political tension had escalated between the North and South with the passage of time, and the whole thing seemed no longer so far-fetched. (The Civil War was in fact now 13 years away.)

And so he would take his own advice and wait patiently for Brigham's prediction to simply come to pass. However, in this

case, the engineering saints would have to do their part, digging miles of irrigation ditches from the water-plentiful mountains if they expected to see, as Brigham testified, of their colony
being one of those fulfilled prophecies from Isaiah in the *Bible:*
"The desert will blossom as a rose."

It was now spring 1848. A neighbor brought him word that
a handcart company was arriving shortly, so the next morning
Porter arose early and began the two-day trek to the mouth of
Emigration Canyon. Before arriving, he spotted the first
handcarts of the group. He rode faster toward the on-coming
immigrants, joined by dozens of well-wishers and relatives con-
verging on the new-comers, cheering and applauding them. Porter gazed over the four hundred men, women, and children.

No Emily.

Disappointed, he turned his horse away, figuring to ask a
coordinator in the city if he knew in which company Emily would
be arriving and approximately what day. Certainly she could
not have pulled a heavy handcart by herself, so had likely
teamed up with a family and, for that matter, had more than
likely found a family with a wagon to share with her.

He disappointedly began his ride toward the downtown
commercial district, almost directly westward from the canyon's
mouth. A certain number of immigrants had not made the ar-
duous journey successfully — in fact the route to the valley
was strewn with shallow graves from those who'd been overcome by exposure to harsh elements, starvation, and illness.

He planned to ride out to find her, after he got information from the immigration coordinator on her approximate arrival. And he decided he would first have to pack provisions from his home. He worried about her condition. How could his little girl make the trek across the plains all by herself — with none of her real family to help her — even if she were with an assigned group amidst a company of hundreds? Why couldn't she have waited till he came to get her in Iowa? In fact, why hadn't she requested him to come get her? Was her independent streak that strong at such a tender age?" It dawned on him that this little woman was the complete sum of him and Luana — a mule times two. "Oh brother," he muttered, wiping the sweat from his brow. An exasperated feeling overtook him. Suddenly he heard a girl's voice call out:

"Papa!"

He turned and saw.

Emily, limping towards him, was dropping the front of a tiny handcart she had crafted and was running towards him. But she was no longer the little girl he had left. He noticed immediately that for 15 she seemed a foot taller — and with the face and figure of a mature young woman.

His eyes brightened and he simply stared at her. She rushed into his arms and he hugged her with all the love he had ever felt, and kissed her cheeks and forehead over and over, tears running down his face.

"I'm sorry, Emily," he said. "I'm so sorry I left you."

She hugged even harder and cried.

CHAPTER 2

After showing Emily his small ranch and cabin north of the valley, he proclaimed:

"This is just the beginning."

She smiled appreciatively, proud as always of her papa, then she volunteered to cook dinner.

"First you tell me," he said. "Did you pull that handcart all the way here by yourself?"

She nodded, proudly.

"And I bet you turned down the offer from a few people trying to help you."

She nodded proudly again

"Darn it, girl, you do have my blood."

She nodded proudly once more.

Three hours later, sitting at their table, they feasted — T-bone steaks from his recently butchered steer, potatoes and carrots, and her favorite hot roll and gravy recipes. Porter complemented her on "carrying Luana's recipes in her blood."

She laughed.

"Papa, I'm going to do something for you after dinner. I'm going to braid your hair. I want you to keep it looking nice, in pony tails, if you insist on this Samson thing. And I'm going to comb your beard every day."

He smiled.

"Let me get something for you," she said, and returned moments later from outside, where she was yet to unpack her handcart. She now stood before him proudly, holding his favorite painting.

"That's the one you did in Illinois!" said Porter. The scene was the same, only complete now. It was a picture of her and him in front of the Nauvoo Temple. He noticed for the first time how she looked, in the picture, so very serene. "You carried that clear across the plains to show me?"

"To give you, Papa. Here."

She handed it to him.

He beamed. He stared at it awhile, knowing she had sacrificed by hauling the thing in a handcart in lieu of other necessities she could have brought to make the journey more tolerable.

"What happened to your other paintings?" he said.

"'Left them with Mama. But I knew you wanted this one. It's her favorite, too, and she threw quite a tantrum over it, for such a big girl."

They both laughed.

"You look very peaceful in this painting," he said. "That's the way I always want to remember you."

"But your other memories of the killings and mobs cloud this picture, don't they?"

He was surprised at her sudden, penetrating question. He looked at her and thought a moment. "That's why I need you here," he said. "To keep this image clear, so no memories cloud it."

She smiled. "I'd like to do another painting with me and Mama in it. But you probably don't want a picture of her husband in it, huh?"

He smiled.

She continued, non-chalantly, "He went off and started his own church in Iowa."

He sighed angrily and turned to her:

"If Alpheas Cutler decided to go off and do a fool thing like that, what in Hades did Luana do — stay with him?"

Emily felt frustrated at her father's quick judgment of her mother, despite her allegiance to he pa. She silently sighed, then answered his question. "She joined his church."

Porter stared at her and gulped. "What about the children?"

"She took them into his fold."

He tried holding in his feelings.

But failed.

"What's the matter with that fool woman!"

"Daddy, I don't want you talkin' that way. Mama's a fine woman. Tantrums and all."

"That she is, Emily. So I don't know what possessed her to marry that man — a fellow who'd turn loco and go off and do that."

"Papa, quit! Please!"

Porter jerked his look over to her, baffled by her.

"I know you don't like what he's done, Papa, but he's been a fine father for the kids."

"So what're you doing out here if he's so all-fired perfect?'

Emily quit eating and simply stared, uncertain if she should tell him the rest of the story.

"Emily, you were young when your grandpa Orin died from exposure. That happened 'cause the Missourians drove us from Independence. He died for his beliefs. My best friend was Joseph himself, and look what happened to him. Who did he do that for? You and me. And Luana and all of us. If there is one thing I don't tolerate, it is lukewarm folks not taking advantage of the sacrifice of others," he growled.

Emily softened. While she admired her father's zeal, she interpreted his anger as rising primarily from the topic of Luana. And within that interpretation she felt a wisp of hope. To the extent he was outraged by Luana, she hypothesized, he still loved her.

"I'm sorry, Papa. What she's done must hurt very much. And I have other news for you now. When Luana left you, she was pregnant with another child of yours."

Porter stared at her, stunned.

She continued, "He was born in Iowa and his name is Jacob. Alpheas became his pa, but now Mama has left Alpheas and married another man. They're in a break-off group from Cutler's following, and they formed a caravan and headed north to Minnesota. And took the kids, of course, including Jacob. She'll never tell Jacob about you. She's saying that a plainsman passing through was the father. But we know different. He looks more like you than her. A lot more."

Porter gazed off. He did not know what, if anything, he could do for this 5th child. One he had never seen. He was aghast. He now had a second son! He was inclined to go visit him, but feared the situation would unavoidably turn into a confrontation, one that could turn his other children against him if they saw him fight with their mother. And if he took Emily on the journey he would take the chance of her re-kindling a desire to stay with her brothers, sisters, and Luana. He could not handle losing Emily. He did not know what to do. He changed the subject.

"I think we should see your grandma tonight. She and my brothers and sisters all live just south of here."

He arose, silently strode outside, and noticed a wagon approaching. Momentarily, Brigham Young descended from the buckboard.

"What's the matter, Porter?" said the venerable leader approaching Porter and shaking his hand.

"What Emily's just told me about her mama," said Porter.

"What about her?"

He repeated Emily's news, then added, "Maybe I should go back — for the kids' sakes."

"Believe me," said Brigham. "Barging in on Luana's new life would produce no good results. Maybe she'll come back to us in the future."

"I suppose," said Porter.

"And we're facing new problems now."

"What new problems?" said Porter.

"The ones I need your help solving." At that Brigham pulled out a small tin marshal's badge.

Porter stared at the silver image glistening in a beam of sunlight filtering through the overcast sky.

"Papa," broke in Emily, "what are you waiting for?"

"An outlaw element," resumed Brigham, "has been moving in and taking advantage of our growing community. You're the best man for this job."

Porter wanted a new life with his daughter. He did not know how to put it into words. He was torn as he gazed at the badge, and also at Brigham's expression, and also at her.

"Oh, mercy," he finally said. "Life's a mess, ain't it?"

CHAPTER 3

That evening Porter took Emily to visit his mother, Sarah, and his brothers and unmarried sisters. Three of his sisters were still living in the Midwest — the two oldest were in Ohio and another was in Missouri — with their husbands. His five siblings here each had a cabin near their mother Sarah's home, on the same ranch. Porter had overseen all construction and helped them fence off the property. Now there were cattle and chickens on the ranch and Sarah seemed content. When she laid eyes on her granddaughter Emily, whom she had not seen in months, she cried and hugged her. Emily then noticed the old family dog, Ugly, galloping in through the back door and jumping on her, sending her sprawling. He licked her face with foul breath.

"Papa! Get him to stop!"

They all laughed. The animal had wandered back and forth between Sarah and Porter since arriving West with Sarah. Porter had insisted she maintain companionship with the animal, knowing her loneliness and fondness for the pet, and Ugly had seemed to sense the importance of his calling in that regard. His fading eyesight, however, prevented him from attacking, killing, and aging his prey for perfume, for which he was notorious years earlier. So now he had resorted to rolling in roadkill — the creatures that horsehooves would strike and carriages would run over. With Emily back, all knew Ugly would be shifting his time primarily to Porter's household. Emily hugged Ugly, laughing and crying at the same time.

Porter melted, wanting the moment to never end, nor their circumstances to ever change. The only change he wished he could see was to have his children from Minnesota living him.

He would for years see his mother and some of his brothers and sisters almost every Sunday afternoon for dinner, when he was in town. If only *all* his children could be there as well for the family gatherings.

Emily would often accompany him, but her aunts' and uncles' subtle asides directed obliquely against her mother, even upon this first visit, bothered her. Sarah, however, was always kind about Luana, including today, though she had, of course, been the first of the family to see such problems years earlier.

Riding home with Porter that night, after taking supper at his mother's cabin, with all five of his siblings present, Emily muttered:

"'You ever seen a snail out of its shell?"

Porter nodded, then looked at her curiously.

"I think," she said, "you're sitting beside one."

"You'll get used to 'em," he said.

"I never have felt so out of place."

"Just 'cause they don't like what your mama did doesn't mean they're not your kinfolk."

"That doesn't mean I have to feel like they are."

"I reckon that's your choice," said Porter. "But you remember one thing. Family is the only important thing on this earth. Even the church is only about making better families. Brigham himself would be the first to tell you that. And no one will ever love you more than them people you ate with tonight."

Emily knew he was right, she just wished his family wasn't so hard on her ma. Further, she felt torn, missing her mother already. She knew her ma loved her more than any of these people — although they did now and always had shown her a great deal of attention and concern. She was mainly homesick, she realized; still, she could not get over their verbal digs, even if what they said did possess more truth to it than what she cared to admit.

A year passed. It was spring 1849. Porter arose from the wooden dining table and put on his hat. "That breakfast was a feast, honey. You're spoiling me good."

Emily smiled, but it was broken by her curiosity as she saw him head out the front door. "Where're you going?"

"The horses need fences."

"You don't have horses," she said.

"That's why I gotta build fences," he said.

She rushed to the door as he headed to the just-completed barn.

"Papa, I need cooking and sewing supplies."

"So?"

"So what do you want me to do?" she said.

"Honey, I want you to get whatever you need. Take the wagon in town, but this time don't take cash. I'm low on it right now, so just put everything you need on our account."

Later that morning, Emily drove the wagon into the nearest community several miles north — Brigham City — to not only get the supplies but to get away and think about her life out here. She was still upset with her aunts and uncles since they'd made those disparaging remarks a year earlier, so she had cut herself off from them, and only had her pa to deal with. She had even stopped visiting her loving Gramma Sarah, simply because her aunts and uncles were always around the older lady. She realized she was far too close to her mother — and had more of her mother in her than she really wanted.

She presently arrived at a general store. Inside, she searched through fabric rolls she'd like to someday buy for dresses, then took to the counter a list of items needed for the ranch.

A boy of 17 entered the shop and ambled behind the counter. He replaced his father in helping customers.

When Emily looked up, her face registered surprise seeing an attractive young man standing there smiling at her. As she pulled herself together, she presented the list of items on the counter.

He began whistling as he grabbed the list and took it with him. He retrieved one item at a time and flipped some of the items from behind his back, then juggled them, causing her to smile. As he laid them on the counter he said:

"Heard you was living with your pa."

"How'd you know who I am?" she said curtly, not wanting to reveal her attraction.

He resumed whistling. He grabbed a ladder and began climbing to a high shelf for sewing supplies.

Emily felt uneasy, wondering if she should pursue the conversation. She assessed his tall, robust form, never having found time to be interested in a boy before and actually never having had much of an opportunity until she had moved out here. Now, without a family of brothers, sisters, and parents and grandparents to constantly serve, she had some freedom. She had noticed him a number of times in Illinois and Iowa, but had only admired him from a distance and had never spoken to him.

"How long 'you worked here?" she said.

"Since I got here a few months back," is all he offered.

"You like shopping here?" she said, then turned and caught her reflection in the window and winced, silently berating herself for such inanity: "'You like shopping here?' she thought. "Of course you like shopping here. You own the place!"

She turned quickly around and looked up, attempting to back-track: "I don't mean do you like shopping at your own store — I mean . . . do you like shopping here in the city?"

"Well, since we're the only store I've been in, I'd have to say I think it's OK. 'You?"

She turned back to the window, saw herself again, and shook her head, swearing she could see the red flush of embarrassment in her reflection.

"I have to do the shopping for my papa and me," she said. "My folks are split up. But I figured everybody knew that."

"Well most people do, but I doubt anybody cares," he said

with a smile.

She felt stupider by the second. Was she seeming sorry for herself?

She shuffled to the door. "If you don't mind, could you please put the stuff in the back of the wagon and add it to my father's account?" She got to the doorway.

"Wait," she heard.

She didn't turn around, but kept walking, wanting to get away from him before she said something stupider.

As he followed her she heard his footsteps clomping on the wooden floor, then coming to a stop. She finally turned and faced him, but shyly stared off to the side.

He smiled broadly. "By the way, my name's Josh Anderson."

"I know."

"How'd you know?" he said.

"Just did," she blushed again.

"Oh, I guess we've seen each other a little back in Illinois."

"I guess," she said, her eyes dilating at the possibility he had ever taken notice of her.

"Well, see ya, Emily."

"Wait a minute," she said. "How'd you know my name?"

"Just do," he smiled.

She blushed again. "Oh."

He was amused by her vulnerability. "What do you say we take a buggy ride to my ward picnic two weeks from Saturday?"

She thought a moment, still too shy to look at him. She felt he was entirely too confident and handsome a boy to be interested in her, a poor farm girl who had never had a boy show interest in her. She felt further flustered by the fact she had always noticed him with much prettier girls hanging about him.

"So what do you say?" he said after the long reflective non-response to his question. He enjoyed looking at her face. Considered somewhat cute by most boys' standards — though not actually pretty — her face was full like her father's, and her eyes equally blue. The long dark brown hair framed her in an attractive manner, but she thought of it as mousy.

"I reckon," she said, "I'll have to think about it and let you know in a couple days. That's when I get back to town." The truth was, she knew she needed her father's permission. No, she couldn't care less about his permission, she realized. The real truth was, she couldn't believe this was happening, and as flattered as she was, she felt simply out of her element. It involved more than her poor background: The boy was obviously from a solid family while her parents were divorced; they had fought; she was caught between them; her mother had told her she was selfish for ever leaving her and her brothers and sisters in Iowa. She wandered if indeed she were, and especially if she somehow were not as good as other people . . .

Although she could not look at his face directly, she forced a small, quick smile and darted out the door.

Outside, she climbed up the buckboard and grabbed the reigns, ready to snap them, when:

"Whoa!" yelled Josh, coming out the door behind her. "You forgot your goods!"

She never felt so humiliated. She saw him bringing the first load of supplies outside. Her eyes then searched nearby businesses for somewhere, anywhere to go until Josh could finish loading her wagon. She stepped down from the buckboard and headed across the street. This way, she would not have to talk with him and say anything else foolish. She headed toward a busy doorway on Main Street where a piano was playing a lively tune and people were laughing. The large, dark room held a strange, undefinable invitation to her. She entered the doorway and stopped, gazing around. Smoke filled the air and the casual atmosphere made her feel relaxed. Something whispered to her to stay put at the door, but she went inside anyway and looked around more.

A stranger inside with long, brown sideburns and a short, sharp chin caught sight of her from deep within the bowels of the tavern. She could not see him, her eyes still adjusting from the brightness outside to the darkness within.

She finally stepped back to the door, turned, and left. Her wagon was loaded now, so she headed straight for the buckboard.

The tavern's stranger, a man twice her age, slid out of his chair and strode to the doorway, watching her wagon disappear down Main Street.

As Porter built more fence in his field, he noticed a young man riding up to the cabin. Emily came out to greet him.

Tommy Clayton was scruffy and thin, and obviously liked her. She looked him over and was not at all attracted to him, but felt unintimidated. He was there to borrow butter for his mother. As she went to get it he asked her out for the same Saturday afternoon as Josh Anderson had. Despite her comfort level around him, today the boy was somewhat annoying, asking incessantly about her house, just to make small talk while she thought of an answer about the date. She finally told him she would let him know the next day. As he left, she reflected how strange it felt having two boys suddenly showing such interest.

The next day, sitting in church alone as people poured in, Porter beheld Emily again talking with Tommy Clayton. She had initially decided to turn Tommy down in order to attend the picnic with Josh but, upon seeing Tommy's puppy-like expression and anticipation, felt sorry for Tommy and without any warning to herself she suddenly agreed to go. She kicked herself all the way back to her pew. As she returned to sit with her father, Porter overheard two teenage girls talking about Emily and Tommy. Emily was already anguished over her decision, and spoke with Porter in harsh whispers:

"Where's the stupid hymn book?"

"You seem friendly with that boy — the Clayton kid."

"Yeah," she said, "he's nice."

"Nice, but no account."

"I take that to mean you don't approve of him?"

"You can say that," said Porter.

"So why don't you?"

"All right — he's lazy and I don't want you getting involved with boys with no ambition."

She boiled with sudden anger. "Mama says folks may've

looked at you like that."

He exploded, "You think I'm no account?"

"No, just gone every second. What am I supposed to do around here?" she whispered louder.

They noticed a dozen people staring at them. Most could not overhear their words, but read their intensity.

"At least Tommy Clayton gives me attention," she continued, softer. "And I am old enough for that. And maybe even for starting my own family."

"You're too young."

"Sixteen isn't too young."

"You're a kid."

"Then I was too young to come West . . . and die of boredom."

"Boredom? You never told me you were bored."

"I'm sorry." She caught her anger, realizing she didn't want to hurt her father. "I'm glad I did come West, Papa," she said, with a mischievous smile suddenly tugging at her lips, "except when I'm bored."

He looked at her and they both chuckled. But beneath her laughter broiled a faint rumble of depression . . . with its core fissured to thoughts of her mother. Despite Luana's manipulations, and her father's mysterious behavior, Emily knew she was loved by both parents — and could not shake the obsessive yet impossibly unrealistic desire to see both of them together again. All she wished for most days was a cure for the pain. Thoughts of running from her life seemed to be increasing daily. She felt from the conversations she had overheard between her parents while growing up that her father's intransigence — his willful refusal to bend toward Luana' will — was the deeper root of the problem, and that perhaps he *was* to blame, although she had herself suffered from her mother's difficult and sometimes impossible demands, so she was not overly harsh in her judgements of her father; nevertheless she was painfully frustrated with him that he had not kept the family together. She simply did not understand him and his desire for freedom, and the more she attempted to — by studying him and analyzing the situation — the deeper her confusion and anguish. She wanted immediate answers and resolutions, and they were not coming. Brother Brigham was visiting the congregations in the area that day, and was sitting on the stand behind the pulpit. He took note of Emily's inner discord, and gave Porter a wink of encouragement.

After church, Emily rode with her father into town. On the buckboard they sat, quiet and pensive. As Porter went to visit Brigham at the local bishop's home, Emily took a folded note to the general store. It had Josh's name on the outside, and respectfully declined his offer for the date. It was hard leaving the note, but she figured he probably had a dozen girls chasing him anyway. She told herself she could not compete with other, prettier girls, so she felt a certain sense of relief as she slid the note under the front door. She was especially grateful it was church day, so the store was closed and she would not have to face him personally. She felt her heart twinge, but brushed it off. To court him would have been too nerve-wracking for her, she told herself. As she walked away from the door she felt another pang. She hoped deep down he would ask her out again, but forced the thought away. Just then, she was tapped on the shoulder. She turned and saw . . .

A scruffy-looking stranger smiling at her.

"Ever seen the inside of one of them?" It was the stranger from the tavern who had studied her earlier.

"What?" said Emily, startled by the question from the strangely magnetic fellow.

"Inside there," he said, nodding toward the saloon. "Inside the darkness."

She slightly trembled. She immediately noticed he was considerably older, and that he had a personal interest in her. his eyes were intoxicating and she forced herself to break the spell by looking away.

Porter emerged from the bishop's home and noticed Emily sitting alone on the wagon. As he walked up to her he observed her staring off as if she'd seen a ghost. She was still amazed that the man, only vaguely handsome, had a power she'd never before felt.

As Porter and his daughter pulled off the main road onto their dirt driveway, he finally spoke:

"He's still trying to get me to take that badge. But I just can't be away from you, honey." He noticed her still staring off.

"You sure look like you' been snake bit. Must be a boy, huh?"

"No boy will ever interest me."

"Not even the Clayton boy?"

"Not even the Clayton boy." She did not tell him about Josh — nor especially the stranger from the tavern.

The next day Emily cleaned the crude iron stove her pa had bought. Porter meanwhile had returned to town to meet again with Brigham. The pioneer leader was still trying to persuade him into accepting the marshal's badge he had twice turned down.

Suddenly she heard a horse whinny outside. Figuring her father finally home, she rushed out with a smile to greet him, badly missing him, when suddenly she beheld two horses hitched at the front fence — and no riders. Her eyes scanned the horizon. She suddenly felt the hair on the back of her neck standing on end. It was a feeling of sheer terror. And she could see no one. But she knew she was in danger.

She was grabbed from behind.

Unable to see the man who held her, she heard a gravelly, high-pitched voice, "How many Missourians did your pa kill, little girl?"

CHAPTER 4

She heard laughter from two men. The one holding her whipped her around to face him. It was the stranger from the tavern.

"Allow me to introduce myself," he said, laughing. "I'm Nobody from Hades. We've met before — but not formally." His smile was crooked and she felt chills. Then he pulled a bowie knife from an old scabbard loosely fitted to his belt.

Emily saw only one avenue of escape: She tried kicking him in the abdomen, but her foot caught only the crude, hard-leathered scabbard of his bowie knife.

"Ow!" he yelled.

His partner laughed.

"Let go of me," growled Emily.

Porter arrived home with his old dog, entered his cabin, and found Emily missing. A sudden sickness gripped his heart.

He ran outside. Seeing signs of a scuffle, he ran to the road and discovered horse hoof prints. His heart shouted in pain. He searched for other clues and almost immediately discovered a scabbard. Apparently it had been hit loose and dropped on the road. He picked it up and pocketed it. The he noticed the hoof prints of *two* horses. Ugly came ambling up.

"Ugly, smell their tracks, boy. We gotta follow 'em."

Ugly sniffed around but was confused. He had come from a visit to Porter's mother's, sensing something wrong as animals often do. Unhitching his horse, Porter rode off in a fast trot, following the prints. Ugly rode behind him. On occasion over the last year when visiting his mother, he had trained Ugly to ride behind him horseback. The first time the dog had ridden horseback was when Porter had tied him to the saddle a few years back, taking him from his burned woodland hideout to his mother's home in Nauvoo, when the dog was wounded. Riding hard now, Porter inspected the scabbard closer and found initials engraved on the crusty old leather. The belt loop was worn, no doubt accounting for the reason it had fallen.

Presently he noticed a thundercloud rolling in. "What're we gonna do, boy?"

He followed the prints to the top of a crest, stopped his roan, and scanned the vast expanse. He could not see Emily or her abductors. What he could see was rain pouring from the sky a few miles ahead, shifting his way. The refreshing smell came stronger, but when the rain hit around him, it washed the terrain, removing almost all signs of the hoofprints. He then rode down the crest, westward.

Traveling through the cold rain he descried a hundred yards ahead a light reflecting from a window.

Arriving there he knocked at the heavy wooden door. Ugly stayed on the horse, whining with concern, knowing what was going on. A man swung the oak door open and peered into Porter's anguished face, lit by the fireplace.

"Porter, what's wrong?" said Tom Huntington.

"They've taken her."

"Who?" said Huntington. "What're you talking about?"

"Somebody's kidnapped my Emily!"

"Porter!" shrieked Mrs. Huntington. She ran to the door, leaving their son Lot at the dinner table. "What happened?"

"Come in and have a seat," said Tom.

"'Ain't got time."

"What can we do to help?" said Tom.

"Her tracks."

"Tracks?" said Tom.

"The kidnappers' tracks are here. Did you see 'em?"

"They came past our place?"

"Hours ago — but the rain washed away most of the tracks. Have you heard of any strangers abouts?"

Tom gazed at his wife. Both could think of no one. Then their son Lot spoke slowly from deeper in the cabin:

"Two of 'em from the gold fields have been hanging about town lately."

Porter and the boy's parents studied the 15 year old.

Porter spoke gravely, "How did you know about that, son?"

Lot looked at his parents and did not answer.

"Answer him, son," said Lot's father.

"I saw them," said Lot.

"Where?" said Porter.

Lot refused to answer.

"Answer Porter's question, Lot," said Mrs. Huntington.

The boy kept his head bowed.

"I think he answered it," said Porter. "You've been hanging about the tavern, haven't you, boy?"

Lot's parents gazed at each other, concerned not only for Porter and Emily, but about their son.

Porter walked inside and right up to him. "What else do you know about them?"

"Just loud talk, and that they're heading back to pan gold in Sacramento."

"Anything else? What did they look like? Did you get a name?"

"They're about 30, 35, scruffy, blonde, my height. 'Didn't get a name."

"Anything else?" said Porter.

Lot just stared at him.

"For heaven's sake, son — it's his daughter we're talking about — what do you know?" said his father.

"Nothing!" Lot said, then he shifted his look from his parents to Porter. "They bought me a couple drinks. 'Wanted me to join 'em on the ride."

Lot's mother was shocked her son would have imbibed — and with strangers such as these. "What did you say to 'em!"

"I told 'em no. They showed me a bag of gold dust. 'Said I could get some too if I went back to the gold fields with them. I still said no."

"And what else!" said Porter.

"They bragged about Lilburn Boggs planning to hunt you down."

"Governor Boggs?" said Porter.

"Yeah — he's got two sons in California with him, and they're in the gold-mining district somewhere. They plan to get you. I got the feeling these two were in cahoots with them — but I ain't sure."

Porter was amazed how he was still haunted by past problems — and the irony of being at independence the very night Boggs had been shot.

"One other thing," said Porter, showing the scabbard to Tom. "What're these initials on the scabbard?"

"It says, 'H.G.,'" said Tom.

Lot chuckled again. "What're you laughing at, boy?" said Porter with anger.

"Nothing. I'm just glad somebody in this valley can't read besides me."

Porter's glare at the boy quickly turned into a smile. He liked this lad — and his honesty.

Porter and Ugly rode in the moonlight, the storm having dissipated. They were able to follow the few remaining tracks.

What went through Porter's mind was the searing pain over Emily being used by Boggs in some sort of revenge scheme — or as bait to trap him. Whatever was happening, he was determined to get her back at all costs. Ironically, he had no desire to pursue Boggs otherwise. On the trek West he had released the hatred that had enveloped him after his pa had died from hardships due to the Boggs' expulsion order of 1838.

On his trip to Sacramento he and Ugly picked up the kidnappers' trail — but lost it again. After a sleepless night he guessed where the fugitives might have gone next. He gambled and ceased looking for the tracks, in order to make up lost time, by simply riding straight for Sacramento as fast as he could.

There, he would simply inquire about Emily, hunt down her kidnappers and, he figured, have nothing left to do but dispatch them without further notice to the Spirit World.

CHAPTER 5

As Porter and Ugly arrived in Sacramento, a small crowd of 12 men gathered around a skinny drunk fat fellow. Porter thought to himself, "A skinny, drunk fat fellow? How can he be skinny and fat, this fellow?"

He studied the man further and realized he was in actuality both skinny and fat — his legs were thin and his belly huge. He resembled an egg on toothpicks. He was leading a small white dog in performing tricks. The street audience laughed and threw coins at the drunk. The pathetic chap finally waddled inside the saloon and re-emerged with a bottle.

Porter finished hitching his horse and ambled past the drunkard. Ugly walked with him, growling at the man, possibly for mistreating the little dog.

"I'll take care of this, Ugly," said Porter. He turned and faced the pathetic drunk: "Awfully smart dog you've got."

"Cause he hangs around me."

"And awfully skinny," added Porter. "Is that also 'cause he hangs around you?"

"I reckon."

"Don't you ever feed him?"

A 12 year old boy with long blonde, scraggly hair piped up:

"His old owner fed him. But he died last month. So this man took him. Wish I had him."

"I use him for drinkin' money," laughed the man.

Porter shook his head, hating to see animals in any way mistreated. He entered the tavern, knowing he would have to do something about it when he left. "Ugly, you stay out here and guard the horse. Bark if there's trouble."

Five men sat at a single table in the back, while two other tables were occupied by only two men each. A tall, scrawny fellow in dusty ripped clothes ambled in behind Porter and sat with the table of five. Porter glanced at each in the tavern, then in his heavy-sounding boots he clopped across the wooden plank floor to the bar.

The bartender scowled, facing the tavern mirror behind him:

"What'll it be for you?"

Common with bars in the West, free crackers and sand-wiches were for the taking. Porter grabbed a handful of round, hard biscuit-shaped crackers and began chewing one.

The bartender snorted, his back still turned to Porter. "I said, what'll it be for you?"

"This," finally said Porter.

The bartender turned and noticed him plopping a scab-bard onto the cheap, rough-hewn wooden bar.

"Never seen it before," said the bartender, not even looking at it.

"It's initials say, "H.G.," said Porter.

The bartender's eyes widened. "So?"

"So why don't you tell me who it is, and I'll be on my way."

"Sorry, mister." The bartender walked to the other side of the bar. "I don't get involved."

Porter sighed, grabbed the scabbard, and clopped away. As he arrived at the end of the bar, he suddenly reached across the counter and with his left hand grabbed the shirt of the bartender. With his right hand he drew his pistol and stuck the barrel against his nose.

"Now do you wanna get involved? My little girl got herself kidnapped and this is the only clue I got."

The bartender broke into a cold sweat. "I told you I don't know."

Porter pulled back the hammer.

The bartender's uncertainty to divulge anything forced him to stammer. "I s-s-s-said, I-I-I . . . " He finally blurted out, "I reckon I do know a H.G. or two out in the gold fields."

"And who might they be?" said Porter.

"'Don't know their names. Only their initials."

"That don't sound very convincing to me," said Porter.

"I'm telling the truth!"

Porter studied his eyes and believed him. "So you heard anything about a kidnapping?"

The bartender stared at the gunbarrel and shook his head.

Porter uncocked the hammer and stuck the weapon back in his belt. He heard Ugly barking and he hustled out the door.

The tall, scrawny fellow arose from the table of five and ran past him out the door.

As Porter arrived outside he was surprised to discover his horse being taken. Three dusty, dark-haired young men were leading it around the corner and away. The scrawny man from the tavern jumped on a small horse and galloped to the others to join them. They quickly turned and discovered Porter staring at them.

Porter merely raised one hand to his mouth and whistled. His roan bolted from the thieves. This caused the fellow holding Porter's horse to fall off his own.

Porter broke out laughing. Ugly, sitting and staring from outside the tavern door, wagged his tail in apparent amusement.

The four thieves stared at Porter laughing. Frustrated and angered, they pulled out weapons and decided to charge him. The one on the ground glanced up just as an associate tossed him a rifle. He caught it, sprung to his feet, and walked quickly toward Porter beside the others, all sporting rifles.

Still laughing, Porter pulled two single-shot pistols.

The dozen men on the boardwalk watching the drunk's dog show now scattered.

The four thieves, charging at Porter, lowered their rifles and fired. All shots missed.

Porter aimed at the thief who was without a horse, and fired, hitting him in the shoulder and knocking him to the ground. He fired his other pistol at another, hitting him in the arm and knocking him off his horse.

As the last two horsemen continued towards Porter, they came within 30 yards and fired at him. He quickly pulled two

small derringers from his boots and fired simultaneously —
knocking both men off their horses. They crashed to the dust
10 feet from him.

The unmanned horses rode past Porter on both sides of
him.

All four men lay wounded on the street as a man in the saloon
came running outside, yelling to the crowd to get the doctor.

Porter ambled up to the youngest thief and shouted, "Who
sent you?"

The dark-haired, 16 year old boy refused to talk.

Porter picked up one of the thieve's rifles as the barkeep
appeared at the door.

"Don't kill the lad."

"Nobody said I was," said Porter. "But maybe you oughta
tell me what's going on here before somebody loses a body
part."

Porter aimed at the young man's ear, and the fellow
trembled.

The bartender gazed at all four wounded men in the road
and realized he had said too much already, but his short breaths
told Porter he would say more.

Porter faced the bartender, the pistol still pointed at the
boy:

The bartender breathed heavily, torn, but knowing he had
no choice now.

"My life's been threatened if I tell you anything."

"So tell me anyway." said Porter.

"We all know who you are," said the bartender. "Every last
man on this side of town hails from Missouri, and we know you

by your hair. Also, Boggs said you'd be coming this way."

"It's nice to be so cared about," said Porter. "But you ain't answered my question. So quit killing time."

"'Lots of these fellows lost kinfolk in the Missouri Wars to the Mormons."

"Thanks for the history lesson, but tell me what you know about my daughter," said Porter, "so more kinfolk don't get lost in my own war."

The barkeep trembled. And finally mumbled:

"That's my son, mister. Please let him go."

"Where's Boggs — I think he might know something. Then I'll let him go."

"I couldn't tell you."

"You ever see him?"

"He comes in for a drink once a week. I've told you all I know. Please, mister, don't hurt him."

The barkeep was relieved when Porter placed his pistol back in his belt.

"You shoulda told him nothing, Pa!" said the young man.

Porter walked to his horse and spoke softly to the bar- keep as he passed him. "You might wanna get your boy in a new occupation."

Then Porter whistled at the small white dog. It ran to him and he picked it up and petted it. He said to the animal, "Looks like you've got a friend who'll take care of you again. Here," he said to the blonde 12 year old kid behind him who had spoken of the animal. "Do you know how to take care of a dog, boy?"

"Yes, sir, I reckon," he said excitedly.

"Well you better know, 'cause he'll be the best friend you'll ever have." He smiled. "Remember my words on your 13th wedding anniversary." He handed the little dog over to him and the boy beamed.

"I'll take good care of him, mister. Mama said I could have a dog."

The drunk fellow was too busy drinking himself into semi-consciousness to even notice. Porter picked him up, put him over his horse's rear, and carried him out of town amidst stares from the 20 townsmen, including his attackers who had witnessed his arrival. They were amazed at the scene they had witnessed — and at what they saw now — as Ugly also rode off behind Porter, perched atop the drunk fellow draped over the horse, wagging his tail.

News would spread like wildfire, and Porter was absolutely certain Boggs and his boys would receive it . . . news of the gunfighter nobody could kill — and his big dog riding horseback perched on the town drunk. A sight over which more than one man was shaking his head as Porter and Ugly rode away. A sight that left the bartender mumbling, "Mercy. That's the weirdest thing I've ever seen."

CHAPTER 6

Porter hauled the drunk to another town 20 miles away. The next morning the fellow awakened as Porter deposited him on Main Street.

"Where am I?"

"Far enough away from that dog to never bother him," said Porter. "But if you do — and I get word of it — I'll track you down myself."

"So what's it to you, mister?"

"That dog now has a boy, and there's nothing more sacred than a boy and his dog. Are we clear?"

"Yes, sir," he sighed. "I'll stay away. All I want's a little gold so I can get more whiskey."

"There's plenty of gold out here," said Porter. "A lot more than in Sacramento. You can drink yourself to death now if you wish, by just working that stream over there. Or you can make something of your life. Build a fortune and share it with people."

"So," said the fellow with a casual, assessing smile, "what's your downfall to be, mister?"

Porter looked at him, taken back.

"Your Achilles heel?"

"What do you mean?" said Porter.

"Someday you'll find it," said the drunk. "But I do appreciate you getting me away from Sacramento out here where I can make a new start." He actually extended his hand to Porter to shake it. Porter looked at it a moment, and did so. But he was again disarmed when the man said, with piercing eyes, "Just watch your backside. It'll sneak up on you from the backside."

CHAPTER 7

At a campfire that night, Porter fed a roasted rabbit's hind-quarter to Ugly while he chewed on another section. The dog ate appreciatively as Porter fed him seconds.

"That's your reward for being a good guard dog."

Ugly beamed.

"Now what I taught you tonight is the only other thing you'll ever have to learn. So, what do you do if you hear a person approaching?"

Ugly licked him on the face.

"That's good — but next time don't drown me."

Ugly wagged his tail.

"I'll lay asleep like this, and close my eyes."

Porter pretended to be asleep when he tossed a rock over his head 40 feet behind him. The dog licked his face again.

"Good boy."

The next day Ugly rode behind him atop the saddle. After a few minutes Porter asked him, "Now what happens when you sniff someone in the wind?"

Ugly licked the back of his neck.

Porter jumped. "Good heaven's you've got slimy slobber." He shook in disgust.

The dog gazed in the direction of the road ahead.

"Good boy," said Porter. "You are the smartest pooch I've ever known. Now shake hands, partner." Porter turned and shook his paw.

Suddenly he felt a lick, then saw two riders approaching from the distance.

He rode off the road. He and Ugly hid behind trees. Shortly after the riders passed them, they re-entered the road.

The horsemen heard Porter's horse whinny, whirled their heads back, and saw Porter's pistols aimed directly at them. They raised their arms.

"'Ain't got much money," said one.

"What you got, you can keep," said Porter.

"Then what do you want?" said the other.

"A little information. That's all."

Porter pulled out the scabbard and tossed it to one of them.

The man caught the scabbard, turned it over, and his eyes widened.

"You just told me you know who owns that," said Porter.

"No, sir, I don't know."

"I think you do." Porter cocked back the hammer of his pistol.

"Well you can't tell anyone we told you," said the same rider.

"No problem there — I don't even know who you are. Now tell me who it belongs to."

"Hyrum Gates," said the rider. "He puts his brand on everything."

Porter's eyes burned. "And where might I find him?"

"One of these mining areas, I reckon."

"That don't help a lot," said Porter, pointing the pistol directly at his face. "Which mining area?"

At a mining creek were 50 goldpanners spread over a hundred yards. Porter and Ugly rode past one panner who just happened to be talking about the long-haired outlaw from Brigham's empire. He was laughing, when Porter appeared behind him.

"Mornin'," said Porter.

The man turned, saw, and froze. His eyes went lunar-like — as wide and yellow as the moon. "Don't kill me!"

"Nice day to die though, ain't it?" said Porter.

The man grunted.

Porter smiled. "I reckon my legend's growing far and wide. I like that." He suddenly shot a hole through the man's gold pan.

The man jumped back. He looked down at it and in a flash Porter was out of his saddle, grabbing the fellow from behind and shoving his face into the stream. He felt the man struggle to reach air. The man's friend reached for his knife, and Porter flashed his second pistol on him. Ten seconds later Porter pulled his victim's head out of the water.

"Sorry to be rough with you, stranger, but I got a missing daughter on my hands, and I ain't in the mood to be laughed at. I've got the fondest of memories for Missouri pukes, however," Porter smiled. "Now just tell me which one of these panners is Hiram Gates, and I'll be on my way."

The fellow stuttered, terrified.

"I ain't gonna hurt you if you just tell me, so quit doin' that."

His teeth chattered, and finally he simply pointed at Gates' cabin downstream.

Porter rode downstream, keeping his horse no more than 20 feet from the water, when he came to within clearer sight of the property.

He dismounted. "Stay here, boy," he said to Ugly. He hid his horse from sight of the cabin, then snuck around to the rear of the property.

Seeing a large rear window of waxed paper, he charged the cabin and dove through the window.

There was a woman's scream. He rolled over and jumped to his feet, holding both pistols on her. Then he quickly lowered them.

"All I want," said Porter, "is to know if you've seen my daughter Emily."

The haggard woman calmed down and moved her eyes from one of the lowering pistols to Porter's face.

"She's 16," said Porter, "with blue eyes and long, brown hair."

The woman nodded, "At my nephew's cabin."

"Gates?" said Porter.

She nodded again. "He lives here with the clan. That's his cabin," she said, pointing through her ripped-out, wax-papered and now open window. Porter handed her a small gold coin. "This should more than pay for the window."

Porter's eyes then shot to the cabin — a crude structure one hundred yards downstream and only 15 feet from the river bank. He wondered if Emily were all right. He feared the very worst had happened to her. His heart churned with anguish. It was time to take her home — and kill anything that got in the way.

CHAPTER 8

Porter snuck through brush towards the distant cabin. Behind him were a number of goldpanners standing at the stream and peering through the bushes. He turned and noticed them. Frustrated, he motioned them with his revolver to get down. He felt the scene looked ridiculous. "Some surprise attack," he mumbled.

He decided to just charge the cabin. He took out running. Breathless, he came to a quick stop outside the front door. He took a deep breath and kicked it in. He rushed inside, holding up two revolvers. And there he saw her.

She saw him and gasped. "Papa!"

He then heard fast footsteps of a man approaching. He swirled his gun onto the figure entering the back door.

"No, Papa!" yelled Emily.

"You Hyrum Gates?"

"Yes, sir."

"I've been waiting for this moment, mister," said Porter. "You don't know how hard I've waited."

"Papa . . . don't!"

"What's the matter with you?" said Porter to Emily.

"Don't hurt him!" screamed Emily.

"What's he done to you?" said Porter.

"Papa — no — you don't understand . . . I have fallen in love with this man."

Shocked, Porter turned his face from the kidnapper to Emily.

"And I married him."

Porter gazed at her, stunned, then at the kidnapper again. The fellow half-smiled and extended his hand to shake Porter's.

"Pleased to meet you," said the kidnapper.

Porter glared at the fellow's hand, refusing to shake it, then turned to stare at Emily again, while slowly lowering his gun. After a moment, he came to his senses.

"Get packed," he said.

"What?"

"You're coming with me."

"Papa . . . "

"You heard me!"

"Papa — I'm married! I want to stay with this man."

"You're coming with me."

"I really am in love with him."

Bewildered, "You're in love with him?"

"Yes!"

Angered, "Oh, well in that case everything is different. He may be a low-life cockroach that kidnaps 16 year old children but, since you're in love with him, I'm supposed to give my blessing to the both of you to live happily ever after. And I just can't wait to have grandchildren, fathered by a bonified, first-rate, felon."

"Things happen when you're with someone awhile," she said.

"Yeah, I reckon you're right about that." He cocked his second gun.

"I didn't want to go with him," she explained. "But after we were on the trail a couple weeks I began to see deep down he really is something."

"I have no doubt of that," mumbled Porter.

"And he is what I want," she continued.

"What you want? How do you know what you want?"

"He's what I've wanted my whole life!"

"Your whole childhood?"

"Ever since I've even looked at boys!"

"Oh, since you were 12, huh? That's a life-long experience, all right."

"My heart has experience in knowing what it wants."

"Yeah, well I predict you'll have more than a lifetime of experience, Emily," he snorted with disgust.

"Papa, I know this is it. I want him . . . and the boys."

"Boys?"

Suddenly two 10 year olds came crashing through the house, hollering like Indians, in one door and out the other, disappearing behind the hut.

"Those boys," smiled Emily.

"They're Zeke and Tork," said her husband.

"No one's given you permission to speak yet," said Porter. He turned to Emily. "Why in tarnation would you not want to come back home now?" I thought we had a special family — you and me."

"We do — or did — but I love him and want my own family here."

"What's wrong with the boys back home?" said Porter.

"You wouldn't approve of any. And in any case, don't you think that's a little late? We got wed a week ago!":

Suddenly Porter noticed 20 adults — the same clan who had watched him back at the creek — approaching the cabin now and entering. One man took Porter's hand and shook it, another patted him on the back.

"Good to have you aboard, cousin," said one.

"Let me shake his hand!" shouted another.

"And me!" said another.

Porter was astounded and simply let them pass by like a reception line. They all enthusiastically shook his hand. Ugly then sauntered in and Emily's eyes widened.

"Ugly!" she shrieked and hugged him.

Moments later Porter found himself outside watching the clan eat fried trout and corn on the cob. He had no appetite and simply stared off, sitting at one end of the table as a guest of honor. He had retrieved his horse which now ate next to the hut. Ugly sat beside him.

"We hail from Kentucky!" piped up Emily's father-in- law. "You've heard of Daniel Boone and his Tennessee buddy, Davy Crockett!"

"I reckon."

"Cousin Sal over there actually saw Dan'l once — riding through Lexington."

"I'm impressed," said Porter, staring at this clan of semi-in- bred misfits with strange facial features, wondering what the devil his daughter had gotten herself into. He now knew what happens when family multiply and replenish the earth with family.

A plate of biscuits and honey was then passed in front of his face. Some cousin with unusually shaped ears and a huge bump on his nose, which gave one the impression he was sporting a horn, urged Porter to take a biscuit.

With even less appetite, he took it and simply sat there holding the thing.

"Well, what do you think?" said Emily's mother-in-law to Porter, "of your new son-in-law?"

Porter stared in horror at the woman: She had no teeth, grinning wide. Her hair had not been brushed in a month. It fell twisted and matted, and it smelled. He noticed a flea jump from a loose strand on her forehead, down to her eyebrow. Porter suddenly felt nauseous.

"Are you all related?" said Porter softly to the older woman.

"What's that?" said the groom's mother.

"I said are you all related?"

The groom's mother stared, then broke out laughing. She repeated it for the whole clan and they cawed and howled.

"That's a good one!" said the groom's father, slapping Porter's knee. "We're more than related!"

They all laughed harder and louder.

Emily glared, terrified for her father who still looked shell-shocked.

Ugly meanwhile seemed disconcerted by the looks he was getting from one member of the family. The old fellow sitting across the table was actually licking his chops.

"I like him," he muttered to Porter. "You ever had it?"

Porter stared at the backwoodsman, astounded.

The fellow then winked at Ugly.

Porter mumbled to the man, "Would you stop eyeing my dog that way?"

"Mister," said the in-law, "you obviously have never had a good marinated dog steak."

"Mister," said Porter, "if you wanna live till breakfast, you'll stop eyeing my dog." He turned to Ugly. "Stay with me, boy."

Presently Ugly needed to relieve himself, and so indicated to Porter with a whine. Porter stood.

"Cousin," said the old fellow. "I'll go with your dog if you like."

Porter glared at him, "Not in this lifetime." He then tramped away into the woods. "C'mon, Ugly."

"Where's he going?" said the toothless lady.

"Into the woods so his dog can crap."

They all laughed.

"Cousin Cecil?" said another. "Is he onto you already?"

They all hurled harder laughs at him.

Presently, down at the river 50 yards away, Porter passed a dozen children staring curiously at him. The children, Porter noted, all possessed the unusual genetic trait of missing eyelashes. Confused at the sight of the long-haired stranger walking past them, they gazed at each other and blinked.

"Lovely children," Porter mumbled to Ugly.

The dog saw them and whined, disconcerted by nature gone so doggone awry.

Together alone now, Porter and Emily walked along the river bank away from the clan, which had found in Porter an excuse to booze it up, yelling and laughing harder than ever. Porter's dog stayed close at bay, never more than a foot from him in this neighborhood. He had found another cousin or two who were eyeing him as well.

"What've you truly got yourself into?" said Porter.

"I know how bad this looks," said Emily.

"You don't know what bad is."

"Time will tell," she said.

"Yeah, in all your wisdom you can tell me that."

"But I know what I'm doing," she offered.

"If you knew what you were doing you'd be coming home with me, and writin' this whole thing off as one big, ugly short mistake."

"But I know where my heart tells me to go with this," she said.

"Into one long, ugly mistake?"

"Well if it is, I'm really happy with it, Pa. This is home for good now. And I have never been so happy."

"And you've never been so stupid," he said, "but don't take it personal."

"Why do you have to make me feel guilty over this?" she shouted.

"Cause I raised you better than this!"

"Than what!" she said.

"Are you serious — better than 'what?' You would actually marry this kind of rabble and even ask me?"

"Why didn't you at least get to know him?"

"Pa, I know him! You don't know him!"

"Who wants to know rabble who kidnap young girls, much less that don't even ask their pa for your hand in marriage. And you didn't even have a decent ceremony with all your people present."

"Did Mama's parents approve of you and her?"

"I did all I could, and we did have a decent ceremony."

"That's about all you had," she mumbled.

"What do you mean by that?"

"Look where it ended, Pa!"

"At least I tried! And I tried to do it the decent way — with a proper ceremony. But your marrying an outlaw without me even knowing — you call that decent? I didn't think you would ever do this to yourself."

"You mean to you," she said.

He glared at her, and strode immediately to his horse and mounted up. Without even looking at her again, he turned and rode away.

Emily stared, crushed.

Ugly stood, looking back and forth between the two, torn over who to follow. Finally he looked at Emily, whined, and took off with Porter.

CHAPTER 9

Porter stopped at a tavern for a drink. He also ate free, large crunchy crackers with jam. He fed his dog exactly what he ate. As he left, he unhitched his horse and recognized a woman walking down the boardwalk with a young man.

"Agnus?" said Porter.

The woman turned and glared. She flushed with embarrassment and began running toward her carriage parked at the end of the block.

The young man ran with her and blurted out, "What's the matter?"

Porter trotted behind them horseback and caught up as she dashed into the carriage. As the young man closed her door, Porter jumped off his horse and bolted to their door.

The young man yelled in his face, "Is there something I can do for you?"

Porter did not answer — he simply stared at the lady through the carriage window and she gazed back. He noticed she wore a bonnet tightly around her head. Something did not seem right.

The young man — of 16 — spoke again, this time to the lady:

"Mother, do you want me to get rid of him?"

The lady stared at Porter a moment, then finally spoke:

"You could never get rid of him, dear. This is Porter Rockwell."

The boy's eyes widened.

The lady stared at Porter. "Would you like to join us for supper?"

Porter nodded.

"Son," she said, "this is as close of a friend as we'll ever have. No man was closer to your uncle, the Prophet Joseph, than this animal-looking creature. "Porter," she said, turning to him, "when're you ever going to cut that mange?"

Inside Agnus' shanty cabin, a quaint structure which held the remnants of culture and wealth with certain furnishings and vases on the mantel, Porter realized this woman was suffering from the onslaught of poverty.

"Where's Don Carlos?" said Porter.

Agnus answered by clearing her throat and turning to her son. It was obvious she was too proud to look at Porter directly to relate her story:

"Son, I may have never told you, but I was the belle of Nauvoo at one time. Porter, here, remembers me in that light. But life has never-ending twists and turns."

She then pulled off her bonnet — and Porter was surprised to see her head stark-naked bald.

"Typhoid fever," she said. She looked closer and saw a tear trailing down his cheek.

As she cooked supper, she didn't know Porter was returning to town, passing a certain shop, stopping and staring at the proprietor through the window, torn as rarely before in his life and taking thirty solid minutes before making a decision.

Just as Agnus and her son set the table with steaming boiled beef and potatoes, they heard a knock at the door. Agnus opened it and Porter held out a gift-wrapped box with a smile on his face. She opened it and burst into tears. It was a long, beautiful wig. When she looked up, Porter pulled off his hat and opened his collar — he was as bald as she was! She burst into laughter.

As she invited him inside, he sat and began eating heartily, while Agnus would break into more laughter and sobs at the same time.

His soul soared for the sacrifice he had made for her — but it was a sacrifice whose consequences would be steeper than he had ever imagined . . .

He left that night hearing echoes of faint and distant laughter . . . and whether from angels or devils, he was not yet certain.

He went to sleep that night at a campfire, the sparkling embers mixing with his thoughts and creating a maze of conflicting emotions. He had helped a wonderful, proud and beautiful woman — whose life had once been devoted to service to her people before retreating from society, while at the same time breaking a promise given him from Joseph — and in actuality — as he felt in his heart — from the Lord Himself.

CHAPTER 10

Porter rode past a crude wooden sign. It read, "Murderer's Bar . . . pop 980 and growing." Seeing a crude tavern ahead, he realized how depressed and . . . empty . . . he felt. He stopped and stared from atop his saddle at the men laughing inside and enjoying themselves.

He sat inside the small, crude wooden saloon swatting flies and drinking a bottle of cheap whiskey. He poured a dab into a shot glass and his dog lapped it up like water, then whined for more. Porter poured him another glass, then one for himself. He talked to Ugly of his woes, and Ugly whined for another drink.

The two finished off the bottle and staggered outside to urinate in the woods, then returned. As they sat at the same table, Porter considered buying another bottle, when he overheard at the next table a story that nauseated him:

"I reckon I ain't no better than Samson. You know why?" he said to the group of six men gathered at the table, not really interested in him. "I was a-preachin' up the coast a year ago. I was a strong man. But I fell from grace. I was caught without my Bible one night, and I walked into some old saloon. I gave in to my thirsts that had ruined my life before. As I took the first drink, I heard a man laughing. I looked around and no one was there except the barkeep — and he was sober as a judge. I got chills. I knew who was laughing at me. When I walked down the street I heard him again. And I've been in his clutches ever since. I'm as useless to the Good Lord as useless can be — 'cause I'm just another drunk. And here I am today."

A dark-mustached, bald fellow at the table said:

"Preacher, you think we're supposed to feel sorry for you?"

The other five at the table laughed and the bald fellow poured another drink for him. "But that was entertaining. And for that you deserve another round." The others snickered.

The drunk proclaimed, "It's the truth, I tell you."

"Sure it is, but you wouldn't turn down a drink for telling that little story, now would you?"

The ex-preacher looked at it a moment, torn because he had a message but no one believed him. He trembled and grabbed the drink and downed it. The others cheered. He set down the glass, ashamed at himself, and then shot out of his chair and left. The others laughed.

The bald man called after him, "Good story, preacher. Tell us another sometime."

Beside them, Porter stared, distraught. He was suddenly in terror. He stared at the liquor, feeling an indescribable weakness towards it, an out-of-control yearning gripping him, one he had never before felt. He gazed in the window beside him . . .

and then caught his own reflection of his closely sheared head, a stark reminder of his broken promise to Joseph, wondering for an instant if he had lost any kind of strength, then he quickly dismissed it . . . until he heard laughter behind him. He looked behind and no one was there . . .

Lying in a gutter during a rain storm, he curled up like a child and shivered, clutching a near-empty whiskey bottle. Ugly meanwhile sat comfortably beside the horse on a bed of dry straw in the stable, sleeping out a drunken stupor. Porter mumbled Emily's name over and over, then mentioned Luana and each of their children — Caroline, Orrin DeWitt, and Sarah Jane. And the child he had never seen — Jacob.

A boot stepped in front of his face. His eyes went up the boot, up the wool trousers, and up the fine-twined suit coat and vest to a familiar face with a neatly-trimmed moustache. It was that egg-on-a-toothpick fellow, only he had lost his ponch, and was trim, slim, and healthy.

"I remember you, mister," said the stranger. "I was that drunk you took away from that little dog. You saved my life."

"From the dog?" drawled Porter, three sheets to the wind. "He didn't look that dangerous to me. Let's go rescue that boy! C'mon."

"No, mister," smiled the fellow. "You planted me next to a motherload, and the next day I struck it rich. Since then, I've invested in mining equipment, and tripled all that money. And I even pulled my life together and never again touched a drop —

all cause you pulled me outa that town and I never again saw myself as a gutter rat."

Porter held up a shot glass full of rain water. "Speaking of which . . ."

The well-dressed fellow found him amusing, and continued, "So I started over. You dropped me on the right street. Now I wanna do the same for you."

"You wanna drop me on the street?"

"Here," he said, dropping a bag of coins beside his nose. "That's five thousand in gold. Start yourself a business. Good day." The fellow whistled and walked off.

"Wait a minute," said Porter. "What about the Achilles heel business?"

But the man was gone.

Porter heard the fellow's cheerful whistling echoing from the far streets of town. All he could do was stare at the bag of gold. "I'll just leave it here," he thought to himself aloud. "What good is life — even with money?"

He began sobbing. He pulled himself together enough to finally mumble a prayer:

"What can I do, Lord? There's no love, only . . . hunting. I'm sick of it. Show me what I can do, please."

Porter was amazed when — directly across the street — a lightening bolt crashed.

The tavern at which he had drunk himself into oblivion was struck through the window and a fire ball exploded, sending the place into splinters. All its patrons stumbled out in a panic, charred with darkened clothes and faces.

"Lord," he said. "I think I have the answer to my prayer. I have seen the sign. I will start a new establishment for this city to help the drunken and downtrodden. It will be called . . . The Round Tent Saloon."

Porter stood in his large round tent, pouring drink after drink for dozens of miners. He had spent every last ounce of that gold on barrels of whiskey; shot glasses; a thick, new, brightly, striped canvas tent; and a beautiful wooden redwood bar that attracted miners near and far. He then poured a drink for a fat-faced gold panner as he heard:

"You've got the best bar in these fields, son. It'll serve thousands of panners. You sure happened to be in the right place at the right time on this one."

"I reckon," said Porter.

The miner added, "Before anybody else even got the idea to replace the old saloon, you were up in business."

A large, red-headed fellow with a hooked Scottish nose overheard them and uttered, "How did you come by this idea so fast, stranger?"

"Prayer."

The portly panner, serious and contemplative, mumbled aloud, "That is one inspiring story."

"Thank you."

"What's your name, barkeep?"

Porter gulped, realizing he dare not state his name amidst so many Missourians. He caught himself and muttered:

"Brown."

"That's it? No first name?"

"Naw, just Brown."

"Well, Brown, when I strike the motherload I will buy a round for everyone in this place — including you!"

Porter smiled.

"Barkeep," yelled a stranger at a table nearby. "Don't I know you from someplace?"

"I reckon so," said Porter. "I been there often." The men laughed. Porter studied him closer and realized the man did know him, and so did his son seated beside him: They were the two deputies in Missouri who had escorted him from Liberty to Independence Jail.

"Did you ever live in Missouri?" said the older deputy, curious.

Porter nodded, responding, "You prob'ly seen me behind a few bars there."

The younger deputy nodded, "I reckon that's it. I bet you've been a barkeep coast to coast."

Porter was uncertain if the fellows would any time soon have their memories jogged. His now, clean-shaven face did seem to throw them, yet he felt uneasy, knowing both men possessed the ability to blow his cover. They had in fact the power to have him lynched.

The older deputy piped in, "You've done such a service here, we couldn't hold nothing against you! Ever! And that's a promise!" The room full of miners nodded to Porter and gave him a thumbs up. Two dozen of them lifted their glasses to him in a toast.

One day, the older deputy approached Porter with the idea of holding a shooting contest. Porter liked the idea. He and Porter nailed up posters near the saloon and two weeks later a thousand miners showed up for the event. Porter was given a "hip, hip, hurrah" by the crowd for holding the event. He had by now easily become the most popular man in the county, owning the biggest and best tavern. He charged a fair price, and now he was about to prove himself the best shooter this side of St. Louis.

He sailed through the elimination rounds. His popularity reached a crescendo by the third round. At end of the 10th round, the thousand men were all cheering only him. The two finalists, after 12 rounds of the event, consisted of only him and a young man from the former Mormon Battalion who had been dismissed at San Diego. The miners did not know that Porter recognized the boy and the boy recognized him.

When there was only one target bottle left, the lad went first but only grazed the glass — it did not shatter. Porter then aimed and, with a pull of the trigger it blew apart. The crowd went wild. The boy seethed with jealousy. As the crowd followed Porter, he glanced over at the boy he'd just beaten. The youngster quickly downed a huge swig of whiskey. Unable to hold in his feelings and prompted by the courage of the bottle, he yelled out, "Porter Rockwell . . . you cannot fool these people!"

The crowd practically gasped into silence. The old deputy was the first to stare at Porter with shock. He suddenly recognized his old prisoner he'd escorted from Liberty. He had never disliked Porter, so now said nothing, hoping the boy's comment would pass. But the fat-faced regular to Porter's saloon felt the hackles rise on the back of his neck and, despite the fact it was he who had led the toast to Porter, it was now he who was the first to break the silence as he yelled, "It's *the* Porter Rockwell. Get him!"

Porter glared at his young competitor of the final round, who immediately realized his unforgivable mistake and softly muttered, "Sorry, Port."

Porter decided he had only one option left: to get the devil out of there. He walked quickly through the stunned crowd. His dog stayed right at his heels. As he reached his saloon, he looked inside one last time and sighed, then grabbed a sack of gold dust he'd saved stashed under some bricks on the floor, and suddenly took off running. The crowd came to a conclusion and took off chasing him.

With the crowd catching up to him, he glanced at the bag and realized it was either it or him — so he dropped the heavy gold dust and picked up speed. He then outdistanced the mob, which came to a stop and lustily scooped up handfuls of dust, putting it in their pockets and beginning to fight over it. Within seconds the gold dust had been confiscated, and the mob resumed its chase. Porter saw his horse at the stable. He dashed inside, unhitched it, quickly propped his saddle on it, and jumped on. He rode back into the street and glanced downroad at the crowd. It was just coming around a corner after him, when his large friend shouted:

"Seize him!"

The fat fellow was the first to grab a rope hanging on the outside stable wall, as another yelled:

"Lynch him!"

The mob surged forward and Porter turned his horse. They almost surrounded him, but he dashed through a small opening and made his way on a gallop to the edge of town. A thousand miners — half of whom were Missourians — screamed for his neck and yelled oaths that echoed off the huts comprising the city district.

Porter realized, as he heard gunshots in the background and a thousand angry voices, that it was probably time he look into a new occupation.

On the other side of Sacramento, heading toward Salt Lake Valley, he spotted a tavern. He felt once again a strange, strong urge for a drink, one he had not felt since his night in the gutter. He dismounted, entered with Ugly, and ordered two whiskeys. The cavernous room, filled with talking men, turned quiet. Curious, he turned.

There, seated across the uneven wooden floor, sat Lilburn W. Boggs.

CHAPTER 11

No one could have ever been able to tell, by just looking at him, that Lilburn Boggs was the former governor of Missouri. He sat in work clothes, hair disheveled, playing poker with his two youngest sons who were now young men, and cramming crackers into his mouth.

Porter smiled, set down his whiskey glass, and sauntered across the crowded saloon, his boot steps echoing off the quietened walls. One of the Missourians had recognized him upon entering the saloon and mentioned his name — at which the place had suddenly hushed.

All knew Boggs was present, and all were anxious to see the outcome of this moment. Porter arrived at Boggs' table in the back corner of the room and stopped. Ugly meanwhile remained seated atop a stool at the bar, lapping his whiskey from a bowl.

"Sit down," said Boggs, noticeably greyer since Porter had last seen him as Lieutenant Governor in Independence, and somewhat more portly in the mid-section.

Porter complied and sat, noticing in the mirror to his side the two boys with concealed weapons.

Boggs smiled.

"I hear," said Porter, "you have a complaint or two against me."

"Well I have to admit," said Boggs, "that the lead ball in the back of my head wasn't the most comfortable experience in my life."

"And it shouldn't have been," said Porter, "from what you did to my people — and especially to my pa."

"Life is filled with its little inconveniences," growled Boggs.

"As well as its little discomforts," added Porter.

"That amounts to a near confession in my book," said Boggs.

"Not in mine."

"Then who shot me?"

"Ask any of your enemies," said Porter. "My people had nearly all fled the state when it happened."

"Nearly all?" said Boggs. "It just takes one, and I heard you were one who happened to be in my state."

"With thousands of your personal and business enemies left behind, don't you think it'd be a Missourian?" said Porter.

"Well, if you're not going to confess, we're not going to get anyplace," smiled Boggs, downing a shot glass.

"And what am I supposed to confess?"

Boggs studied him. "Well, your friend Bennett told me — "

"Bennett? You'd believe his story?"

"Certainly. He was a top henchman of Joe Smith's."

"Don't you look at people's motives?"

Boggs seemed satisfied. "Let me buy you a drink. I wonder if I should have had you hounded all those months by bounty-hunters."

"And jailed for nine," added Porter.

"What do you want me to do — apologize?" smiled Boggs, looking around.

"I guess that'd be beneath you," said Porter.

Boggs looked down. "We all have a political agenda, my friend."

"And I guess we also know how far some will go to get that agenda done," said Porter.

"Boggs' lip quivered. "We do what we have to."

Porter suddenly pulled both pistols out and aimed them at Boggs' sons:

"Yeah, we do now, don't we? Tell these boys to drop their pistols they're holding under the table."

Boggs' eyes widened.

"And if they don't?"

"They'll lose more than their pistols."

Boggs nodded to his boys and they dropped their weapons.

Porter said, "Now tell them to put their hands up on the table."

Boggs nodded again and the boys obeyed. Boggs smiled, "You've got steel nerves, friend, I like you. But as you've figured, these boys're likely to get you before you exit the saloon."

"That's fine with me."

"You don't care if you lose your life over treating my boys like this?" said Boggs.

"I thought I was done with my feelings for you, but I reckon not. Not after you're showing all the remorse of a rattle snake after what you did to thousands — including my pa."

"What's your real anger, boy?" said Boggs.

"What do you mean?" said Porter with a smirk.

"Brigham's trying to hire you as a lawman."

"I'm not a lawman yet. I didn't take his badge. And how did you know about that?"

"Process of elimination. And we both know you're going to take it, don't we?"

"How do you figure that?" said Porter.

"Process of elimination."

Porter was ever so slightly shaken by Boggs' cool analysis.

"I'm leaving," said Porter, realizing the scene had no positive, potential outcome.

"Come, Mr. Rockwell," chuckled Boggs. "Does it disconcert you that much knowing what I know?"

Porter's lips quivered ever so faintly.

"You can't stay away from it, lad!" said Boggs. "You're a natural born hunter of bad wildlife. You will own that badge."

Porter peered at Boggs' big eyes. They assessed him like a cagy animal, and it unnerved him. He hated admitting to himself that this genocidal manipulator had a handle on his soul. He fought it, but could not help being mesmerized by the fellow.

"Most lawmen I know have something stinging them inside. That's another reason you won't turn away the badge, good brother," proclaimed Boggs confidently. "They're stuck with a scorpion in their gut — maybe something from what happened to them as kids. That's what'll help you take up the badge, isn't it?"

Porter was losing his concentration, and finally looked down and lowered his weapons.

In that instant, Boggs' sons grabbed their pistols off the floor but Boggs motioned to them to not move.

Porter fought the spell overpowering him. He muttered:

"I dealt with that hand a long time ago."

"But it's still there, isn't it?" said Boggs. "Like four kings you just plain can't get rid of."

"I don't even want to be deputized — so you don't know what you're talking about," said Porter. "I even told Brigham I only wanted to stay a rancher."

Boggs wasn't dissuaded. "Maybe you tried telling him that — and even yourself. But deep down you don't want to just ranch. One side of you couldn't wait to get out here and hunt me down. By the way, I heard about your daughter — " he probed, playing with Porter's mind further while studying his every reaction, his every nuance of motion, his every twitch.

"— Did you have anything to do with it?" belted out Porter, trying to break the spell.

"My, we are getting delusional, aren't we? Next, you'll be seeing mirages on the horizon. To answer your absurd accusation, Brother Porter, of course not, but that only substantiates my point here, doesn't it? We both know you wanted me tied to it. Deep down you wanted to confront me. Actually kill me. I know you fought this craving for a showdown — perhaps even successfully for a season — but I also saw that smile on your face when you walked over here. Your inner soul finds the concept of dispatching me downright succulent, doesn't it? Let's be honest here, Mr. Rockwell, your hatred is as intense as ever — and that conflict — given your Christian upbringing — is what is causing you to shake in your boots at this very moment, isn't it?"

Porter stared at him, and quietly quaked.

"Would your father want it this way? Is there any chance you promised him, or someone else perhaps — even Joseph — that you would just let this go?"

Porter trembled even harder.

"You can't kill me, Porter, nor my sons. In fact, as much as you hurt inside, you can't pull that trigger 'cause you promised someone, somewhere, you would not avenge what happened in Missouri. While that's admirable, to many of these old Missouri pukes, it's really just plain ole chicken, ain't it boys?"

The tavern full of 40 men broke out laughing. Several yelled cat-calls at Porter while a couple squawked like hens.

Porter turned and stared at them, then glanced back at Boggs and noticed a look of absolute contempt. Finally Porter holstered his pistols and strode straight for the doorway.

The miners taunted him and laughed as he passed them. His dog jumped down from the stool and followed him. They trod outside, leaving the door swinging.

There, he heard them all still laughing inside. He heard one say, "So here came and went the mighty Porter Rockwell." They all cackled and cawed even harder. Porter realized at that very moment Boggs never needed to shoot him; he had humiliated him so thoroughly that, in every corner of his soul and in every respect imaginable, he had won both his battle and his revenge against Porter a thousand times over.

Outside his cabin, which sat on a small elevation overlooking most of Salt Lake Valley, Porter sat in a chair on his porch and stared at the vast expanse. His ranch took up the first few acres on the horizon westward, and while he was proud of it, he was still feeling sick over Boggs' — a battle that to him represented the entire anti-Mormon movement and their victory over them. He wondered if he would ever have a chance to — in some overt or subtle manner — strike back. Sweeping such unrealistic thoughts from his imagination, he now simply pondered over Emily. He gazed straight into the horizon where the sun had disappeared into the Western sky. Disappearing inside his cabin, he returned to the porch with the portrait of Emily and himself at Nauvoo, and he nailed it beside the door. He then sat on the porch and stared at the painting, lit by the last remnants of twilight.

"A beautiful young lady, ain't she?" he said to Ugly seated on the porch. "'Looks just like her mom."

At midnight he finished brushing down his favorite horse when he noticed a rider in the distance. He ambled curiously forward as the figure came closer. He was stunned when he recognized the rider.

It was Emily.

CHAPTER 12

Not knowing how to react, and hardly believing what he was seeing, Porter remained on his porch staring at Emily as she dismounted from her horse.

She led her horse to the water trough, then walked with indecisive steps toward her father.

With her face full of hope, she immediately lost her smile when she noticed his crestfallen countenance.

With emotions tearing from all sides, Porter stared off, stoic and cold.

"I suppose you're wondering why I'm here," she said, surprised and disconcerted over his refusal to look directly at her.

"My husband Hiram died from a fever, and soon his two boys I was raising were killed by Indians."

Porter still just stood there, fighting his feelings. She arrived beside him, hurt over his continued coldness, and turned to look off in the direction he was staring — at the west horizon. She thought a moment and spoke:

"Papa, I want to stay with you."

He finally looked at her, in turmoil, and managed to only nod. She turned and hugged him. He finally hugged back and she caught him wiping away tears.

Days later fall began turning bright colors. It was October 1851 and Porter drove the buckboard, with Emily beside him, toward a huge barn dance. Ugly, quite aged for a dog, if not now downright ancient, was content to stay at the ranch and visit the baby horses. Emily of course loved the animal and fed him dinner scraps before they had left.

Porter and Emily arrived at the dance just before sunset and observed 200 wagons and horses hitched around the barn. Hearing banjo and fiddle music blaring from the giant doorway, Emily's heart pounded at the prospects of picking up where she had left off before the kidnapping: Two young men interested her — the confident, handsome attendant at the general store and the neighbor boy with his child-like charm. What made her nervous was the time that had passed and if the boys could accept her now. She was now a war-weathered 18 year old widow whose family had been ravaged by disaster — nursing a husband till his death, and discovering the arrow-riddled bodies of her boys — not much younger than she — in a nearby field. When leaving California, she had determined to never marry again, but upon working for her father at their ranch, thoughts of settling her own home had begun seeping in; additionally what haunted her was the fact she still had no children of her own . . .

Upon entering the barn, Porter and his daughter were amazed at the energy inside — the cheer, noise and laughter of over 400 people — clapping to music, dancing, talking, and eating. Soon, dozens flooded onto the "dance floor," and Porter was surprised to spot Emily's hand almost immediately grabbed by a young man. She was practically dragged onto the floor, where the band struck up a spirited rendition of "Turkey in the Straw."

While dancing, Emily caught sight of the young store assistant across the room. He glanced at her and away — then back — surprised to see her. Her eyes also searched for the neighbor boy but, not seeing him — and remembering him as mostly just comfortable anyway, she decided to focus on young Josh who, a couple years previously, had made her feel self-conscious and uncomfortable but also who, now with a few life-toughening experiences under her belt, she no longer felt fearful of — or of practically anything.

Porter scanned the crowd. He discovered himself searching for women who looked only like Luana. Cursing himself for it, he glanced back at Emily. The song was ending and he noticed her eyes on someone across the room — Josh — making a beeline through the dance crowd and arriving at her side.

Emily smiled confidently, straight into his face. He was surprised, and asked her to dance, wondering for a moment if this were the same shy girl he had thought she was.

As the music slowed, they attempted an awkward, country waltz and, while dancing, Josh realized how self-assured Emily actually was.

"Are you the same girl who came to the store, then broke a date with me once upon a time?"

"Yeah," she smiled, "I reckon I am . . . once upon a time."

"What've you been doing since once upon a time?" he said. "And how come you stood me up?"

"What've I been doing?" Emily repeated. "Oh, nothing. 'Got kidnapped, married, raised some kids, and watched them get massacred by savages. 'You?"

He stared at her, stunned. "Your pa never said nothin' about any of that." He stammered, "I-I reckon he's been gone most of the last couple years though himself."

"Busy family," she smiled.

Porter watched disapprovingly as not only Josh continued dancing with her into the second slow song, but three other boys waited on the sidelines to make their moves.

Emily felt happy over this new confidence she possessed — so much so that it staggered Josh. He felt himself for the first time in his life shaking, attracted to her yet actually feeling inferior to her.

"I still think," he said, "we should try that date we talked about. Would you like to come to the regional dance with me next week?"

"No," she said. "I don't know," she added. "Maybe."

The boy realized he was going nuts around this young woman. She knew something about herself she did not know before, he sensed, and that further both attracted and intimidated him.

Porter's scowl was evident only to Brigham. The pioneer leader ambled up to him.

"'Any of these ladies interest you?"

Porter kept his eyes protectively on Emily. "Not a one."

Brigham smiled and said, "Well I'd like you to talk with John Neff over there. He's looking for a partner to sell lumber from the canyon."

"I'll think about it," muttered Porter, eyes still on Emily.

Suddenly a beautiful, blue-eyed young lady with flowing blonde hair danced in front of Porter, half way between him and Emily.

"That," said Brigham," is Neff's daughter."

She was fuller in the face now and inches taller than Porter's last encounter with her. This was the same lass in Nauvoo who had fed him in his wet, muddy longjohns after the Missouri sheriff had chased him through thick woods. The years had been good to her.

"I'll definitely think about it," said Porter, amazed at how she had grown up and out, every which way. "Every which way," he muttered.

She glanced his way and smiled — a mischievous smile that delighted him.

"John Neff is over here," nodded Brigham. "You're still look-ing at his daughter," he teased.

As Porter turned to walk toward Neff, Emily stopped her father:

"Pa, I've got a ride home for later." She strode toward the refreshment table with Josh, hand in hand.

Porter watched her stroll away, and he scowled.

"He's a nice boy," said Brigham with a twinkle.

Porter grunted, gazed at Brigham and smirked, snatching his fatherly possessiveness right in its tracks.

"I guess I should stop it, huh?"

Brigham smiled, and added, "By the way, what did you think of that play you performed in back at Nauvoo — *Pizarro?*"

His mind raced with curiosity. "I didn't mind it, but I wasn't real busy then."

"Well you've been volunteered for the same part. The play's in two weeks." Brigham walked away.

"Is this your idea?" called Porter after him.

"Actually," called back Brigham, "the play's director — he asked me to ask you when I saw you again."

"Well still nobody's asked me yet," said Porter.

"That was my way of asking you," smirked Brigham, then he disappeared into the crowd, chuckling.

Porter approached John Neff and re-acquainted himself with a handshake. They spoke of lumber and the necessity of building a road to haul it from the canyon south of Mill Creek, so the townspeople could build bigger cabins, fences, and barns. Presently, John caught Porter staring at someone on the dance floor.

"Did you hear the last thing I said?" said Neff.

"Of course."

"Who were you looking at?" said Neff. "That's my daughter you've been staring at!" he chided.

"Now why would I look at your daughter?" said Porter, embarrassed.

"Aren't you a little ashamed? Your own daughter's only a few years younger."

Porter found the fellow's humor abrasive. "Can we talk about the business? I'm not interested in your daughter."

"Yeah, you are." He chuckled and winked. "Everybody is."

"All right, I won't look at her again!"

"Well her name's Mary Ann."

"What?"

"In case you're wondering," said Neff, who winked again and walked away to the refreshment table. He turned his head back. "And she's 22, you old goat; you really ought to be ashamed."

Porter stood there a moment thinking, then began treading his way through the dance crowd closer to the lass . . . but only to observe her, too embarrassed to actually ask such a pretty young filly to dance.

John Neff watched from the refreshment table and smiled, shaking his head. His wife had been too tired to attend the event; so at her insistence, he and his daughter, Mary Ann, had ridden to the dance together and now he was enjoying every second, most especially mingling with friends, though they were decidedly not as excited to see him, due to his strange personality.

Porter arrived closer to Mary Ann and glanced at her through the crowd. Suddenly she locked eyes on him, surprised to be stared at by such an older fellow. Then she recognized him — even with his hair much shorter — and her mouth literally fell open.

Presently a 23 year old stud swaggered in front of her and grabbed her hand. She laughed with the boy as he dragged her onto the dance floor. Apparently they were close friends, Porter surmised, so he shrugged and walked away, figuring to watch more from a distance. Then he toyed with the idea of actually asking her to dance. The idea appealed more and more to him as the seconds ticked by, until . . . in the window beside him . . . he caught his own reflection. He studied it a moment and saw an aging veteran — of both battlefields and domestic warfare — who was not only 38 but a 38 with sunken eyes and a heavy soul. His eyes then focused on the scene reflected in the window behind him — Mary Ann, laughing with a young, handsome buck, while several more of the same waited in the wings. Porter's eyes floated down with increasing self-consciousness from the mirror-like window, and he slowly retreated toward the wide door. He was ready to go home.

Just as he passed under the giant portal to leave for his ranch, someone stepped in front of him. He was taken back to see . . .

Mary Ann standing there, blocking his path, sporting a huge, charming smile. While momentarily flattered, he shrunk from embarrassment, realizing he looked like an old man compared to this 22 year old beauty.

"We haven't danced yet," said Mary Ann. "My father wanted to introduce us. I guess he and Brigham told me about you before the dance tonight."

Porter glanced over at John Neff through the crowd — who caught sight of him and flashed a big smile. Porter smirked back, realizing Neff's teasings were only for his own amusement.

"So, I'm Mary Ann Neff," she said, extending her hand forward to shake. "And I remember you well," she giggled. "I believe the outfit you wore was . . . red . . . wasn't it?"

After turning that color himself, recalling with too much clarity the longjohns incident, Porter laughed for a moment like a youngster, delighted with the effervescence in her voice. But when he saw several people nearby staring at him, he realized he had blurted out a silly, school-boy giggle, and he flushed with embarrassment. Getting control of himself, but distracted by the curious stares of several older women, he shook her hand formally and felt a tenderness and warmth of spirit underneath the handshake. Then, still feeling incredibly shy, he muttered, "Yeah, nice to see you," then he excused himself.

She watched with curiosity as he strode past her through the portal and outside.

As he approached his carriage he decided to glance back . . .

And there she was, leaning against the doorway outside, still studying him. Another young man then grabbed her arm and led her away, to the side of the barn.

Porter continued walking toward the carriage. When he arrived there, he unhitched his horse and glanced back again at Mary Ann, who was now arriving with the boy at the porch of a house near the barn.

Porter climbed onto his buckboard and looked again at her. She was now leaning forward on the porch railing, with the boy beside her. Then another young suitor arrived. All three talked and laughed. A couple seconds later another fellow arrived. The three boys soon seated themselves on a bench at the edge of the porch, while Mary Ann sat on a chair facing them.

As Porter pulled up the reigns, he noticed a long rope on the ground below the porch. Then he glanced again at Mary Ann and the boys and noticed they were at the edge of a virtual lake of mud. His eyes scanned quickly left — to one end of the long porch — and there he spotted a horse hitched to it. He recalled the time years earlier when he had used a similar rope to shake off the competition. But he shook his head, talking himself out of it. As he prepared to snap the reigns for the ride home, a thought hit him. He lowered the reigns, and glanced again at the rope on the ground . . .

At the porch, Mary Ann laughed and talked to the three young men who were vying for her attention.

Nearby, a hand whacked a horse's rear.

The horse moved forward, tightening a rope. As Mary Ann stopped talking, the rope began moving the boys' bench. Suddenly, their bench jerked backwards — and all three went flying into the lake of mud.

Mary Ann shrieked with surprise — then caught sight of a figure standing 70 yards away in the doorway of the barn. She squinted and realized who it was . . .

Porter was leaning inside the portal, smiling at her, with arms confidently folded. She stood there a moment and gawked at him, amazed. Then burst out laughing.

The three boys were meanwhile slipping and sliding, trying to make their way back to the porch. One suddenly lost balance and knocked over the other two. They all fell into the deep, soupy mud with another loud splash. All three boys angrily snapped at each other, then good-naturedly broke out laughing. But they stopped laughing when they looked up and saw she was gone . . .

Inside the barn, Porter and Mary Ann danced. A fast waltz played as they stared like children into each others' eyes — and laughed.

CHAPTER 13

Next day, Porter played with Ugly in the corral, tossing sticks for him to fetch. Leaving the animal with Emily to keep her company, he rode to the ranch of John Neff, two days south at the mouth of Big Cottonwood Canyon in Salt Lake Valley.

"Come in," said Mary Neff, his wife, repairing the corral gate, "and have refreshment." Porter may have had a difficult time recognizing Mary Ann's mother, Mary, even if they had been better acquainted: Mary Neff was now almost totally grey. Her hair was grey, her face, her eyes; she looked as though the desert sun had baked the very color out of her. Even her voice was grey.

"My daughter will get us drinks."

When they entered the cabin, he got a better look at Mary Ann — without her face powdered nor her hair fancily combed. She was every bit as beautiful as at the dance.

Mary Ann stared at Porter, surprised to see him with no advance notice, but she said nothing.

He perceived in her a faint tremble.

Her mother noticed nothing going on between them. She had heard her daughter talk of Porter years earlier and laugh about the longjohns incident.

"John told me he talked with you at the dance," said Mrs. Neff. "He's looking over the canyon south of Mill Creek today. I guess he talked with you about the lumber there? He could sure use a partner. The mill keeps him busy enough. I tell him he needs help."

"Yes, ma'am."

As Mary Ann and Porter glanced at each other, Mary Ann flushed.

Her mother did not see that either. She began setting the dinner table. "Can you stay for supper, Porter?" said Mrs. Neff.

Mary Ann broke in:

"I really need to tidy up a little, Mother."

Porter was feeling more and more awkward before blurting out, "And I really need to get back to breed the horses. I mean feed the horses."

"Perhaps some other time," said Mrs. Neff. The living room sunk into deathly silence, but she still did not see anything going on between the two.

Mary Neff then studied her daughter, wondering what the devil all this silence was about.

"Honey," she finally said to her daughter, "do you remember Brother Rockwell from Nauvoo?"

She practically whispered. "Sorta."

Mrs. Neff still could see nothing unusual.

Porter studied Mary Ann in fuller light — compared to the torch-lit barn — and realized that with several more years to her, she had attained more character to her face, and even a great beauty, but none of the coldness of great beauty.

Her smile turned to a warm gaze.

His smile turned into a stare — a clear, piercing glint, and the girl's mother cast her eyes back and forth between the two.

Mrs. Neff was surprised at what she was finally seeing.

Leaving the canyon, Porter ran into John Neff and solidified the partnership with a handshake. "We'll make decent money," said Neff. "When can you move down?"

Porter had thought over the need to move into the valley — he wished to be nearer to Brigham since accepting the badge, although he was not very active chasing outlaws as yet, and he primarily wanted to be near Mary Ann; in short it was time to move from Porter's Springs and return to civilization.

Over the next couple weeks he and Mary Ann moved their belongings and few animals down to the mouth of Mill Creek, only a mile from the Neffs' ranch.

Porter sat on his porch and gazed over the new property — with its new fences having gone up quickly, and he smiled, patting Ugly on his grey fur.

"Beautiful, huh, boy?"

"Thank you," said Mary Ann, entering the porch with a smile. "You're right, Papa."

"What're you so happy about?"

"Ten families moved down to the valley here from Brigham City, and two of them are Josh and Tommy's families — from what the paper said.

"Wonderful," scowled Porter. "Just wonderful. Just what I needed to hear." He had hoped those suitors were history.

Mary Ann smiled. "Life's looking pretty good right now, I'd say."

Porter also suddenly smiled. If only she knew how much.

Ugly saw his smile and wagged his tail.

Porter drove his wagon to pick up Mary Ann for a play. It was January, and he shivered in the icy winds. But not from the cold. He held a lead part in the production.

Not that he wasn't prepared. Indeed, as Brigham had noted to ease his nerves, he had performed the same play at Nauvoo years earlier — and in fact the very same part — but tonight was opening night and the woman by whom he happened to be smitten would be sitting on the front row staring at his every flaw.

As he arrived at the "John Neff Mill" he found that Mary Ann, in a yellow dress with olive skin and long, Scandinavian blonde hair, looked stunning. He also found himself wishing she had been struck with a mild case of malaria.

"Hurry up, Port," she said, climbing onto the buckboard.

He climbed beside her.

"I can't wait to see this," she said.

"Neither can I," he mumbled. Adding to his consternation was this bold and naked fact: His daughter did not yet even know of young Miss Mary Ann Neff . . .

He hesitantly snapped the reins and his wagon pulled away from her cabin. Of further distress was the fact that Emily was going to the play also . . . on her first date as a divorcee, with some hot-shot, good-looking kid about whom he knew absolutely nothing. Josh Anderson.

———————

Porter was dressed as a Spanish conquistador. He peered from behind a stage curtain at 500 people packing the theatre. He then discovered Mary Ann sitting on the front row, dead center. Three rows behind her sat Emily and her date, Josh. Porter's face blushed with nervousness.

Suddenly, he heard his cue. The play was a half hour in progress, and he was about to make his entrance. He felt his throat tighten. He scuttled away from the curtain toward center stage. All eyes were on him. The walk seemed endless. He tried to not look at Mary Ann, but when he heard whispers, he wondered if they were disparaging, if they were about him, and most importantly — if Mary Ann had heard them.

Before him now stood a Peruvian warrior sporting a spear. On cue, Porter drew his sword. The Peruvian performed adequately, finishing his impassioned speech, and Porter readied himself for the reply.

He forgot his reply.

He glared in horror at the Peruvian.

He broke into a cold sweat.

He heard a whisper behind him.

The director backstage tried prompting him, but Porter could not understand the man, who was burdened by a French accent thicker than horse glue.

Porter would rather have faced a thousand screaming warriors, he thought to himself, than this. The director's words came louder. People in the audience overheard the director and began to chuckle. The director modulated even harsher. The French accent downright comical in its exaggeration. Additional chuckles.

Still unable to hear his director, Porter decided to do the only thing he could. He faced the Peruvian and exclaimed, "Excuse me." He then turned to the audience and said with an embarassed smile, "Escuse me." The nervous chuckles in his behalf began to increase.

He lumbered over to the curtain where the director whispered his line loudly. The audience politely held back its laughter, although a few more giggles escaped.

Porter then clumped back across the stage to the Peruvian. He stretched forth his sword and boldly proclaimed, "Another word, grey-headed ruffian, and I strike!" He sounded wooden and over-dramatic.

The audience began to snicker.

Porter cringed. He sought out Mary Ann's eyes and within them found sympathy. He thought he found sympathy. He then caught her laughing at him also.

"Do something," said the Peruvian softly.

"Do what?" whispered Porter.

The audience now began to laugh heartily. The Peruvian character blushed with embarrassment for Porter, then unexpectedly also began to laugh. Porter, seeing his laughter, was caught completely off guard and suddenly gasped with stage fright. He was completely frozen. Hearing one loud belly laugh however at the back of the auditorium — belonging unmistakably to Brigham — caught his fancy and suddenly he relapsed, seeing the absurdity and the levity of the whole thing — and his anguish completely melted. He broke into a smile. And then began to laugh also. The audience howled.

The other actors on stage kept their laughter silent however. Their shoulders merely shook. Then Porter collected his thoughts. He was supposed to do something. What was he supposed to do?

He turned to the director behind the curtain and finally proclaimed loudly above all the laughter, "Shall I stick him?"

The audience exploded. They stamped their feet and clapped and cheered as they laughed. Porter focused right in on Mary Ann and saw her practically falling out of her seat.

The audience now rocked with laughter and simply could not stop — and neither could he.

Backstage, as he washed off his make-up, he relived the entire scene and, in anger, he kicked a table. But again broke out laughing . . .

As the crowd dispersed from the Social Hall theatre, Porter and the other actors greeted the audience in the lobby. He waited for Mary Ann, anxious to laugh with her over the incident, but simultaneously wondering if she would even accompany him home after such a disaster. Emily suddenly appeared with her date, Josh. She quickly hugged Porter and then introduced her young escort to her father.

"I reckon I need boning up on my Thespian skills," he admitted aloud sheepishly.

Josh shook hands with him, but all Porter saw was a blur for his face, such was his self-consciousness. He was additionally distraught that both young women would any minute meet and possibly be overwhelmed by the existence of the other . . . and especially with the fact that both were essentially the same age.

"Porter, you were so funny!" cried out Mary Ann.

He noticed Mary Ann through the crowd, and winced. He looked right at Emily beside him and forced a small, agonizing smile. Mary Ann then made her way through the crowded lobby and grasped his hand:

"Where did you learn to be so funny?" she laughed.

He presently realized he was funny, all right. He was practically the town clown, and in a second would be forced to introduce his 22 year old date to his 18 year old daughter.

"Uh, Mary Ann, this is Emily."

Both young women eyed each other curiously, forced a smile, and shook hands.

"Well, Papa," said Emily, visibly taken back. "I've got to go."

Emily and her escort then got swept away in the crowd and out the front doors as Mary Ann spoke up, "I suppose she's the same age as me." She thought a moment. "Doesn't that make you feel weird?" she teased.

Porter stared in horror at the chandelier. Straight up.

CHAPTER 14

Taking Mary Ann home that night, Porter rode on the buckboard with his arm around the young lass's shoulders and realized how good — how comfortable and natural — it felt to have a woman beside him again. Especially this particular woman. If only he weren't shaking from embarrassment, he realized, he'd feel a bit more comfortable and natural.

He then cleared his throat and told her he would not be seeing her a few days. He feared moving too fast with her, but did not explain his reasons.

She turned quiet.

After he took her home he returned to his cabin, realizing all the way home he had just made a supreme, once-in-a-lifetime blunder to his possible, once-in-a-lifetime love. His dog waited by the glowing fireplace, and wagged its tail when he arrived.

"Tell me this night didn't happen," he said to Ugly.

Porter lay in his bed while Emily fed the horses a hundred yards from the cabin. It was just before sunrise. Ugly slept on the floor in front of the still warm fireplace. Window shutters flapped in the breeze, banging the wood, and Porter slept right through it.

What awakened him was the caress of a gentle hand. Mary Ann was seated on his bed.

"What're you doing here?" he said, startled and sitting up.

"Brought a surprise for you." She pulled from behind her back a bunch of freshly picked wildflowers. "What an adorable dog. Where'd you get him?"

"Stole him from the wilderness."

Ugly extended his paw, and she laughed, then shook hands with him.

"He's the smartest critter I've ever seen," he said.

Suddenly she sneezed all over the dog's face.

"Whoa," said Porter, smiling as Ugly shook his head.

"I can't help it," said Mary Ann. "Whenever I'm around dogs, I sneeze."

Porter sat up straighter and noticed her staring at him. "What're you looking at?" he said.

She smiled, "Your longjohns. They look the same as the last ones I saw you in. Now it's your turn."

"What do you mean?"

"To tell me what you're staring at," she said.

"I reckon," he said, not certain how to phrase it, "you're the most forward female I've ever met."

"Thank you."

"I wasn't complimenting you," he said.

"Yes, you were. I can only take that as a compliment."

He arose and gazed out the window. He reaized that the soft demeanor of this woman — her gentle inner nature — contrasted the semi-aloof, mysterious nature of Luana that had so attracted him upon first meeting. He noticed Emily outside watching the cabin while feeding the cattle. She obviously was concerned over Porter's visitor.

"Don't worry," said Mary Ann, "she doesn't bother me."

"Well she bothers me," offered Porter.

"Are you relieved?" said Mary Ann.

"Over what?"

"That she doesn't bother me?"

"Yeah," he chuckled, "I guess I am."

"Well, to be honest, I guess she does bother me."

Porter stopped chuckling.

"Not her age being close to mine or anything like that — but the fact you'd let what she thinks upset you."

"Well, she's my daughter. So I reckon I do care what she thinks."

"You miss my point, but I won't argue," smiled Mary Ann.

Porter sighed silently and glanced back at her, then sauntered toward the kitchen table. "She even laid out a meal for me," he said. "She's somethin', ain't she?"

"You must be very proud of her."

He nodded. "Have a seat."

"I've eaten, thanks," she said. "And Pa is expecting me back at the ranch to help out." She sneezed again. The dog looked a bit frightened and backed away.

"Tell him I'll work on the road this week," said Porter.

"That's what hired hands are for," said Mary Ann. "Pa admires you for working along side them, but he thinks you're a little crazy doing it."

"Oh," he grunted, digging into his buttered fresh bread, bacon, and scrambled eggs.

"Why're you that way?" she added.

"What way? Working with farm hands? I like to work with the boys. Just 'cause I hire 'em doesn't mean I'm above 'em."

"No, I mean restless?" she said.

"What do you mean — restless?"

"I see it clear as sunshine in you."

He stopped eating and stared at her.

"But there's no reason for it anymore," she added. "None at all."

"Well I'm glad to hear that, whatever it means," he said.

Emily suddenly entered the cabin. "Well, Papa, what have we here?" She smiled, stepped towards them a few strides, and extended her hand to Mary Ann.

Mary Ann smiled warmly and shook Emily's hand. Mary Ann glanced at Porter and noticed beads of sweat on his forehead.

"My, the morning's passing quickly," said Emily. "I must be getting back to Pa. I'll tell him what you said, Mister Rockwell." To Emily, Mary Ann then added, "We have something in common."

Porter looked down, wondering what in tarnation she was going to say next.

"It looks like our fathers are partners," said Emily as she stepped towards the door. She looked back at Porter and winked.

"Bye, Mr. Rockwell."

Emily, catching her overt flirtation, gazed at Mary Ann's swagger out the door, then glanced at her father.

"Uh, yeah, bye," managed Porter.

Emily sat at the table across from Porter and sighed, then spoke:

"*Mister* Rockwell?"

Porter sheepishly looked at Emily, then stared at his food. He could not eat for a few moments until he could catch a second wind.

CHAPTER 15

As Emily planted crops in a small, plowed field west of their cabin, she noticed her father arriving horseback with Ugly seated behind his saddle. Presently, she was in his shadow as she stared up at him. His face was a darkened silhouette against the blaring sun behind his head.

"Where're you going?" she said.

"Town. For supplies."

"Be back this afternoon?"

"Or tonight," he said.

"Must be getting lots of supplies," she probed.

"Maybe. Will you be here when I get back?"

Shaking her head no, she replied, "But I'll have supper waiting for you on the stove. We're having stew."

Porter cleared his throat. "Well take some in a covered mug over to him."

She smiled, "What're you talking about — him?"

"I think we both know Josh will enjoy your special stew — all red-blooded boys would."

"I guess you don't mind me seeing him, then?" she said.

"I didn't say that. But I can read your mind."

"How do you always know what's in my mind?" she said with another smile.

"Half of it's mine."

She rolled her eyes, "That's scary. Papa, what do you have against Josh?"

"He looks too good for his own good," he replied. "And he's never had to use other parts of his soul to get places with people."

"He's far deeper than that," she said.

"Yeah, I'll believe it when I see it."

"Well you don't worry about me," she argued. "Josh is only a friend. Do you have a special interest in anyone yourself, Papa?" She dreaded her father wanting any woman except the one in Minnesota, and still hoped deep down Luana would leave her third husband and come West to reconcile with him.

"I have no interest in anyone, honey," said Porter, "except maybe as friends."

From his parroted response, she suspected differently. On the horizon she noticed a horseman approaching. Porter followed her eyes, and immediately recognized the old neighbor boy, Tommy Clayton. Porter glanced at Mary Ann, who winced. He could sense his daughter felt torn. "Excuse me, honey," said Porter to her as he waved at the boy and took off on a fast round trot toward the city. "You sort out things and I'll sort things out," he said, his voice fading away from her. "And together we'll sort through things," he chuckled.

Tommy Clayton rode up to Emily, who politely smiled.

"It's been awhile," said Tommy.

"It has," said Emily.

"I heard your Pa telling my folks yesterday about your experiences in California. I'm sorry."

"That's life," she said.

"And death," he smiled. "I'm so sorry. I didn't mean to make light of that. I reckon it's all still pretty close to your heart."

"I reckon," she said, forcing a smile and looking up. "I didn't see you at the stake dance last night. Or the one up at Brigham City."

"Didn't have much reason to go," he said. "I mean I've been busy with the new ranch — moving and all."

"Did you finish?"

"Did, in fact," he said. "Which gives me a reason to celebrate. You feel like going to another stake dance up the valley? That way I could celebrate with you."

She collected a mouthful of air in her cheeks and blew out a long, silent sigh. "Let me think on it," she said.

"I reckon you're busy now that you're back, huh?" he said. "Maybe I'll check back in a few weeks," he added, turning his horse.

Emily was surprised to find how much she liked him. She felt caught between an over-confident charmer who excited her, and this lad who, although just this side of homeliness — and terribly insecure — tugged with equal strength at her emotions. Tommy had an honesty and vulnerability portrayed in a manner that she could easily discern and find disarmingly attractive, a trait most never-married girls her age would readily shun for the charismatic, clever Josh.

"Father doesn't approve of either of you," she mumbled under her breath where he could not hear. "What am I to do?"

"What's that?" he said.

She shook her head and smiled. "I'd be glad to go with you to that dance."

"I'll see you there then," he smiled, starting to turn away.

"Maybe you better pick me up in your carriage," she offered.

"Yeah, of course," he said, flushing. "I'll see you tomorrow at sunset. I mean if you're ready. I mean of course you'll be ready. I mean if you don't have to do chores for your pa that'll cause you to change your mind. So, right when the sun sets, I'll see you — unless it's cloudy and we don't know right when the sun sets, and — "

"Tommy?" she said. "I'll see you tomorrow."

"Right," he replied, then turned his roan and in his excitement broke straight into a gallop, his horse's hooves throwing up dirt clods on Emily's dress.

She smiled, watching him ride away. She was even more surprised feeling her heart waiting with anticipation to see him the next day.

"I'm thrilled to be caught between what Pa sees as a no-account — and a shallow good-for-nothing with only looks," she said aloud to herself. She chuckled, then, turning toward the house and walking towards it, she kicked a loose rock, angry over wanting to please a father in whose eyes she could *never* win.

———

Hours later, Porter walked through an aisle of farming equipment in a hardware store. Ugly followed several feet behind and explored the interesting odors a general store could offer. Suddenly Porter glanced out the open door and caught sight of Mary Ann. He decided to study her, so he meandered closer to the doorway. She did not see him inside. A remarkably handsome fellow, about 22, soon strode up on the street and began flirting. Behind the boy waited two attractive young ladies. Mary Ann smiled in response to a question from him but shook her head.

Porter barely heard the boy speak: "How about Saturday? I haven't asked these ladies because I've had my eye on you awhile."

Porter stared curiously as Mary Ann turned the fellow down. Not giving up, the young man circled her. She ignored him while she resumed her walk towards a nearby shop.

But the boy was apparently not used to being shunned, so he followed her, then confidently reached his hand up to her face and caressed it while he spoke further.

Mary Ann stopped, made a half-turn to face him, and suddenly slapped him.

The young stud flew to the ground, and the girls giggled.

Porter was impressed, and slowly shook his head, realizing he felt a bit more secure about Mary Ann. Indeed, she had passed the faithfulness test with flying colors. Walking outside, Porter pulled gold coins from his vest pocket and handed one to each of the participants. The two young ladies and the young man took their pay as the fellow nursed a bloody nose.

"I deserve two of these," said the boy, rubbing his face.

"Two bloody noses?"

"No — two coins — she packs a wallop, mister."

Porter smiled as he walked past him, and flipped another gold coin to him. Flying end over end, the coin sailed high in the air. The boy watched it disappear in the blinding sun, then suddenly reappear right in front of him. He reached out with his hand and snagged it in mid-air.

Porter smiled with hope.

As Emily stirred beef and vegetable stew, she heard horsehooves approaching. Assuming the rider to be Porter, she continued stirring. Soon, footsteps across the porch entered the front door. Realizing they sounded differently than her father's, she turned.

There stood Mary Ann, with eyes of red from either restlessness or anger.

CHAPTER 16

After a long pause of assessing one another, Emily Rockwell invited Mary Ann Neff inside.

Mary Ann stood inside the door somewhat nervously, staring indifferently at the stew pot on the stove. She wondered if Porter's daughter knew much — if anything — about them seeing each other, and even hoped to get some "inside information" of what her pa thought of her.

"Have a seat," offered Emily.

Mary Ann did. Both women waited for the other to speak. They each had a question in mind.

Finally, Emily broke the silence. "'Here to see Pa?"

"Well outside I could see his favorite riding horse was gone," said Mary Ann, "so I thought I'd just visit you while I was here."

Emily liked her honesty. "Did you come here because your pa wants to get my pa a message?" probed Emily.

"What?" said Mary Ann, surprised.

In that response, Emily had her answer. And from Emily's reaction to her response, Mary Ann had her answer: She knew Porter had not divulged to Emily any of the progress of their relationship.

"I was just wondering," said Emily.

"Yeah," mumbled Mary Ann, both realizing the other had her answer. Emily then delayed the inevitable, feeling the air was simply too awkward to level with Emily as she had hoped. "Well . . . I reckon I . . . "

"Would you like to stay and eat?" said Emily, angry at herself for making the offer.

"Sure. I guess. Well actually . . . I'd best be going."

"Well thanks for coming," said Emily quickly, wanting to get her out the door.

As Mary Ann walked toward the door, she stopped and turned to face Emily:

"Thanks for being a new friend."

Emily stared at her, wondering what the devil that meant. She had no intention of being friends with this forward young lady.

"I mean," clarified Mary Ann, trying to make headway into a realm of friendliness, "it's good our pa's are friends and I thought maybe — "

"Yeah . . . sure," said Emily with a bit more warmth, trying to cover the critical glare she had just given her.

"Well, I'm sure we'll see more of each other," said Mary Ann, continuing toward and out the door. Leaving the porch, she stopped and studied Emily's self-portrait. She finally turned and left, fighting a whirlwind of conflicting feelings.

Emily stopped stirring the pot and felt overwhelmed by the thought that indeed maybe she would be seeing more of Mary Ann — too much of her. "How could Pa even look at a girl just older than me?" thought Emily. Feeling sickened, she walked to the doorway and stared at Mary Ann riding away on the road northward. Suddenly from over a bluff, Porter appeared, riding homeward on the same road. Emily watched them in the distance as Mary Ann stopped to chat and laugh with him, then ride together off to the east, toward her ranch. Emily felt a knot in the pit of her stomach.

At the modest cabin beside the "John Neff Mill" at Mill Creek, seated inside at the dining table, Porter finished eating.

John Neff spoke up, "I am frankly amazed . . ."

Porter thought, 'All right. I am about to be chewed out for courting his young filly. He didn't mind me getting to know her, but now that he sees how dumb it looks — with me actually seated with her here, twice her age, and eating like I'm trying to be one of the family — he's fed up. He must be fed up. He's so fed up he's sick to his stomach.'

"Yeah," said Neff. "I am truly amazed. You fit right in with us and look downright perfect for Mary Ann."

"Papa!" shouted Mary Ann, blushing.

"But I tell you what I'm also amazed by, Porter," continued Neff. "It's that you put in so much time with the road crew."

"It goes faster that way."

"He just thinks of himself as one of the workers — and not the supervisors," said Mary Ann. "I like that."

"Right now I think of myself as full," said Porter, rising. "Sister Neff, thanks for the feast."

Mary Neff beamed.

John Neff continued, "Mary here talked me into staying on with just the mill part of the company, so I want to turn over the papers to the sales and foresting to my kin, Franklin Neff. He'll be a good partner with you. Is that all right with you?"

"Yes," said Porter. "I know Franklin. He's as honest as they get."

"Mary Ann likes him, too," said John. "So I'm glad we can keep it in the family, so to speak."

"I'm family already?" said Porter.

Mary Ann blushed. "Let's go outside, Porter."

Mrs. Neff piped up, "Honey, are we embarrassing you?"

Mary Ann stood. "Of course not," she said, turning even redder. "I just want to show Porter the mill — and how it works. Yeah, that's it. C'mon, Porter." She smiled at her own humor and practically ran to the doorway.

Porter also smiled, looking at John Neff, and realized it was his turn to wink.

Porter and Mary Ann walked moments later in the moonlight. Ugly was waiting patiently by the house and whipped his tail back and forth as he observed Porter approaching with a meaty bone. Feasting away moments later, he watched Porter and Mary Ann ambling toward the stream.

Porter told her he may have to hunt outlaws that were plaguing their people down in Utah Valley, 40 miles south of her ranch around Point of the Mountain. "I heard they're stealing horses," he said.

"You just want to get away from me," she half-joked, probing for his degree of interest.

"I think I may be taking up marshalling," he said. "I was officially elected in '49, but now it's time I work at it."

"The deadly brotherhood of the gun?" she said pointedly through a forced smile.

"Even though I told Brigham I don't wanna fight, I reckon deep down I do."

"Why?"

"What I went through growing up — seeing bullies have their way, and later seeing the lawlessness, and the mobs."

"But is that an excuse now?" said Mary Ann.

"I've had a couple things awakened in me since I ran into him."

"Who?"

"Boggs."

"What're you talking about — when?"

"California."

"You actually saw Governor Boggs there?"

Porter nodded, "But he could see me a lot better."

"What're you going to do about it?" she probed.

"Prove him wrong."

"About what?"

"He said I got an anger that'll drive me to kill. And I am proving him right about one thing. I am taking the badge."

"Maybe he knows you would, and he manipulated you to accept it because he wants you dead."

"Maybe — but I don't care what he thinks."

"So why do you want to do marshalling?"

"To prove I can be a peacemaker. With no anger. I feel plenty of anger towards injustice so I need to prove to myself I can work free from it and be what Pa wanted me to be. But I can't prove anything unless I'm in the thick of the battle — can I?" he smiled.

"You're really confusing me," she said. "Why not just give it all up?"

"If you look at Mount Timpanogos over there," he said pointing south, "you can't just sit still and admire the tallest peak in the mountain range."

"Why not?"

"I guess that's the difference between you and me. I can't just look at it."

She knew what he meant, and nodded, but feared how numbered his days might be.

"There's outlaws here that are so ruthless — and skilled at killing," she said, "they could take on any of the cowardly mobs you've faced before. I don't think you know what you're up against now."

"Well I guess I'll find out," he said. "Somebody's gotta do it." He gave her a long hug and mounted his horse.

"Have you got an assignment?" she said, looking up at him in the moon's reflection.

"Not yet, but Brigham's been sending down messengers the last couple days about the Utah Valley outlaws. I reckon he wants to know if I'm taking the badge or not."

———————

Mary Ann's face registered pain as he turned and rode into the night with his dog.

CHAPTER 17

Brigham Young sat in his study sifting through papers on a hot afternoon. He heard a knock at the portal of his office. He looked up and saw Porter in the open framework.

"Come in, Porter. Have a seat."

He entered with Ugly and made his way to one of the leather-backed chairs across the desk from Brigham.

"Is that dog still alive?" said Brigham.

"Naw, I carry his corpse around. Taught it how to walk."

"Very funny," Marshal. So . . . can we call you that?"

"There's something else about that animal," said Porter. "He's the best friend a marshal could have."

Brigham nodded, smiling. He opened his desk drawer, took the badge, and tossed it across the desk to him. Then slid a neatly designed wooden box across the desk to him. "Here's a couple other friends you might find handy."

Porter studied it curiously.

"Open it," said Brigham.

Porter did, and his eyes lit up. It was a pair of new Colt Navy 1851 revolvers. Porter had heard of them, but he was now among the first in the West to own them. Unlike the earlier pepper shot revolvers, they could fire six reliable shots as fast as one could fan the cylinder.

Porter pulled one out and spun the cylinder. "This is a beaut."

"The best there is," said Brigham. "For the best there is," he winked.

Porter sat back, amazed by the weapons. They were the most artistically attractive revolvers he had ever seen as well, and had a feel and look of perfection. In his free time he would practice shooting them before breakfast each morning, he decided.

"And here's a bag of lead balls and a bag of powder," added Brigham. "We'll provide all you'll need. I assume you'll practice."

"I'm planning that already."

"Good," said Brigham. "So you got the word from my messengers?"

Porter nodded.

"I mean about the horsethieves assignment."

Porter nodded again.

"So?" said Brigham.

Porter grabbed the box under one arm and arose. With his right hand he held the silver badge at waist-level and inspected it carefully. A sunbeam coming through the window hit the badge and cast a glow on his face.

Brigham noticed it and sat back. "Isn't this a bad time to finally like that badge?"

"How do you mean?"

"Don't misunderstand — we need you — but it seems to me you have more important things to be doing with a daughter at home right now."

Porter appreciated his concerns, but shook his head.

"Don't you think she needs help being raised?" said Brigham.

"She's raised."

"She strikes me as having had a few rough years — a *difficult* life in fact — and perhaps she needs to be emotionally nourished by a strong parent for awhile."

"You don't know how independent she is."

"I do know she needs you."

"Well I think she doesn't want that."

"It's your choice," said Brigham. "But I hope you don't do anything you'll regret — either from her standpoint in your relationship with her — or from what you do under the stars with that badge, trying to prove something."

Porter looked at him curiously.

"I don't know what your inner concerns are," said Brigham, "but I do not want them getting you in trouble flirting with death."

Porter stared at him, amazed he seemed to see the same things Boggs saw.

"Why do you look so surprised?" said Brigham.

"Not only can the devil's anointed see through me, but so can the Lord's."

Brigham stared at him curiously as Porter arose and left without another word.

CHAPTER 18

Porter entered his cabin, freshly back from seeing Brigham. Emily had waited up for him, reading by candlelight and petting Ugly's head on her lap.

"Did you think I'd ever get back before you?" she said, "Even though I had an evening out on the town?"

"Yeah, I reckon it's a little surprising to see you back this early," he smiled. "Where did you go tonight?"

"A play at the Social Hall. It wasn't as funny — I mean — good — as *Pizarro.*"

"Thanks," he said, rolling his eyes.

"So where did you go?"

"Brigham's place. And before that to the Neff's for supper."

"Oh, so you and John Neff spent the evening together talking business?" she probed with a smile.

"Not exactly."

"Then what exactly?" she said, still maintaining a smile but her heart now churning.

"Well I've become friends with the whole family."

"Oh, the whole family."

"Actually, his daughter Mary Ann."

"Oh?"

He felt cornered, so he attempted casualness in his voice:

"We've become fairly good friends."

"Fairly good?"

"Pretty good."

"Pretty good?" she said.

"Very good."

"Close friends?" she said.

"Very close."

"Extra special, close friends," she said, losing her smile.

"So what's wrong with that?"

"What's wrong?" she said. "You're courting a girl, Pa. Not even a woman. A girl only four years older than me! How am I supposed to feel?"

"You weren't calling yourself a girl in California."

"Well it's a different world back there — and maybe I married a little young."

"Well that's the first time I ever heard you admit a mistake about all that," said Porter, still hurting over it.

"I didn't say it was a mistake," said Emily. "I said maybe I was a little young."

"So you still did nothing wrong marrying who you did or when or how you did it?"

"That was my business," she said. "And it still is!"

"Then it's my business who I marry!" he exploded. "So I want you to keep out of it!"

"You're marrying that girl?" she said incredulously.

"I didn't say marry."

"I heard you say marry."

"I said the wrong word — I meant court."

"Don't we marry those we court?"

"I don't know — do you have wedding plans with Josh then?" he said.

"Why do you have to attack me?"

"'Cause maybe I ain't perfect when somebody attacks me," he said, calming. "Maybe some folks want to fight back at everything," he added introspectively. "And maybe I'm falling in love with her, and maybe I shouldn't do that."

"I don't believe you could do this," she muttered.

"What right have you to say what I feel?"

"What right have you?" she demanded. "You disapprove of all the boys I've ever liked!"

"I have the right — you're my daughter — and I have experience knowing who would be good for you and who won't!"

"So, you want to run my life?"

"Only protect you."

"Well I'm protecting me now," she said. "And I know I can't handle having this girl in my life."

"I'm sorry," he said after thinking. "Emily, if you don't want me to see her again, I won't."

Emily blew out a sigh of thoughtfulness. "Papa, I don't want to stop you from her . . . I just want you to not want her — on your own."

Porter was torn. "This is the one chance of happiness I've got."

"Aren't there other women — your age?"

"'Haven't seen any."

"I see dozens of widows."

"They bore me."

"What about Ma?"

He glared at her.

"I'm sorry. I shouldn't have said that." She thought a moment. "Papa, I will give up marrying again if you'll do the same."

Porter was surprised. "Why are you saying this?"

"If you marry anyone — especially someone who captures your heart like this girl — that'll destroy any chance of you getting back with Mama."

"What?" Porter gazed at her, astounded.

"I reckon that's all I have to say."

"Emily, come here."

She walked to him. He put his arms around her and hugged her like when she was a little girl. "I once loved your mother very much — and she'll always hold a place in my heart. But that chapter is over."

"Papa," she said, backing away from him, "I'm part of that chapter. So it'll always be there."

"You don't understand," he muttered, fighting tears springing from both hurt and anger. "I didn't take that chapter out of my book. She did."

"But didn't you drive her away!" Emily said.

Porter angrily held his voice low. "Who drove who away?" he said. "She pushed me out of her life with constant complaining." His got loud again. "I still tried keeping our family together because of the kids — and mostly you! So how dare you say I drove her away! She booted me out! And I will not stand for your trying to make me feel guilty for wanting to get on with my life with someone else!"

"Mama has a different story."

"Who is she to tell only her side of things! No wonder the other kids won't write me!"

"Mama should be able to tell us what she felt."

"I know she should," said Porter. "But what about the truth?"

"Her truth is what matters most to me — and to all of us," said Emily.

Porter felt a bolt of anger surge through him.

Emily added, "She raised us. Not you." She looked in terror as he reared back to slap her.

He caught himself and lowered his hand.

She strode away from him, hurt and angry, then disappeared into her room where she slammed the door.

Porter stared at the closed door.

CHAPTER 19

Lot Huntington had last seen Porter just after Emily's kidnapping. It was he who had shared drinks with the kidnappers in a Salt Lake City tavern, and then given Porter the tip under pressure from his parents.

He had continued to enjoy his camaraderie with young rowdies in the saloon he liked to frequent, but after drinking too much one night, then being talked into participation in an armed robbery, he had high-tailed it to southern Nevada, breaking his parents' hearts. That's when he was 15. He was now a couple years older but had not grown an inch. He acted cocky for a man five feet tall, so in the mining camp near Las Vegas Springs where he worked, his fellow miners referred to him chidingly as the camp dwarf.

He seethed inwardly, so was determined to show them his worth: He would at the first opportunity dispatch the first gunfighter he'd come across — and it did not matter on which side of the law his target hailed.

He recalled not disliking Porter Rockwell personally, but since turning to a life of crime and realizing he was already the family "black sheep," he would not mind taking on Porter to win his respect.

"Are you loco?" said one miner at the hut beside the river after a hard day's mining.

"No, I'm serious," said young Huntington, approaching his 18th birthday. "I'm sick of old Brother Rockwell getting all the stories in the newspapers. He ain't nothin' since Illinois — I don't think he's killed one soul — but the papers are still writing stories, saying he's the man to be a'feared of. It's time I got my share."

"What's this 'Brother Rockwell?' Are you a Mormon too?"

He said nothing.

They laughed and whooped it up for 20 minutes that he'd even think of taking on the notorious Rockwell, then, sensing his determination, they curiously watched him set up bottles for target practice. Six shots from his Colt Army revolver took out six bottles at 30 yards. They gasped at his accuracy and the rapid fire of his new-fangled "six-shooter." They also realized he wasn't to be joked about anymore. Not only did he have a dead-eye aim, he was the only person in camp with a real revolver.

Soon Lot Huntington was headed northeastward to the land of his former home. He decided he would hunt Porter down and either put an end to his legend or die trying. His fellow miners wondered if he indeed could take out the long-haired gunfighter with his accuracy and advanced weaponry. Rather than making a joke of him, they bade him a sincere farewell, and began looking up to him already. He glowed as he rode away from Las Vegas Springs, receiving the respect that he so much craved.

Mary Ann Neff lay asleep in her cabin when she heard a metallic click on the front porch.

As she donned a gown to inspect the noise, she suddenly had the vague impression that it was *not Porter* . . . She stepped outside and shivered.

Suddenly someone grabbed her from behind.

She gasped. She was turned to face the man and she beheld his eyes glistening in the moonlight. He quickly pressed her face to his, and before she could pull away . . .

She was melting under Porter's kiss.

"Why did it not feel like you?" she asked, concerned.

"Maybe I'm a little different since I left. I've had time to think."

"You've changed about us?"

"No. Just thinking about things."

"What things?"

While I was gone, I thought about how much I'm needed. I heard complaints about robbers taking advantage of the settlers down in Utah Valley — I reckon it's everywhere. And I reckon it's time for it to come to a stop."

Mary Ann breathed out, concerned.

"But it'll be different than Illinois. I'll only go on overnight trips. A few days at most."

Minutes later they were walking to the creek where they had often sat on the fallen tree and thrown rocks into the water.

Ripples spread under the moonlight, and on this particular night he told her of his deepest feelings.

He added he was now on his way to perform a short assignment for Brigham — to find the location for a new penitentiary. It would last less than a week — and then he would return to talk to her more about something "very serious."

Mary Ann was both ecstatic over the prospects and uncertain.

A month passed, and no word from Porter.

At the Neff cabin she waited agonizingly for his return. One night, her father John Neff carved a wooden totem as he sat before the fireplace.

"One thing, Mary Ann, I gotta hand to ole Port — he's been honest with me and gone the extra mile by working — and that's saved us all a lot of money."

The county had required a road to be completed before Porter and his new partner, Franklin Neff, could sell lumber from the canyon just south of Mill Creek. The canyon was now under full operation and both men were profiting well from their investment. John Neff had second thoughts about giving up the sales and wood harvesting operations of such a lucrative business but, agreeing with the admonition of his wife that "extra hours should be spent with the family," he was managing only the mill the operation in his spare time when he wasn't ranching, while a foreman actually supervised. Porter meanwhile had evolved into a silent partner.

Throughout this period Mary Ann found her father encouraging their relationship, and over the weeks he had advised her to not give up on him, even though she now often wondered if Porter were not indeed a silent partner with her. "Don't know if you'd find another like him," he said this evening as he carved, reading her thoughts.

She said nothing. She was frustrated with his long absence and was angry.

"So where do you think he is?" he added, sitting at the silent embers of the fireplace.

Certainly Porter had completed his location-scouting for the penitentiary by now, she mused, so why hadn't she heard from him?

"I suppose he's gone off to hunt outlaws again," she snapped.

"Honey . . ." said John Neff, lifting his eyes from the totem and noticing her face set firmly on the flames, "Maybe you oughta look elsewhere."

Mary Ann lay asleep when she was startled awake by a tap at the window.

She glanced outside and saw Porter smiling at her.

She walked hand in hand with him, under the moonlight, toward her drinking well. She pumped him for answers like she would within seconds begin pumping the well handle.

"Sorry I was gone so long," he said. "I was location-scouting."

"How come so long?" she said, torn between her feelings of love for him and simultaneous neglect.

"'Seems no one wants a penitentiary in their back yard, and that's why it took so long, but I finally found a spot that'll work." He told her the details of his trip.

He was in a talkative mood. She noticed him rarely in-between: He was either as open as an hour-glass or reticent as a rat. She further observed he was usually most sharing after long departures, but within days would retire into his mind and there hibernate. His excitement for her was as strong as ever, he told her, and he assured her he needed only to accept occasional assignments for Brigham in the future. What he did not tell her was that another fear about their relationship had cropped up: He wondered about their future; specifically, if she would retain her feelings for him over the years if certain lengthy assignments did crop up, despite his representation to her a month earlier of likely seeing only overnight tasks in the foreseeable future. Since then, reality had settled in, and now he doubted that his occupation could support such a commitment. Further, he could not put himself through the anguish again of loving a woman who refused to support his lifestyle, he told himself. To the very extent he was attracted to Mary Ann, he feared her.

And deeper: Luana's words still haunted him . . . he wondered if he were not indeed an "incurable adventurer." What if, after establishing a life with this woman, and despite all the feelings he had for her, the voice of the wild wind happened to beckon him again? Perhaps he could not stay on a ranch, imprisoned to only his acres and his children, when he was used to his freedom and being accountable to and responsible for no one.

He wondered if — when it might come down to his sanity — she would accept him chasing after that freedom, and basically if she could simply accept who he really was. He wondered if he could be loved *unconditionally* — as he had been only by Joseph, by his parents, and by Emily at one time.

But he knew that, despite his uncertainties, he loved her too much to not marry her. As they continued walking toward the well, he now told her things she substantially already knew: that she had the "beauty of a prairie dog" and "the attraction of a she-bear in season," terms that she would have otherwise found highly insulting had they come from another man but which, from Porter, seemed almost romantic. His flair for waxing poetic during courtship had obviously taken a downward turn since the riverbarge days with Luana. Mary Ann, nevertheless listened to his heart, and found herself trembling as he asked her to "tie the final knot."

At his cabin Porter arrived at midnight. He entered and found Emily, as usual, up late reading with Ugly's head on her lap.

"Sorry the trip took so long."

Emily stared at him, seething and hurt.

Porter cleared his throat. "I have news for you." He sat at the kitchen table and faced her across the room.

She looked at him, expecting the worse.

"As I told you, I have become very close friends with the Neff's daughter, and we're talking about getting married."

Emily said nothing.

Porter read the shock on her face and he looked down. "Actually, uh, we are getting married."

Though not surprised, she held back a silent gasp, hearing the reality of her worst fears confirmed. She stared at him a half minute in silence.

Porter continued. "You'll really like her."

"Yeah, a step-mother my own age."

"Then you'll have some things in common."

"Right — you," she said.

"She and I really like a lot of the same things."

"Pa, I've been running this ranch just fine without her."

"Well, now you can share."

"If I have to share, I'll do it with my own family."

"Emily, she is our family — or will be."

"Not *our* family."

Porter looked at her, surprised.

"Never."

Emily arose and went directly to her room. Porter followed her and stood at the doorway, astonished to see her packing. He was angry that she would not comply with his wishes; basically, that she was no longer the obedient child he had raised that would do *anything* to be with him.

"Emily, who do you think you are, telling me who I can and can't have in my life?"

"I'm not telling you anything. You can do whatever you want. I clearly belong near the ocean where I can start over."

Porter stared at her, not knowing what to say. He felt too angry and proud to beg her to stay, though that's what he wanted to do.

She ripped through her belongings and packed them in a bag, then brushed past him and outside.

Porter looked down, hearing horsehooves galloping away. He felt his heart breaking once again . . .

CHAPTER 20

Lot Huntington wore his pride on his holster. The camp of Nevada miners was waiting his return. When Lot arrived in Salt Lake Valley he had learned the lawman was gone several weeks, so he had camped in the wilds south of the city and occasionally entered to learn if Porter were back.

He slowed his horse near the general store, the one which he had learned Porter most frequented. "'Know where I might find Porter?" he said to the proprietor, slapping change on the counter for chewing tobacco.

"You haven't heard?" said the proprietor.

"I wouldn't be askin' if I had," said Huntington.

"This afternoon he gets tied up," he laughed. "Like a knot."

Inside Brigham Young's house, Porter and Mary Ann Neff stood before the Mormon chieftain and exchanged vows of love and loyalty. It was May 3rd, 1854. After placing a modest gold band on her finger, he took her in his arms and kissed her. The feelings of his wildest dreams were complete. Tears came to her eyes, and he finally pulled away from her. Then the thought of Emily's absence from his life tugged at his thoughts and he lost his smile.

George Bean let out a whistle and neighbor Lot Smith began applauding. A dozen Neff neighbors joined in and the cheers were spontaneous. Even Ugly joined the verbal fracas and broke out barking.

"I'm surprised she's even here," said Lot Smith.

Porter glanced at him curiously.

"Don't feel bad, brother," said Smith chidingly, "It's just that you have the hardest time keepin' a woman of any man I ever met."

Porter glared at the blunt — but in his own way, likeable — old scout.

Brigham Young smiled at the unusual proceedings and soon saw the couple stride out of his house to Porter's wagon, accompanied by Ugly.

Across the street, leaning against a hitching post and staring at the couple riding past, was Lot Huntington. His parents had not seen him because, as they had left the wedding and walked to their carriage, he had hidden behind a barn.

Porter did not see Lot either as he and Mary Ann mounted their buckboard and rode back to their ranch.

Lot remounted his roan and followed. He had been planning for weeks to halt Porter's legend that so rankled him, and he would just have to follow Porter and dispatch him and his Samson-like superstitions all in one gunshot.

Mary Ann slept soundly. Porter stared out the window at the moon. Outside on the porch slept Ugly, since Mary Ann sneezed whenever he was inside. She felt sorry for the old dog and made a bed of blankets on the porch. She even fed him all the beef and buttered bread he could enjoy. Ugly thought her a strange creature, emitting such wet and loud, explosive discharges from her nose whenever he came too close. He knew she was the reason for his exile, but she grew on him nonetheless. Sometimes he preferred sleeping in the barn with the other animals if he felt like company, whereupon he would nestle in the hay, but he liked Mary Ann and Porter both, enough to usually bed down in the blankets on the porch just to be near them.

Meanwhile, Porter still could not fathom the fact that through all the torment of his life he was finally settling down with a peaceable and kindly woman. The stars he then studied took him, as it were, to other times, other places, distantly. Then thoughts of Emily cut into him like a bowie knife. He felt consumed with the desire to find and reconcile with her. He determined to track her down *en route* to California, where she no doubt was heading. He then realized that, despite this being his wedding night, he was unduly haunted by that precious, precocious daughter. He felt a paternal obsession to make her happy, and even pictured her in a wedding gown beside a decent young man with numerous friends greeting them, all smiling, with himself beaming, knowing they'd live next to his ranch the remainder of his life. This, he'd always dreamed, was earth's equivalent to heaven. But first he had to bring her home. He knew the trail to Sacramento was fraught with hazards. Robbers, rattlesnakes and rockslides were bad enough, but Indians were attacking travelers all the way to California's Humboldt Valley. He pictured her being ambushed by white robbers. He sat up. He was not sure if he were dreaming this, when through the window pane he suddenly heard noises.

He grabbed his gun.

Mary Ann asked him to not go outside.

Outside, he stepped towards the well, when he heard footsteps behind him. He twirled and saw a man staring at him, eyes wide.

"Porter!"

"Brother Larson?" said Porter. "What can I do for you?"

"Heather, my 15 year old."

"What do you mean?"

"The gold-seekers," said Larson breathlessly. "She gave water to a bunch the other day and they began teasing her. I reckon they came back for her."

"Kidnapped?"

"I reckon."

Porter's blood boiled. "Where're they at?" he boomed.

"The emigrant camp, south of Goshen." Larson was a blue-eyed, light-complexioned, first-generation Scandinavian who had lived in North Carolina and converted to the fold. This was his first trial of faith in his six months of Mormon living.

And now as Porter looked into his eyes he knew he could not let the man down. Nor could he stay away from the danger.

"Don't worry," said Porter. "I'll get her back. You go on home now."

Larson's pleading eyes revealed anguish. "Let me go with you!"

"No, I have my own methods — and I don't want you getting hurt."

"Then don't let my daughter get hurt!"

"That's why I'm doing this — now go on home before I handcuff you."

Larson blinked and came to his senses. He realized finally that he had confidence in Porter. He nodded, turned, and remounted his horse, then left.

Porter glanced back at the porch and saw Mary Ann staring at him. Her eyes penetrated his thoughts.

"After you find his daughter," she said, "you'll be getting Emily back here?"

Porter felt torn over pursuing his daughter right after the wedding, but was convinced her life was at stake, so he could not let her continue to California. He would have to bring her back. Nevertheless, the kidnapped Larson girl was in *immediate* danger, so despite that fact that he was torn, he knew he had to rescue Heather Larson immediately. Yet as he gazed into Mary Ann's eyes, he knew without a word spoken that she wanted him back for herself immediately, and that she disagreed his daughter was in any true danger or need for him. Their eyes read each other and she turned away, frustrated not only with his hanging onto his former family so strongly in his heart, but mostly upset with herself for not wanting him to go after Emily and protect her in every way possible.

Porter rode into the night wind, Ugly on the saddle behind him for not only protection but companionship. The moon lit a golden pathway on the desert sand before him, and he followed the tracks of the young woman's kidnappers. He worried over what Mary Ann was thinking and wished he had reassured her more thoroughly. Tumbleweeds blew across his path with increasing numbers under the full moon.

Suddenly he heard a voice behind him and up a gully. When he heard two clicks of hammers drawn from two revolvers, he quickly assessed an ambush. Ugly had not smelled the attacker, since a stiff wind was blowing the other way. Porter then heard a voice:

"Welcome to the wild West, Brother Rockwell."

He turned and beheld Lot Huntington behind a boulder. When his old neighbor stepped forward, Porter studied carefully the young man of small stature; the weapons aimed at him commanded his immediate respect, one being a repeating Colt Army.

"I reckon you call that drop on me fair and square?" said Porter.

"What do you mean?" said Lot, noting an ironic dryness in the voice that mocked him.

"How can I prove to you how good you are with those," said Porter, "if I don't even have time to draw?"

While Lot wanted to win respect at the mining camp, he knew he'd lose his own if he just opened fire on his old neighbor without even giving him a chance. He realized he had not fully thought this through, even after all these weeks.

"All right," said Lot, putting both revolvers into his belt. "You draw first."

Porter read his eyes. "You're braver than most men I know," said Porter. "In fact I've never seen a murderer put away his guns after he had the drop on someone."

"Who says I'm a murderer?"

"Ain't murder what you're here for?"

"Kind of."

"Kind of?" said Porter.

"Yeah, I am."

"I don't think so."

"What do you mean you don't think so?" said Lot.

"I mean your mind might think so, but your heart ain't exactly in this, is it?"

Lot was taken back by the lawman's kindly eyes. They were not what he had expected or remembered. The crow's feet around Porter's eyes also displayed a kindlier countenance than his memory had served him, mainly because of the notoriety of Porter's legends.

"How old are you now, boy?" said Porter.

"Almost 18."

"I've got an idea. Let's you and me sit down over some jerky and fresh brewed coffee and figure out what you really want."

Porter knew a killer by his coldness. Something he exudes. Over the years he had learned a rattlesnake radiates a different attitude — a different aura — than a farm dog, and this kid was no rattler.

Porter's approach was intentionally gentle. "You remember crossing the plains with your folks and how hard they tried keeping you alive?"

Lot nodded. He perceived Porter's intention by the question.

Porter read his mind, shook his head and smiled. "Your pa's been worried sick three years over you, boy — ever since you left. And you put your ma nearly in the death bed with worry too."

Lot looked down.

"I'd hate to see all that work your folks put into keeping you alive on the plains just get buried, but that's what'll happen if we shoot it out. No doubt you're a faster draw than me," he said, attempting to both flatter and placate him, "but after you put me away, a posse would have to hunt you down and put you away — probably into a stinking little jail cell a few months, until the court decides to put you further away, into a hangman's noose."

Lot glanced up at him, then down again.

They sat at a campfire and sipped coffee. Ugly lapped some from a bowl, but found it rather dull and looked up sadly at Porter, who read his mind and laced it with a shot of whiskey. The man carried a metal flask with whiskey next to his chest, hung from a leather strap around his neck, just for such moments. And Ugly was very pleased he did. Yet Porter felt somewhat guilty now that Ugly was becoming apparently too attached to the stuff. The dog lapped happily as the two men spoke:

"I never had my folks or anyone else treat me like I deserved," said Lot.

"How do you mean?"

"Like they treat others," said Lot.

"You mean with respect?"

The young man nodded.

"You got wagers from some town on this thing — shooting me?"

Lot again nodded. "Couple dollars."

"Face up to 'em, boy."

Lot gazed at him curiously.

"Go tell them you got the drop on me, but I wasn't half bad, so you ended up taking a job with me."

"Job?"

"As my deputy."

Lot was astonished.

"For one day," said Porter. "But don't tell them that it's only for one day. Then you head back to my ranch and be my foreman till I get back. Tell my wife she'll cook your meals and you can sleep in the shed. We'll build fences together when I return. But first you gotta face those fellows you made the bets with."

Lot Huntington's head was spinning. "I'm up for armed robbery of a liquor store awhile back."

"How much?"

"Ninety dollars. It's all been gambled away."

"You'll work it off and I'll see that the store drops charges. Meanwhile you can keep a roof over your head while earning spending money. I'll take care of it all when I get back."

Lot sighed, and tried to hold back grinning and sobbing simultaneously.

"Porter?" said Lot.

Porter read his face, a mite embarrassed, and looked down.

"Porter," continued Lot, "this is the worst coffee I have ever tasted."

Porter and Lot Huntington rode till midnight. Ugly stayed on the saddle behind his master, somewhat drowsy from the whisky, yet wide awake from the coffee. The discordance in his head was making his brain buzz with strange noises. The dog whined. Porter understood and smiled.

"We gotta get you on the wagon, boy."

They discovered, in the bright moonlight, tracks leading over a bed of rocks. Although the kidnappers had taken a route to evade pursuers, Porter picked up the trail without even slowing. He arrived atop a knoll and spotted glows from the kidnappers' campfire a hundred yards ahead, then noticed farther away — about a mile — 50 wagons circled about a bonfire.

"They're emigrants," mumbled Porter. "You stay here and fire two quick warning shots if anyone comes from that camp," he told Lot. "We don't need these kidnappers getting reinforcements." He then rode down the hill towards the kidnappers, with only Ugly joining him, now seeing the world somewhat out of focus.

Lot beamed, staying atop the knoll. "I can't believe I'm Porter Rockwell's deputy!"

"Neither can I," said Porter back in a harsh whisper a hundred feet ahead. "Now keep quiet!"

The eight kidnappers ate near a campfire. Twenty yards away a bearded chap sat beside Heather Larson, a distraught, disheveled 15 year old, as he tied her wrists to a stake.

"Hurry up," called another at the campfire. "We need help with this ransom note."

"I'd say you need help," laughed the tall, bearded leader. "You're the only one that can write!"

While Heather was staked to the ground, the bearded fellow leaned forward and teased her, making silly faces. She noted the man smelled like horse sweat. She loosened a leg and sent her foot into his fat belly. He lurched backwards and plopped to the ground.

While the other men laughed, the fat one returned with a branding iron.

"Go ahead, honey, try kicking again," he chuckled, moving the branding iron towards her forehead.

She could see its red glow. "Don't . . . " she begged.

"Don't you want to be branded like them steer your papa raises? Maybe we need to teach you compassion!"

The branding iron came slowly towards her forehead. She felt heat from the metal as it approached her skin . . . and just as the fat fellow was about to thrust the rod forward, she felt him jerk forward as they heard an exploding crack.

The fat fellow dropped over her, and the iron sizzled up into his face. Heather heard another shot and simultaneously saw blood fly out the side of his fat torso.

A horseman with long hair came flying into camp, and the blinding sunlight behind him kept her from seeing who it was. The remaining six kidnappers ran for their weapons.

Heather saw the silhouetted long-haired horseman fire again. One emigrant was hit and spun on impact, landing face forward into a scrub oak. Another lead ball fired from the horseman's barrel — flipping a fellow over a tree limb in a somersault.

Heather saw two of the kidnappers aim point blank and fire — but the long-haired horseman answered with two more shots — and both men tossed over backwards, straight into a vat of fresh buffalo dung.

The other three ran for cover. The long-haired one reloaded one revolver, then took three, studious, carefully aimed shots.

All three runners fell forward, one dead, the other two wounded. Those two began crawling agonizingly for cover.

Heather saw the horseman take aim again and, with four last fast shots, stopped their crawling cold.

The long-haired man gazed across the now peaceful camp and beheld blood flowing from every corpse. Most of them still had their eyes open. The horseman slowly rode towards Heather.

When he halted, she could not at first make out who it was, then she beheld the kindly smile of Porter Rockwell, and she broke out crying. Relieved and free and completely in safe hands.

Immediately, Porter and Ugly rode horseback together while Heather Larson and Lot Huntington rode on Lot's horse. At the bottom of the hill, Porter glanced up at his compass —

the stars. He stopped and gazed two directions, torn over whether to ride westward immediately to find his daughter or to return Heather to her father. He spotted a camp miles away of a hundred men.

Porter, Lot, and Heather came closer and recognized them: It was Brigham Young with an entourage of 100 people and 34 wagons heading south through dangerous Indian territory to St. George.

"Come join us," bellowed Brigham. "We need your hand to ward off attacking Utes. We also need your help for George Bean and me to meet with Chief Walkara for peace negotiations." Bean was like Jacob Hamblin, who worked on faith that they would receive Divine protection if they showed supreme trust in their native neighbors. "He doesn't even carry a gun," smiled Brigham. "So you might say we need you for back-up."

Porter explained his dilemma about leaving his bride to find and return his daughter.

Brigham studied him thoughtfully. He finally advised, "Stay clear of Emily awhile. It's Mary Ann that needs you now. But first, we have lives at stake — and this is your job with the territory — to protect lives."

Porter took comfort in listening to the one whom he considered the bearer of inspired advice. He would return Heather immediately back to her pa. One way to accomplish this was to send her with Lot but, although he felt the boy was perfectly capable, he did have warrants for his arrest and, certainly the last thing he needed now was to be mistaken as Heather's kidnapper and he shot on the spot. Despite his spiritual desire to obey counsel, Porter still fought an emotional battle inside and thus wanted to go after Emily. He was torn several directions as he studied the stars.

He also felt a dissonance over whether or not to continue the campaign of clearing up the territory vs. staying at home with his new bride. Brigham had indicated he could balance both tasks, but he felt a determination to completely cleanse the territory — and that would take more time than he wished to be away from Mary Ann. He felt terribly guilty leaving her high and dry, yet felt a passion to do his job right and in the process cleanse his soul of the anger Boggs and Brigham had discerned was a driving factor in his life. True to the governor's prediction, while rescuing Heather, he discovered a hidden resurrected anger towards the lawless. He wanted perfect, cool control over those passions, as taught by both Joseph and Brigham, but as yet had not achieved it. Until meeting Boggs in California, he had not even been aware of such sinews in his soul. He finally made his decision to simply obey Brigham.

He took Heather home himself. She sat directly behind him with Ugly walking beside them. When Heather's father saw her in the distance, coming home on the back of Porter's horse, he burst into sobs of joy and ran out to hug her. He then hugged Porter. Ugly, also jumped on him, wanting to be included.

"We gotta give credit to Ugly," said Porter. "He sniffed the trail and helped me find her."

Larson hugged the large grey dog.

"I'd say that was a mistake," chuckled Porter. "That dog rolled in something awful ripe on the way here."

Brother Larson nevertheless rejoiced, hugging Ugly, after which, his joy was quickly fused with nausea.

"Heather," smiled Brother Larson, "get the bath barrel ready.

"Papa, have you got any water heated?"

"Nope. Cold will do."

Porter and Ugly rode away, silhouetted against the moon as Heather and Brother Larson (anxiously awaiting his bath) waved tearfully to them from the doorway. Through gritted teeth, Larson muttered, "My word, that dog packs a wallop."

Porter and Ugly would ride all night, then catch up with Brigham's group in two days. Meanwhile, Lot Huntington headed southwest to Las Vegas Springs to finish his business at the tavern, and clear both his reputation and his conscience.

"Better take this with you," Porter had told him before they parted, pulling off his badge. It had his name engraved on it. "This badge will help prove to 'em what you say."

"I don't care if they believe me or not," said Lot. "I know it myself."

Porter knew all Lot needed was someone to believe in him, then he'd find faith in himself.

"But you better give me the badge anyway in case they don't," laughed Lot.

Porter chuckled and tossed him his badge. He was still chortling as Lot had disappeared around the hill. Lot meanwhile was amazed at the hand the last few days had dealt him.

On their ride to catch up with Brigham, Porter suddenly halted. He felt overwhelmed by his desire to find and protect Emily, despite Brigham's admonition. He fought it, but finally could no further, and turned his horse due west, hoping to catch up with her. He realized after several hours that she had fled at a pretty good clip, and had caught up with a California-bound Mormon wagon train which had left the day before she had gone, and whose tracks were still fresh. Knowing she was far safer now, and feeling his conscience tugging at him to help Brigham's expedition, he decided again to let her go for now. He would get to California later, he decided, and hope she would realize life there without family or parents was too lonely an existence. He fully expected her to miss him as much as he missed her. Feeling confidence and a hope to that end, he turned southeast to catch up to Brigham's group, sensing it was laid open to recent warring Ute Indian attacks. Brigham had told him his reputation was such that Indians respected both him and his six-shooters, as well as his uncanny ability to read the terrain. They also bought into his growing legend that he was impossible to kill, believing the stories of trappers, traders, and others who dealt with them.

By sunset the next day he arrived in Goshen on the trail to southern Utah. There, he found Brigham's party on its way south.

"Did you get Heather safely back?"

"Yep."

"And young Lot Huntington — did he take off to see the miners at Vegas Springs?"

"Yep."

"'Suppose he'll return?"

"Yep."

Brigham could read his mind. "I appreciate you letting her go — for Mary Ann's sake — and also for her's."

"Maybe so. But after we visit Walkara, and I get you safely to St. George, I'll be headed to California."

Brigham gazed at him analytically.

"What's wrong?" said Porter.

"That's not the best thing."

"It's the best thing."

"Not for her. You're dealing with a young lady's feelings — confused feelings," said Brigham.

"So what do I do? Let her mess up her life again?"

"It is her life."

"You told me earlier I needed to be in her life more — and that she needed a strong parent."

"Only if she chooses to stay with you."

Porter looked down.

"Now if you'll listen to me, you'll stay with your bride a few months, then I'd like you to help Colonel Steptoe of the U.S. Army. He's looking for the quickest way to California and it'll do us well to extend a peace offering to the Government. But I suggest strongly for you to not see Emily while you're there. Just dictate a letter and send it to the bishop in Sacramento, and he'll get it to her. She's probably in the gold mining area again, since a number of our people are there, and I saw her at a dance, talking to several young people who were moving there. In your letter, just express your love for her. Let her decide if she wants to return home."

While Ugly slept soundly on the saddle blanket laid out by the campfire, Porter could not get his mind off his daughter. He walked to a ridge where he studied the sunset. Brigham's counsel two days earlier was hard enough to follow — but now this — of not seeing her after he would already be in California — seemed too difficult a trial. The sunset turned to twilight, and then to a bright starry canopy that held his soul.

What would he do? He didn't know, himself.

And would he succumb to the temptation of drinking himself into the gutter again? Had he lost all control over himself that way? The thirst for liquor grew stronger some days than others, so much so that it frightened him. Never, before cutting his hair, had he that problem in his life. What had he done, he wondered to himself, by disobeying Joseph's promise and blessing? It occured to him in a whisper the good Lord had traded one consequence for another — he would still be protected in fighting for justice — but no longer would be projected from the wiles of the Adversary in his personal life. Not, at least, in the world of strong drink. He feared and knew it would be a weakness till his dying day. And how, in the end, would the Lord look upon his worthiness on that last day? The answer, he felt, would come in this life, through someone close to him. Those keys to heavenly secrets are often forged from trials with those most closely bonded to us, and then revealed at some unexpected moment.

PART II

Judgement

CHAPTER 21

A buggy rolled into the valley one fall afternoon of 1854 and the man who stepped out was William W. Drummond. He took one look at the expanding town of Salt Lake City and mumbled:

"Quaint."

He could not wait to sink his teeth into the territory's judicial concerns, since he was now the territory's *bona fide* federal judge. And whether or not Brigham Young and his people wanted him, here he was, with a mandate from the federal government and the power to perform it.

Drummond had irreconcilable elements co-existing within him. He sought to be his own man, but in order to be so, he had to compromise. He knew clearly the Eastern mining interests had been watching — drooling, as it were — over Brigham's desert kingdom. Gold in California had recently sent thousands of immigrants through the Great Basin, making the Mormons far better off financially, with factories and mills now operating 24 hours a day. Great Salt Lake City — recently shortened to

Salt Lake City — was teeming with industry. As was all the Territory of Deseret, being dubbed "Utah," after the Ute Indians. Various precious metals had since been discovered in Utah as well. So, the large companies, he suspected, were putting pressure on Washington to make things happen.

Drummond despised taking orders, but his first phase of directives would not be that distasteful. He agreed wholeheartedly with what was expected of him: to cut the powers of Brigham Young and turn them over to the powers in the East. He only feared one thing, being told what to do the remainder of his life . . . particularly down the road when he would replace Brigham as *Governor of the Territory.*

No one had actually informed him that would be his scepter, but it had been implied. He would now have to carry the banner obediently during his judicial reign to prove how invaluable he was, and make for himself a reputation that exemplified how deserving he was of the crown.

He had not even met those from whom the directives had come. In fact, all had been communicated by subordinates. In Chicago he had the strange sense he had been "interviewed:" Lower-level executive branch administrators had spoken with him vaguely, informally, while "happening" to run into him at Illinois taverns. At first he thought they were curious strangers, but one day when he came home from work, he was astonished to receive a letter of appointment promoting him to the federal judgeship of the Territory of Deseret. Most of his years had been spent in Illinois, and now he would spend a majority of his judicial term (or "sentence," as he dubbed it) in Fillmore, Utah, the territorial capitol several days south of Salt Lake City;

but whenever he could, he would perform duties in Salt Lake Valley itself just to be near civilization and to visually remind Brigham of his presence and power.

Drummond's gift of repartee was celebrated. He was widely traveled and spoke several languages.

What he lacked in looks he made up for in persona. As with DeBergerac's plume, he carried a special panáche of which only he seemed aware that made him feel superior to women. This infused into his psyche a mysterious air of confidence which intrigued them — especially those who saw in his eyes a mischievous sparkle. A sparkle, coupled by power, which excited the opposite sex.

He was short, plump, and balding.

Women fought over him.

His wife adored him.

He was bored out of his wits with her.

In order to maintain his sanity, of their 23 years of marriage he had for 22 of them sent her off to relatives for the summer. Upon leaving Illinois for Washington in order to be briefed on his new job, he had met a stimulating woman named Ada Carroll who was active in Washington social circles. Ada was genuinely charmed by him, yet not particularly bright. That, in itself, he realized, was not a shining endorsement of his social prowess, but, he figured, what the heck, she was pretty and outgoing — and that alone qualified her for the upper echelons of the District of Columbia. He was to leave for his desert outpost soon and had one minor predicament. He was already married. His wife was anxious to join him West once he was settled down — but he was not particularly looking forward to that. Especially when Ada decided she wanted to go. Mrs. Drummond's arrival in Utah was to take place in a few months (she had pushed for weeks, he had talked her into months). However, just prior to his departure from Washington, he decided to take Ada with him. When his wife *would* arrive, he knew a sticky situation lay in store, but his decision was based primarily on the subject of boredom. It was bad enough to be exiled to the desert while a future promotion ripened, but to be imprisoned in marital monotony for heaven knows how long in that desert was more than he could stomach. In any case, out in the wilderness he would be free to spend his time with whichever woman he wished. His promotions had been and would be predicated on performance, not puritanical morality, and the fact that it now happened to be in the hotbed of Mormonism made him smile all the broader. He would indeed have his fun with them. While still in the stagecoach, he stopped a stranger on the street.

"Where's Brigham Young?"

"'Round the corner."

"Get him a message for me."

"You tellin' or askin' me?"

Drummond was surprised at the man's insolence. He had heard the Mormons were sheep-like. Their new-found freedom had made them a bit raw, he thought to himself, but he would match their vituperousness and, if necessary, raise them one.

"Tell him I'm not interested in meeting him," said Drummond, "nor in being interfered with." He then explained who he was. What he did not explain was his intention: to step on Brigham like a slug in a garden.

The stranger nodded with a scowl and reluctantly shuffled toward Brigham's office with the verbal message.

Drummond's chief concerns were those on which he had been briefed by certain secretive Washington messengers. In addition to various documents, he had been lent newspaper clippings from the Mormons' last area of residence. Having resided in Illinois during the Nauvoo period, he had followed the Mormon problem in Hancock County with some degree of interest, but now knew more fully from the newspaper articles what to expect from these rebels. They were all from the *Warsaw Signal*. He couldn't wait to establish an office and courtroom a stone's throw from Brigham's high command just to make a statement.

His most enjoyable moments, however, would be found in his favorite Salt Lake tavern. Most active Mormons shunned saloons, as the decree had the year previously come from Brigham (and, to a far less extent years earlier by way of suggestion from Joseph Smith) to abstain from liquor — although it would take decades for some active Mormons to catch onto the practice. Thus, inactives and non-Mormons alike flocked to the place. There, Drummond would be esteemed as a hero even more than he would in his own courtroom.

Soon in fact, he became the respectful recipient of an increasing number of tavern toasts. Occasionally he would include Ada in his tavern jaunts, but usually he'd leave her at his hotel room when in Salt Lake Valley or in Fillmore.

It was on one such chilly afternoon in February 1855, not many weeks after his arrival that, after a day's deliberating in Salt Lake, Judge Drummond strutted into the tavern with his aide, Simon W. LeFevre. There, he overheard for the first time complaints of Brigham's "Destroying Angel."

"I've heard stories about him," said LeFevre.

"Who are they speaking of?" said Drummond.

"Porter Rockwell."

"*The* Porter Rockwell?"

"The Porter Rockwell."

Drummond stared at him, surprised. "Certain people assured me he would've been killed in brawls by now. What's he been doing?"

"Tracking outlaws, I suppose."

"Outlaws? The king of the outlaws himself?" sniffed Drummond. "*Tracking* outlaws?" he repeated incredulously.

"He's the U.S. Deputy Marshal."

Drummond was astonished. "How could that happen? Brigham has stooped that low?"

"Seems to have."

"What else do you know about the rogue?" said Drummond.

"Just the stories."

"He should've been lynched in Missouri. Find out what you can about him by Monday."

"Judge, I've got a busy weekend."

"Drop it; find out everything you can." Drummond knew he needed an angle — something heavy which could crumble the frontier power structure under Brigham's feet — and he sensed it just might be tied to this. "One other thing — find out how closely Mr. Rockwell is tied to the hierarchy itself."

Simon LeFevre was not pleased with the assignment. Having worked as a legal aide in St. Louis, and before that in Boston, he had been highly recommended by certain parties of which he was not even aware, who in turn had recruited him to assist Drummond at the new post.

LeFevre was by nature an obsessive worker. His vitality was immense. But having just met an interesting single woman at the tavern the day before, he had plans to spend his weekend with her and was, therefore, upset by this intrusion into his private life.

As to his feelings about Drummond, within several weeks of service he had realized he both disliked and respected him.

LeFevre, only 27, was considered to possess wide-ranging interests and a dry wit. He also communicated adroitly with older people, possessing the ability to converse on most any topic. This gave him a solidity and an air of maturity that were of service to him.

As a college man six years previously he had been something of an athlete, and had courted women with position and wealth, despite the fact his own family was middle class and had trouble financing his education. Therefore he had received scholarships, and had made something of himself.

Drummond theorized that LeFevre's abilities had been discovered by certain mining interests and that perhaps these same interests were behind his own promotion. He further suspected — which caused a rather uncomfortable pressure — that they would both have to produce, and produce well.

LeFevre's ambition was hard to define. He wanted to work his way up, but to what he was not certain. He seemed to enjoy utilizing his investigative abilities, and even taxing them when possible, just for the fun of it. He rarely found women he could enjoy, since he considered them, like Drummond, his intellectual inferiors. Unlike Drummond, he generally became bored with them very quickly — and therefore sought to lose himself in his work, hoping that one day the perfect match might appear.

He stood from his table, forced himself to thank Drummond for the drink, and left.

Drummond faced LeFevre three days later in the judge's Salt Lake City office.

"I've got that report for you," began LeFevre. "Last month Rockwell was hired by the Army as a guide to capture certain Pahvant Indians involved in a murder. Colonel Edward Jenner Steptoe of the Army then hired him to search out the best route to California by himself and bring back a map. And that's where he is now, due back in March. I first learned of this when his young wife Mary Ann told some of her neighbors. I also talked to the colonel's quartermaster, Captain Rufus Ingalls. According to him, Colonel Steptoe thinks Rockwell is the best guide in the West. Steptoe had been ordered to come in and take over as governor of the territory, but when he arrived with his troops and saw Brigham doing what he thought was a decent job, he left for California."

Drummond gazed at him and sniffed.

"Do you want to know what else I learned about him?"

"I'm waiting," said Drummond with controlled impatience.

"I'd heard the Indians have been an on-going scourge to Brigham, but I didn't realize how much until now. Some time back, Rockwell went south with Brigham and George Bean, a noted Mormon negotiator. First thing Rockwell and Bean did was see Chief Walkara, to prepare him for a meeting with Brigham Young. Brigham would be coming into their tribe in a few hours, so, Porter slipped the chief a bottle of whiskey to soften him up. But the plan backfired. Rockwell got the chief so stoned that the talks were stalled indefinitely."

Drummond chuckled. "What did he do next?"

"He and Bean visited Walkara again and nearly got themselves killed," said LeFevre. "But they escaped, and later talked the old chief into trading with the whites again and halting their attacks for while."

"Did Rockwell's dealings with the Utes end there?" said Drummond.

"No, he and Bean saved eight Mexican Indian slaves from being butchered by their owners."

"Who were —"

"Ute Indians."

"How did Bean and Rockwell save them?"

"They gave the slaves their freedom. That's all I learned."

Drummond blew a smoke ring. "Rockwell interfered with slave trading? That's illegal."

"Why's that?"

"James Calhoun, Superintendent of Indian Affairs, has approved of Indian slave trading with the Mexicans," said Drummond. "So it's none of the Mormons' blasted business. We can nail Rockwell on that alone. But find something bigger. Where is Rockwell now?"

"I told you California — but I didn't tell you he's in some kind of self-imposed Hades."

CHAPTER 22

Emily pulled hot bread from the oven. The California gold streams were practically at sea level, so she found bread-baking an entirely different art than back in Utah at the 4300 foot elevation of her father's cabin. February temperatures were typically mild in the gold-laced streams near Sacramento, and today was no exception.

She heard a knock at the door and turned. There stood her father. Her face quickly lit up, but immediately withdrew, both torn over whether or not he would accept her again and undecided over whether to accept him herself.

"What're you doing here, Pa?"

"The Army sent me out to find the best route to California. I just finished, and I need someone to help me write the map. 'Know anybody who can do that?"

Hours later she finished writing on the map he had drawn. They had talked sparsely — all on safe subjects: the weather, the ward, the dog.

"I guess that's it," she said, labeling the last mountain range on the route East — the Wasatch Mountains. "So tell me, Pa, How'd you find me?"

"It's been the hardest decision of my life," he said, "whether or not to, and then I had to spend awhile looking for you. It seems like I spend half my life out here doing that."

"And the other half?"

"Deciding if I should."

She warmed up to his smile, then noticed Ugly ambling in with tail wagging.

"Come on in, boy!" she said. "Have some supper!"

Ugly jumped on her and licked her.

"I reckon he rates an invitation. Do I?" said Porter with a smile.

"You're a close second," she beamed. She laughed at Ugly's large licks.

"And here I thought he loved me," groaned Porter dryly.

"He does, like I love you and others at the same time," she said.

"Like that rabble husband still? He's dead, honey."

"Like someone else," she muttered, hurt by his comment. "You didn't have to say that."

"You found someone else already?"

She changed the subject, upset he would not apologize. "So why'd you come see me?"

"Emily, I have news for you," he continued. "We went ahead with the marriage — Mary Ann and me — and we're even having a baby soon."

She was devastated, fully realizing his "other family" was now a reality — and in a very real way competing with her and her siblings. She wanted to strike out. She took pleasure in telling him:

"I'm also married."

He stared, stunned.

"You'll be pleased to know he's at least a veteran of the Mormon Battalion."

The battalion, the same that had left from Nebraska in 1847, had made the longest march in known world history, and had finished without fighting in the Mexican War.

"His name's Henry Brizee," she continued. "He stayed behind after the troops were disbanded in San Diego."

"Why didn't he return to the valley with the rest?" said Porter critically.

She sighed silently. "Not all soldiers returned to Salt Lake," she responded.

"Nearly all did," he argued, "like they were supposed to. So how did you meet this fellow?"

"At church."

"Why didn't you do it right? You know I wanted to be there and have him ask for your hand and —"

"We've been through that," she interrupted.

"So why didn't you —?"

"What's there to complain about?" she interrupted again. "He's not a criminal, or a kidnapper. And he's even active in the faith."

"So where is this groom?" muttered Porter.

"Right here," said Henry, entering from outside with a smile. He extended his hand to shake Porter's.

Porter shook uncertainly. "How come you never returned to the valley after the march?" said Porter.

"'Cause I can't be walled in. I love exploring out here. And gold-panning the creeks helps me breathe easier."

"Well I hope you breathe easy enough to provide for my daughter."

Emily rolled her eyes.

"I don't see a problem there," said Brizee, turning to Emily. After smiling at her, he added, "Excuse me, but I'll leave you both to visit while I find supper."

Henry departed. Porter turned to her sarcastically:

"He seems to provide you with a lot of security, huh? I don't see a farm or garden anywhere — so where has he gone to hunt up supper?"

"This is more predictable than I thought," she snorted.

"So where's tomorrow's supper — and next week's?" he added.

"I knew you'd like him," she said dryly.

"How'd you know I wouldn't?"

"Because he's just like you."

At supper Emily and her husband ate, with her father seated at the dining table practically gawking at them between bites. Ugly sat on the floor beside Porter, receiving juicy table scraps from him. Meanwhile, Emily and her husband chatted continuously with each other.

Porter was torn over whether or not to invite them to relocate to Utah or to demand they do so, or following Brigham's mandate to not even touch the subject. Since he had disobeyed

Brigham's admonition to not even see her, he felt uncomfortable offering any opinion. So he simply said:

"I'll be headed back now." He arose and ambled to the door. The desire within him to have Emily live near his home burned so intensely that he was not able to hold back a comment. Yet he feared their reply — so he did not even want to see their faces — as he blurted out, "Brigham wants all the members back home."

"This is our home," said Brizee.

"Not as far as the Prophet sees it."

"You mean how you see it?" said Emily.

"Are you agreeing with this fellow against me?" said Porter.

She stared at the wall, exasperated. "He's my husband."

"How can you go against your own father?"

"We've made our decision," she said, evading his question.

"Then we'll just let life run its course," said Porter, "and see what else happens." At that he walked to the door. Emily stared after him, torn and hurt. She put down her fork.

Porter wished now he had not come to see her, but had instead followed Brigham's advice and merely sent a letter. Now, she would be thinking of reasons not to re-locate to Utah, he realized. Frustrated, he turned to her from the doorway:

"Keep Ugly here as your wedding present."

"I can't do that — he loves you."

"Then make the right decision — come home and bring your husband. That way, Ugly will be happy, and we'll all be together."

She squinted. "So Ugly is to hold out hope we'll be together — just like I have with you and Ma, is that it? I don't want him to know that pain — you take him."

Porter walked to his horse and began unhitching it. Emily appeared at the doorway. "I'll shoot Ugly before I'll put him through that."

Porter sighed and stared at Ugly. He whistled, and the dog came running to him. Porter knelt to one knee and Ugly jumped, using him as a springboard, and landed atop the horse. Porter mounted, then left, angry at himself, and galloped away.

CHAPTER 23

The town ahead was a thinly populated outskirt to Sacramento, whose name he never caught.

As he passed a general store, he spotted a bottle of whiskey sitting in the window. It had a fancy gold ribbon about it and he caught himself jingling some change in his pocket. Torn, he eyed it lustfully. Every sinew in his body began to crave the hard, strong jolt it would give him, the fire he would feel as it slashed like lightning down his throat. He did not even like the pungent, rotten fruit-like flavor of the stuff he had tasted to date, but the effect of the mere sight of it was mesmerizing. He felt chills. He fought the hypnotic-like dream overcoming him. He pictured the relaxing sensation that could overtake him.

Would overtake him. He emotionally castigated himself as he sat on the boardwalk outside the store, unpeeling the gold ribbon. Ugly whined, and he dumped the bottle upside-down a moment into the dog's mouth, then quickly put the bottle to his own lips and proceeded to gulp it down, his dream realized, the effect more powerful than he had even anticipated.

His head began spinning. He awoke, and could not re-member anything afer that first sip. His eye-level was an inch off the dusty road. A boot passed in front of his face, then another. A woman's shoe stopped a foot from his eyes and he followed his focus up the skirt to a woman smiling at him, then dumping the last cup of a cheap wine bottle onto his face, laughing derisively with three other women, and strid-ing away.

He sat up. Ugly sat beside him, whining but now happier to see him conscious. The general store proprietor walked up and stepped over him, offering him coffee, which he drank. Porter then threw up, along with half the previous day's whis-key and food, all over himself and his dog.

Ugly growled and jumped back, but it was too late — he was covered in his master's vomit.

Porter groaned and looked up at the proprietor. "How long I been out?"

"Since yesterday."

"Where'd I go?"

"All over town, mister. You shamed your people, son."

"What do you mean?"

"You wandered up to a wagon train of Mormons heading to Salt Lake City, and you got kinda loud."

"Loud doing what?"

"You sure you wanna hear this?"

"I reckon," he said, not wanting to. He was hoping it was not as bad as this fellow had perceived it

"You yelled around that you should lead the wagon train."

"Is that all?"

"That's just the beginning. You said you could get it faster to Salt Lake than anybody else. The wagonmaster then asked you to leave."

"Did I?"

"Naw. You swore and began shooting your pistols. Everyone dove for cover. You put holes through three windows – one of 'em mine. That'll be three dollars, by the way,"

"Was anybody hurt?"

"No."

"What happened then?"

"Some old lady told you off, then grabbed you by the hair and dragged you to church. All your Mormon folk were too red-faced to even look at the rest of us, but you gathered quite a crowd of townspeople there, and they were all laughing pretty good."

Porter placed his face in his hands, humiliated.

"But it gets worse."

"Worse?"

"At your church — in that big tent over there — you were talking loud and swearing all during the service. So townsfolk all gathered under the canvas just to see the commotion. I don't think the Mormons ever had such an attendance of outsiders at a service — but believe me — nobody was converted that day. They was there to watch you. When Mormon folks would talk at the podium, you'd shout things about the way they looked — one woman you said looked like a pig with a bonnet. The townsfolk howled with laughter as you yelled out cat calls about everything and everybody. The leader of your group finally stood up and said you'd done a lot of good service for Brigham and Joseph, and that they should be tolerant of your whiskey problem. But then you yelled out that you were to blame for Joseph dying — you should've protected him and gone to Carthage with him. Everyone kinda shook their heads, I reckon feeling sorry for you at that. And even us townsfolk did. I know I did. It wasn't right the way the Missourians and them treated you folk."

Porter was red-faced.

"Well . . . the townsfolk left, some sayin' how they felt for you, others just chuckling over the whole thing. The Mormons were left to themselves. I reckon they have mixed feelings over you, judging from their looks, but their leader did say they have a lot to thank you for, and they left it at that. They had a prayer, and then took off for Salt Lake. You wandered back over here to my store for another bottle, but I wouldn't sell it to you."

"Thank you. Here's ten dollars to pay for everyone's broken windows." It was half his savings, and he had hoped to use it to buy Mary Ann a dress. "Now what'll I do?" He mumbled to himself, finally standing up, "buy her half a dress?"

As he walked slowly away, chunks of throw-up fell onto the ground from his clothes. He ambled achingly to his horse, which the proprietor had fed and taken care of. He placed his saddle on the horse. He rode off with Ugly behind the saddle, and never looked back at the town, too embarrassed for anyone to see him. He realized at that moment — was using his own wisdom in making a wig for Agnas Smith been worth it? His compassion, which his enemies saw non-existent in him, was, ironically, the basis for his very downfall. Or was it something deeper? His free will and choice to disobey Joseph's promise by helping another in distress. How exacting of a commandment, then, is the requirement for obedience?

"It's everything," he mumbled to himself. "Everything."

Porter rode eastward, his head low, hoping to make good time back to the Valley, which for him was only a couple weeks away. Bittersweet, dichotomous thoughts enveloped him. He could not wait to see Mary Ann, who was due any day with their first child.

Yet the pain he felt over Emily was equally intense, which tore his heart a different direction. Simultaneously, he wondered how good he was to the Lord's cause anymore and how much he had to fear for his life.

He suspected, based on his previous gunfight in Utah with Heather Larson's kidnappers, that his priesthood blessing of protection was still intact — at least for a time — but what concerned him most now was that it could have a limit on it, much like an hour glass with its finite connection to the time continuim because of its limited grains of sand, which caused an uneasy feeling that at any day his protection could completely run out. The question now overtaking his thoughts was, 'When?'

He stopped at a creek and dismounted. As his horse drank, he dipped his canteen in the clear running water to fill it. Fifty yards to the east sat a mill with a town built around it. Suddenly he felt Ugly licking his hand. He jerked his head up, noticing a metallic reflection. He glanced sideways and caught sight of, across the creek, hidden in bushes, a man wearing a shiny medallion around his neck. The man did not realize Porter had spotted him. He watched Porter a moment and disappeared behind thick brush.

Porter heard footsteps of someone else 50 feet behind him. He realized a trap was being set for him. He backed up slowly, to not raise suspicions and to get an angle on his ambushers, when he heard a third man. Then four others behind him to one side, quietly closing in on him in a semi-circle.

CHAPTER 24

Glancing down at his leather coat, he noticed Mary Ann had proudly pinned his marshal's badge to his saddlebag, and he had forgotten it was there. He had obviously stumbled upon a nest of outlaws who resided near the town ahead and his badge had made him stick out like a sore thumb. He made a quick decision.

He raced across the shallow creek on large stones. Immediately he disappeared into thick brush. Gunshots suddenly rang out and whizzed over his head. In the cover of trees he caught a glimpse of six moving men. His eyes squinted as he saw they carried six-shooters, a newfangled weapon like his own 1851 Colt Navy. He tore into the nearby woods hearing the men splashing across the creek behind him, one yelling orders to the others:

"This way! . . . He's here!"

More gunshots followed. He ran forward and darted left — then right. Seeing the back of stores on the town's main street, he scooted for cover behind a building.

He caught sight of the six outlaws searching the woods to his right. He was momentarily safe, he figured, and sighed. Then a seventh came forward riding Porter's horse.

He was furious. He spotted two large middle-aged ladies entering their house. It rested beside several others clustered behind Main Street.

Minutes later Porter stood behind a draped window inside the same house, with Ugly beside him.

"Lovely dog you've got there, mister," said one of the elderly ladies. "What's his name?"

"Ugly."

"Oh. Uh . . . nice name."

Through the drapes he spotted the seven outlaws posting themselves about town. He sighed, studied the two ladies now seated across the room knitting, and noticed — hanging up on the door — a dress. A large dress.

The seven gunmen took little notice when three ladies emerged from the house. They wore tight bonnets which covered their faces. The nearest gunman became curious when something fell out of the dress of the largest lady. Ambling up to it, he picked it up. It was some sort of cotton stuffing. He was baffled. He reached down, gathered up the remainder of the cotton, and hurried to catch up to the last lady. He poked her on the shoulder, and she turned around. He stared straight into the face of a bearded, long-haired lawman.

Porter smiled. The outlaw drew his weapon, but Porter whipped up his Colt Navy and fired. The outlaw flew through the air backwards, and crashed to the dirt road.

The remaining six gunmen witnessed it in awe.

Porter yelled to the women, "Run!"

The ladies chugged as fast as they could towards the side of a store across the road, for cover.

Back on their porch, Ugly watched the ladies waddling as fast as they could, and wagged his tail, laughing.

Porter dove to the ground, firing at a second gunman. He rolled and fired again, hitting him and another gunman, who flew through a store window. A third and fourth fired at Porter as he dashed to the cover of a tree. A gunshot hit beside his head. Realizing several must have fired from behind him, he whirled and fired again — hitting one, who whipped back and down, dead.

Porter caught sight of the remaining four gunmen charging from behind. In a hail of lead pistol balls he turned and faced the gunmen. Using the tree as cover, he fired his last three shots — stopping three men dead in their tracks.

Now out of ammo, he waited as the last gunman approached. The man studied the scene and smiled, knowing Porter had used all his shots on six fallen victims: The gunman slowly and confidently came forward.

Disarmed, Porter froze and gazed at him. The fellow stared back, and aimed. He fired point blank — but, to his astonishment, missed. It was his last shot. Horrified, he took out running. Porter grabbed a pistol from a nearby corpse and checked it for ammo. One lead ball was in place. He cocked the hammer and began searching for the last remaining gunman. The fellow ran, terrified. He hid first behind one store, then another. Porter kept closing in. The gunman then ran to the stables, shocked to see Porter waiting for him there, predicting his every move. The gunman then ran towards another building.

The two elderly ladies strode quickly towards their house, heading for cover. They noticed Porter disappearing into the saloon, where, from their porch, they heard only silence. Still, seemingly interminable silence. And then a loud crashing, reverberating gunshot. Blood drops splattered across the saloon windows. The women cringed.

Waiting breathlessly to see who came out victor, they beheld the strange man in the dress appearing at the saloon doorway. He swaggered toward their house, right past them to enter their home in order to change back into his clothes, when he muttered, "Ladies . . ."

Passing Ugly on the front porch, he noticed the animal jumping off the floor in circles, barking, and it occurred to Porter . . . he was being cheered . . .

Porter and Ugly approached the John Neff cabin a couple weeks later at midnight. Porter arrived just in time to see Mary Ann give birth to their first child. It was his first time to not wait outside on the porch during a child's birth. Mary Ann insisted he witness the event with her, so he sat at her side as she clasped his hand. It was March 11, 1855 and in the warm, late winter breeze, as the midwife pulled the infant Mary Amanda from Mary Ann . . .

Porter took one look at the bloody scene — and fainted.

Mary Ann had taken Emily's painting from the old Porter's Springs ranch and nailed it up in "Emily's room" in their new home, a sign of support to her husband. When she announced that to Porter, he grunted and refused to even look at the thing.

"See if you like where I hung it at least," she said.

"Naw, that's all right. I'm sure you put it up good. But she don't need a room here."

She felt sorrow for his pain, yet almost pleased about the rift between him and the last holdout of his former family. He never mentioned Emily again. But Mary Ann could see the anguish in his heart.

In her eyes he was a dutiful husband: Over the next few weeks he helped with the baby, tended the ranch with Lot Huntington, and made repairs. He bred his horses, some of the finest in the West due to his idea of buying lame horses cheaply that were once fast and strong, then breeding them for top-notch stock and selling them at a premium price. And he loved being home. He worked hard with Lot Huntington and found him a solid friend and work companion. Lot opened up more about his family, and even his dreams.

After several weeks passed he began sitting in the newly re-named "guest room" and staring at Emily's painting.

His hair was growing toward its original length, and Mary Ann realized she needed to comb and braid it. She received immense satisfaction formulating the new braids of his trademark hair.

Despite his exile to the porch, Ugly also enjoyed life on the ranch, playing "sheepdog" with a small herd of cows. Mary Ann had traded a few horses for these slow, lumbering creatures, and from them Ugly felt a renewed youth, being able to keep up with them, since he had lost a step or two with age. (Horses were out of his league and had been for years.)

"You did what?" said Porter upon learning of the trade.

"This is my ranch, too," emphasized Mary Ann. "More so lately with you gone all the time, and I'll darn well trade what I want to."

He looked over the cows, then at the horse herd, and realized which horses were missing. He smiled, then stepped forward and hugged her. "Good trade."

She calmed but said, "And what if you hadn't liked it?"

"Fireworks," is all he said.

She laughed, then gave him a kiss. "I would say so," she said. "'Cause I never back down."

The next day as they ate at the table, she asked him, "Seriously, dear husband, what would you do if you didn't like my trades?"

"Few years ago, if I'd known you wanted to mess with my stock, I'd prob'ly have traded 'em all away before you could touch 'em."

"And now?"

"It's your ranch too, ain't it? Just like you said."

She smiled. "You've come a long way for a long-haired madman."

Two days later he awakened to birds loudly chirping and he sat up, surprised at the sudden feelings overtaking him. Despite the powerful love he felt for his new little girl and his wife, he felt an old temptation tugging at him. Not liquor. Not since his last binge. but something else equally distressing to a marriage — something he had experienced with Luana and therefore of which he was well aware: He felt an all-consuming craving for a *change of scenery.*

He also knew Mary Ann would not be pleased.

But when neighbor George Bean showed up at his ranch with news of Indian trouble, Porter was ecstatic. Brigham desired both him and Bean to negotiate once again with Chief Walkara of the Ute tribe.

Porter attempted hiding his pleasure, and even acted perturbed that he had to leave his wife and ranch, but Mary Ann saw straight through it.

"You chased away Luana and then Emily with your wanting to get away," she said.

"It ain't that simple," is all he replied. "It's an assignment."

"Assignment is one thing — where you can get others to take your place if you wanted — and could even hire a deputy to do some of this stuff as Brigham told you last week at church — but you're plagued with something far deeper."

"Yeah, I'd say. What deputies can I trust? Nobody knows the land and nobody knows how to fight the way I do."

"Porter, that's an excuse, as sure as you and I are sitting here. You've got something inside that *pulls* you into the wilderness. And it's not right."

As he and Bean rode away on horseback, Mary Ann cried. "I'll be back," he called back out to her.

Lot also watched furtively as Porter and Bean disappeared on the horizon, wishing he had been asked to go.

Porter could not understand himself. The first night under the stars, as he and Bean watched the campfire flames with Ugly asleep, he said nothing. Bean could tell something was on his mind however, and left him alone to his thoughts.

Porter wondered deep down if he were worthy of such a woman. Why couldn't he stay on the ranch and be satisfied with only married life? Had he in fact driven away Emily? He wondered if Mary Ann were right. Before now, when confronted by Luana years earlier, he'd always felt too defensive to address the possibility that he was in the wrong when it came to the topic of his incessant adventures. Tonight, as he began drifting asleep, he became aware of a light before him. Though the only light in the night was supplied by campfire flames, he felt another partially illuminating a road before him. While entering the road he realized he was not entirely justified in all his years of leaving home — certainly on some occasions, yes, but not all. He became aware of a mysterious field that lay on the other side of the road. The imagery reminded him of Lehi's dream in the *Book of Mormon,* which had been read to him numerous times, only these symbols — as well as being different — he knew had entirely different meanings. In his mind he felt bothered not knowing what lay in the field. Down the road ahead he saw a man-made fountain — not at all like the natural fountain he pictured in Lehi's dream. He wondered if and when he would ever solve the mystery of why he felt so compelled to leave home. If he could just arrive at the fountain, he felt, he might find his answer. What drove him to act as he had, which was so ruinous to his relationships? Suddenly he was jolted awake by his horse whinnying. The mystery of his compulsion for leaving home haunted him the remainder of the night, and he didn't sleep a wink.

CHAPTER 25

Porter's and Bean's mission to Chief Walkara was a qualified success. The chief was attracted to Bean's kindly nature, and respectful of Porter's firm hand. The lawman's legend from Illinois fights also carried some weight with him. But the quarrelsome chief did seem to enjoy creating tension between the whites and his people, so Porter knew their problems would continue — only probably at a less severe level. The chief had been eyeing Porter's Colt Navy pistols and had studied the steel-like determination in Porter's blue eyes before clearing his throat a couple of times, then emitting these simple words, "We will have peace. If that's what you want."

Upon returning to his home several days later, Porter was relieved to find Lot Huntington still working his ranch. The boy still hadn't the nerve to visit his parents, but the next day Porter would break the ice for him. On his way home, Porter stopped at the city judge's ranch and persuaded him to allow Lot to work off his punishment for the armed robbery years earlier. Lot had stolen $50 and had by now worked off that amount for Porter. Porter gave the judge $50. The judge told him Lot was to work another 500 hours at no pay tending city gardens for punishment in lieu of prison. Porter convinced the judge that Lot was still a youngster at heart and he'd see to it the boy stayed straight.

Porter visited Lot's folks and gave them the news; afterwards, they rushed off to see their son, his mother crying all the way to Porter's ranch. "Why didn't you let us come before, Porter?"

"He didn't want to see you. A boy has to deal with guilt, and it takes time."

Porter had in fact sent Mary Ann with verbal messages to Lot's family, keeping them apprised of Lot's return and progress since the beginning. With the continuing admonition to give the boy space.

Lot finally had agreed to see his parents. He hugged them and Porter felt his own eyes getting moist. He told the boy's parents that Lot would visit them Sundays and one other day each week until the 500 hours were worked off.

Meanwhile, Porter took care of his wife and infant for two uninterrupted weeks. He considered that mentally as too short of a time to stay on the ranch with a peaceful life — but emotionally it was a taxing, horribly lengthy period to stay home with domestic chores. Spending time in the back fields after dinner each afternoon with young Lot Huntington, however, made the time go easier. As did of course time spent in the evenings with his wife and baby. He and Lot worked the ranch hard, built fences, shoed horses, and sometimes told stories and laughed till dawn.

But in Porter's laughter was an anguish of imprisonment.

It had taken Mary Ann only a short while before she was becoming short with him, sensing his discontent of feeling trapped at home. With such treatment from her, Porter became increasingly aware that he was ready for more adventure, despite what he had convinced himself earlier about his wandering days being over. Of growing emotional concern was what to do with Emily. Thoughts of her could not be extinguished and he finally made up his mind: He would have to try again and convince her and her husband to live on his ranch.

Mary Ann determined the focus of his discontent and finally confronted him:

"You think Emily and her husband want to live here?"

"Why shouldn't they?" Then he realized, 'Why *should* they?' He had to sufficiently soothe out his feelings with his daughter before she would even consider having him in her life again, much less to move home with him — especially from the verdant valleys of California.

What Porter did not realize was Mary Ann's reason for her increasing anguish.

"And if she does move back here," said Mary Ann, "where will you spend your life?"

"What do you mean?"

"People spend their hours where their hearts are."

"You don't have to worry."

"I do that every day."

"No need."

"You don't think so?" she said. "With your every heartbeat centered on that precious daughter?"

"What do you have against her?"

"It's not her I'm worried over."

"Then what's bothering you?"

"Like a large river running through the valleys," she said. "It starts deep in the mountains. Then it goes back to the source, the spring bubbling out of the mountain. I'm speaking of the spring you loved."

Porter understood. "Luana is a different world away."

"And how much like her does Emily seem?"

"My love is Emily only."

"I fear it's deeper."

Porter was surprised at her disclosure, and tried reassuring her with a kiss, but she turned away and melted into tears. He tried comforting her but Mary Ann refused to be comforted.

"I just want," she said through tears, "to be loved as a wife should be."

"I know, and I'm sorry you don't feel that."

"I can't, not with your concerns so centered on your other family."

"Believe me, I love you only in the way of a man loving a woman. Luana is thousands of miles away and a distant memory. But Emily does hold my heart. And only as she can. But you have nothing to worry about."

"Your whole soul is wrapped up in her." She cried more. "I'm important too."

Porter felt tears well up within him as a compassion for Mary Ann overtook him. He hugged her with more love than he'd ever felt for her.

The next day he walked outside with Ugly and mounted his horse. He wondered what was wrong with him — leaving like this and with everything a mess between him and Mary Ann. He did have an assignment — but he hated the fact he *wanted* to go.

Days earlier Colonel Steptoe had offered Porter to guide him and his 300 troops to California, rather than just using the map Porter had drawn for him. At that time Porter had decided to lead the Army to California and also see Emily. Ugly sat in his ever-present position behind him on the saddle. The trip to California would be difficult on his emotions, he realized, as he felt anguish in two directions — feeling the tug to see Emily, but equally pulled by the desire to stay with Mary Ann and follow Brigham's earlier directive to leave Emily alone. Mary Ann forced a smile as he waved. She did at least truly, finally sense his compassion. Only, she wanted far more.

Not only Mary Ann, but also Lot felt lonely as Porter passed him in the fields on his way out of town. Porter knew Lot had no other friends. As he rode away he told Lot he'd take him on a journey sometime . . . but deep down knew that might be awhile. He felt a certain guilt haunting him — actually something *gnawing* in him to include the boy more, even on this journey, but he quickly dismissed the thought, telling himself that part of the reason for being away in the wild was just that . . . to be away . . . from people — period. Porter was beginning to realize he enjoyed his own company more than he had thought, especially the older he got. Still, he loved returning to the homestead and to friends, but being alone was a part of life he now treasured. As for young Lot, he suspected an uneasiness growing in the boy and feared that in later years this loneliness could take its toll. He shook his head to forget those nagging concerns and took in a deep breath of sweet mountain air as he headed straight to the gold fields of California to see Emily. He was determined to get her home if it killed him.

CHAPTER 26

$\mathbf{J}$udge William Drummond sat in a Salt Lake City courtroom listening to spirited arguments of opposing counsel. Bored practically to tears, he was waiting for the day to end. It was an unseasonably hot afternoon when Simon LeFevre entered a side door waiting for the judge to slam his final gavel.

An hour later the two sat at the sweltering bar, cooled by an open door to the dark, windy alley, finding the hot autumn air of that tavern still more comfortable than anywhere else in town. LeFevre wore his clothes well and his clothes were well cut. Drummond admired his polished appearance. He had not seen him in 10 days. During that time, LeFevre had poured himself into more research of Mr. Porter Rockwell.

"I learned everything."

"Everything?"

"Yeah, but they're mostly rumors," said LeFevre.

"Any facts?"

"Some."

"Start with the facts."

LeFevre was self-possessed. He marshalled his facts well and rifled them with precision. He unveiled an account that mesmerized the judge. He told of Porter's arrival in the valley and of his activities since.

LeFevre was interrupted. The tavern proprietor swaggered up and informed them he was closing but, Drummond, in his indefatigable way, talked the owner into performing paperwork in the back room until the judge and LeFevre chose to leave, as they still had a few drinks to finish over important conversation. Drummond tipped him generously. When the two were alone again, Drummond gulped another drink and spoke softly:

"So what has he done since?"

"Primarily tracked cattle and horse thieves."

"Who has he killed?"

"A few outlaws. However, church enemies claim he's an assassin for Brigham. They claim it's the same stuff he did in Illinois — only worse.

"I've heard, but what's the proof?"

"I don't know — people talk."

"What do you think?"

LeFevre regarded the empty room. "Everyone in here thinks so. But then they talk only to each other."

"So find me the proof."

"What if he catches me snooping around?" said LeFevre. "I do value my future somewhat."

"Tell him you're writing an article on heroic lawmen of the West or something — you know, for a hobby — or better yet for a legal journal, since he knows you're tied with me. Where is the fool now?"

"He went to California — this time leading Steptoe and his 300 men personally."

"Why would Steptoe take him personally instead of just using the map?" said Drummond.

"What would you do — rely on a piece of paper or take the author of the map himself? I'm sure it cost the Army handsomely but, in Steptoe's shoes, I would've hired Rockwell. Wouldn't you?"

Drummond thought a moment. "By all means. Lead ball or no lead ball in my back."

Both men laughed heartily.

On Porter's first night of freedom in California, having finished his expedition with Colonel Steptoe, he decided, after further consideration of Brigham's recommendations, to nevertheless go his own way and see Emily in Sacramento.

At his campfire an unusual incident occurred. He slept under the stars and had a dream. He swam in a lake and became hungry. He spotted a fish and swam after it. The fish swam farther and farther from him, but he kept up the chase. He finally stopped, realizing he had to change his approach. Suddenly the fish returned and he caught it. He woke up. He knew it was time to go home.

Despite the dream, as the hours wore on and as he rode eastward, Porter pondered the matter and felt his emotions overtaking him. He had to bring Emily home. He turned around.

He knew that, despite their differences, and in contrast to Mary Ann, Emily would always love him. A wife could come and go, he had learned, but Emily would always be his daughter. He would try anything to get her and her husband to return to the valley. His ride across desert daylight sand and on stark moonlit terrain went quickly.

He found Emily at her hut near Sacramento, nestled in hardwood trees at the edge of a cliff. Despite her guarded feelings, she beamed upon seeing him. Ugly ran around her in circles and barked happily. She pulled a stew bone from the kettle and gave it to him. He staggered outside with a bone the size of his thigh to enjoy the evening. Porter and Emily greeted each other with hesitant hugs. After a few polite words, he slept outside on his saddle blankets, using his saddle as a pillow.

Alone at the breakfast table the next morning with Emily, Porter confronted her:

"Why won't you return?"

"He's been on a lucky streak. Every day he's cashed in five dollars in gold nuggets."

"Is that where he is now — panning?"

"Yeah."

"And what happens when the creek runs dry of gold?"

"I don't know," she said. "Maybe find another creek."

"You call this a future?"

"It gets us by."

"I could teach him horse ranching," said Porter. "Something stable for the future."

"He loves it here."

"And you?"

"I don't mind it."

Porter sighed, then gazed at her. "Don't you want to be with me?"

She studied him and finally responded. "You'd be off all the time."

"I am less these days," he said.

"'Must be temporary. You'll never stay put."

"I will with you around."

"Papa," she moved from the stove to his chair, reached down and kissed his forehead. "I don't know what to think of you. We're always mad at each other." She also felt anguished at the obvious reminder of his new wife:

His hair was neatly braided, but differently than before. It had been Emily's idea for her father to wear a neat pony tail before he had cut it, but now Mary Ann was intruding into this matter as well with a different style, she felt.

"I want you home with me," he said after a moment. "You and the goldpanner."

"He'd never go back to the valley. But you could move here."

Just then, Henry Brizzee, entered.

"Boy," said Porter, "it's time you face your responsibilities and build a future for my daughter and yourself. I'll teach you a solid occupation."

"Are you serious?" said Henry.

"I am," said Porter. "Start packing."

"What if I don't want to?"

"I'm here to help you." At that he pushed Henry toward his clothes dresser.

"Papa!" yelled Emily.

Henry glowered at him a moment, then lowered his head, ran forward, and rammed him.

Porter fell back, the wind knocked out of him.

Emily shouted, "Honey, don't hurt him!"

Henry shouted at him, "You can just get out of my home if you're going to start bossing us around."

Porter then sprung from the ground like a cat. He pounced on him, but Henry punched back.

Angered and hurt, Porter hit him — and the force of his fist sent Henry hurdling out the wax-papered window. And over the cliff beside their house.

CHAPTER 27

Emily screamed.

Porter jumped into the door frame, then leaped outside to the edge of the cliff. He saw Henry eighty feet below treading water in the cold stream. He dove down into the river beside him, pulled him up, and Henry gasped for air.

"Thank you," said Henry.

"You're welcome," said Porter, then pinched him again.

Emily rushed outside and tried holding her father back, but he punched Henry with his left fist, then with his right. Henry crashed backwards into the water, out cold.

Porter pulled him ashore.

Ugly gazed over the edge of the cliff from his bone feasting to observe some of the commotion, but returned to his concentration of the food task at hand, wagging his tail.

Porter saw Emily arriving with a pack mule on the steep, winding trail. He picked up Henry and tossed him on the pack mule, and began walking beside the animal as it returned up the hill. Emily walked on the other side of the mule as she noticed her husband regaining consciousness. "Are you all right?" she said.

"Never felt better," said Henry.

Porter stood over him, continuing to walk as he slowly spoke:

"The Lord wants us in our territory. You know that."

"I guess I do know that," he said.

"Yep," said Emily. "I know that too."

"Good," said Porter.

"But we ain't goin'," she said.

Porter sighed with frustration. He was as upset with this decision as he was with himself for acting as he had, attempting to force them against their wills. His daughter and Henry had obviously thought through their decisions and knew what they wanted. They arrived atop the cliff and Henry slid off the pack mule with a thud. He arose, staggered into the hut again, and sat down at the table, where he resumed eating his eggs and potatoes.

Porter joined him. "Good potatoes," he offered.

"Yep," said Henry.

Neither man looked at the other — both kept eating away as if nothing had happened.

"You reckon to have a mild winter out here?" said Porter.

"'Did last year."

Both chomped away in silence, eating with a good appetite. Emily entered and stared at them, amazed at their immediate, unspoken return to cordiality. She smiled, then sat with them.

"Want more beans?" she offered both.

"Yep," said both simultaneously.

"You first," said Henry.

"No, you first," said Porter.

Henry took a heaping spoonful and passed them to Porter.

Porter took a bite. "Fine beans."

"Yep."

Emily smiled again.

Porter then put on his hat, nodded to Emily and Henry across the dinner table, and left without another word. He then went back inside, shook Henry's hand, and hugged Emily. Still no words spoken. Then left.

Ugly joined him, prematurely ending his stew-bone feast and therefore not entirely pleased with the afternoon's events. When Porter noticed the disconcerted expression on his face he urged him to bring along the huge bone.

"I'll tie it to the top of the horse," said Porter.

Ugly wagged appreciatively.

As they rode away, Porter muttered to his dog, "I just can't seem to get the knack for this social graces thing."

Ugly wagged.

Behind Porter rode Ugly and his bone for the next two days. By the third day it began to smell, and the rest of the week was somewhat nauseating for Porter, but he respected his friend and would not toss the thing overboard, although he was tempted, especially when a good, stiff breeze came up from behind. However, that night Porter urged him to bury it.

"Dogs are supposed to like burying bones," he urged Ugly in somewhat of a pep talk. "That way you can dig it up if we pass this way again." Of course at that point it would be dry and meatless, but that was all right with Ugly. From Porter's gestures he seemed to understand, and commenced digging the soft, sandy California earth. At their campfire, Porter felt greatly relieved, watching chunks of earth being kicked up and behind the dog by his massive paws.

Porter squinted as he was sprayed by flying sand landing on his face.

Months passed. Remaining in California Porter spent his time helping Mormons pack for trips to Salt Lake. Various converts were arriving at San Francisco from Europe on sailing ships. He helped them by giving his considerable earnings from Steptoe to various families in desperate need who had run out of funds for provisions to make it to Salt Lake.

When he ran out of money himself on the last day of summer, he took out for home on the very next day, leading a missionary just returning from Calcutta and several others.

"Can you help us make it fast?" said the missionary, almost completely broke.

"Yes, sir," said Porter. "If you share with me half your provisions, I'll hunt us up the rest and get us there faster than man has ever made it."

"'Deal," said the missionary.

Porter smiled, shook his hand, and both men stuck to their word.

They left Carson Valley September 22, 1855 and arrived in Salt Lake Valley less than two weeks later.

At his cabin Porter told Mary Ann about his trip. She was interested — unlike Luana would have been, but resentful — like Luana would have been. He wanted to get out on the open range immediately, and in conversation he casually alluded to the fact. She demanded to know how long he could stay home before he would have to leave.

He felt imprisoned. Mary Ann should feel secure enough to allow him to leave anytime, he felt. He knew deep down he was wrong, but was tired of this recurring marital problem.

A week passed. He was in a surly mood so Lot did not enjoy being with him. In fact they worked at opposite ends of the ranch.

When Porter announced he would be leaving on not one but two more assignments — for several days each — he expected Mary Ann to seethe.

Instead she said, "Go right ahead."

"What did you say?" he said.

"I mean it. I want you to go."

She had attended church the day before and had heard a sermon from the lay ministry that encouraged spouses to support each other in occupational and church assignments. She felt it her obligation to support him, and she attempted to take on a new attitude. Therefore, he was now eating his favorite meal — catfish, T-bone steak, potatoes, and brown bread and butter, freshly whipped.

He knew however as they spoke after his favorite dessert — Southern-style, warm peach cobbler — that she was trying to cover her real feelings. He did figure out this much: She was the kind of woman who needed him home despite what she learned at church, and she had fairly warned him of that before their marriage. Thus, he figured, she must be growing in her resentments. He could not sleep, sensitive of all these things inside not settling right.

As the night wore on, he could not slip unconscious, sensing her still awake, although she feigned sleep. Actually, she was worrying and was not willing to talk. He arose and walked outside.

The next morning he left for three days, taking Ugly with him.

As before, Lot watched him ride away, and this time his heart sunk when Porter did not even wave. He had no idea of the turmoil brewing in Porter's heart, but from his coldness, the boy's own disappointment sunk into depths he had for awhile forgotten even existed.

Porter returned to his ranch at dawn — only to find the cabin deserted.

Mary Ann was gone.

There was also no trace of Lot.

Porter walked in and out of his cabin searching for notes from her, then noticed in the dust an arrow pointing to George Bean's ranch.

He galloped off and got Bean out of bed.

"I'm afraid she hasn't been feelin' good, Port," said Bean.

"Is that all she said?"

"Yeah, and she's gone back to her folks awhile till she feels better."

Porter knew exactly what that meant, although Bean did not; Mary Ann was not the sort to spread dirty linen in public, although she was known to share with certain friends her deepest, private concerns.

"As for young Huntington," added Bean, "he's back with his folks. I guess he worked off his punishment some time ago but was staying at your ranch 'cause he liked you. When I saw Mary Ann, she said Lot told her you were never around anymore, and he also thought you were mad at him anyway, so he took off."

Porter was upset young Lot had misunderstood him. He immediately mounted up with Ugly and rode off to see Mary Ann.

"I'm afraid she doesn't want to see you," said Mary Ann's mother, moments after Porter knocked at the door.

"Well, I'm her husband and I can see her if I want."

"Not according to her," she said, "and I'd advise you to get out of here."

Porter began opening the door to push his way in, when Mrs. Neff informed him that Mary Ann was not there anyway.

"Then where is she?"

"'Doesn't want you to know."

Porter sighed. He was chagrined by the similarity between her and Luana's mother protecting their daughters. She could be anywhere — visiting or hiding at any friend's or neighbor's home, he figured. And then he realized — if she did not want to see him, why the devil should he force the issue? If she loved him, she'd come back to him. That was that. And so he left.

A fear of her leaving him for good began to overtake him, and it stabbed his heart. He know how much he loved her. But also knew he loved her. But also knew he was too much at war with himself — and too proud — to go tracking her down. When he had put all that effort into tracking down Luana, it had all been in vain — so why bother, he told himself. Mary Ann would have to put up some effort, too. He had been burned on that issue once too many times. The only question was — how long could he wait.

He felt like dying.

PART III

Assassins

CHAPTER 28

"All right," said the bartender, "Who here has the guts to disprove the legends of Mr. Porter Rockwell?"

No one spoke in the Mexican-border tavern.

"A twenty dollar gold piece here says no man can do it." The bartender tossed a coin onto the bar. Another added a ten dollar piece.

Still no one took the bet. Four others threw in gold pieces. Then a wealthy miner threw in a bag of gold dust worth a small fortune. "If any man here has the guts to match this and take on that lawman, they're entitled to it," he said.

"Everyone started to laugh. The gamblers were half drunk and smiled with relief, realizing their wager was safe and that they had been a bit too bold.

Suddenly, from a far corner of the dimly-lit saloon, a slim, broad-shouldered man with a brown mustache arose and swaggered to the table. All eyes watched as he stopped at the bar and threw down three gold pieces and a matching bag of gold dust, all worth $300 — half his life's savings from robberies and shooting contests. The laughter stopped.

"Barkeep, you keep the kitty," said the stranger. "If anything's lost from it by the time I get back, two bullet holes will be where your eyes once was."

That afternoon, the stranger rode north to add another notch to his gun belt — one that would be his most highly prized yet — one worth a small fortune since the town's wealthiest men had taken him on. He thrived on challenges, and already had a dozen notches from similar bets on his belt, ranging from small town sheriffs to U.S. Marshals . . . He had heard of the Mormon marshal who could not be killed — but until now no one had offered betting money. He smiled as he imagined the obvious outcome of his impending confrontation.

The man was Frank Slade. While riding out of town it occurred to him he could double his winnings by betting the other half of his savings at additional taverns near Salt Lake Valley. He figured to stop at all that he could as he approached his destination. He determined them perfectly safe bets. And with his life on the line, what good was his last $300 anyway?

CHAPTER 29

In Salt Lake's largest saloon sat William Drummond at his usual corner table, staring out the window at the street bustle. It was Saturday night and the place was packed. The smoke was so thick it made his eyes smart.

Simon LeFevre strode up and sat across from him. "Judge, have you ever heard of Frank Slade?"

"I'm too busy to know everyone in the territory."

"He's in town on a bet asking about Rockwell," continued LeFevre. "I met him with a couple drinks under his belt and he talked a bit more than was prudent — but the advantage to him is that he came across as some big-talking drinker. I checked up on him at the sheriff's office and learned his credentials. He's got a decent shooting record. More than decent. Brigham's main protector may be falling sooner than we thought. Perhaps with their walking legend gone, the people's faith might get shaken a bit. Even quite a bit. And Brigham's support could even be undermined if the people lose faith that they're being protected. "

Drummond lifted his stare from LeFevre's face back to the window. "Find him and tell him I'll prosecute if there's any bloodshed in my territory, as long as I'm in town. But I'll be vacationing with Ada to the Colorado border soon. Think he'll get my drift?"

"Loud and clear," said LeFevre. "But why do you want the delay?"

"We have homework to do on Brigham. I want a solid case against him and Rockwell first. So when Rockwell does have an accident that catches up with him, we can release our side of his background to the press and watch the locals' faith get shaken. But as it is now — if he died by an ambush, we'd have a martyr on our hands. We need to watch him step into public relations quicksand first — which from his intermittent drinking problem could be happening sooner than we had hoped. So for now we need Slade kept at bay."

In Drummond's mind, what would be left of Brigham's tumbling power structure in the aftermath of the revolution would be a gubernatorial throne. Not even LeFevre was privy to these aspirations. "After you drop this hint to Slade," said Drummond, "begin to interview all local government officials you can to glean what information that will help us bury Rockwell's reputation."

———————

Porter still lacked the courage to return to his cabin, and spent the next two days visiting his friend George Bean.

When he did muster up the courage to face further rejection, he returned home. Mary Ann was still gone. He came to a painful realization of the feelings he had tried dismissing. He had heretofore been angry at her refusal to discuss what bothered her, which was just the opposite of Luana's general overt criticalness. But he was also perturbed by two traits she shared with Luana — leaving him high and dry and attempting to impede his freedom. He knew it was mostly his problem, but it still bothered him about her. Why couldn't the women he fell for be independent-minded and freedom-giving like some women he had met? Then again, he realized, would he really want that? What was wrong with him for wanting women he was no good for? And especially for falling in love with them so deeply? And most importantly — why couldn't he settle down? However, he now felt only one dominant emotion: the fear of losing her.

He rode away from his deserted cabin to the nearby Neff ranch in Mill Creek Canyon. Dismounting, he strode to the door.

"She's still not here," said her mother.

"Where' she at now?"

"Her own cabin."

"She has a cabin?"

"Her father's building it."

"Where?"

"Over that knoll."

Porter galloped across the knoll and reined in at a crude cabin under construction. Mary Ann was busy helping her father haul wood to the site, while the child, Mary Amanda, was fenced in a nearby corral and playing. When Mary Ann beheld Porter, she stopped and stared.

John Neff also gazed in amazement, then quickly excused himself and left for his cabin.

"Sorry I was gone so long," said Porter.

"That's something new for you."

"Being gone so long?"

"Apologizing."

He cleared his throat. "But I did come searching for you."

"Before you took off for George Bean's place?" she said, holding in her anger. "I was just getting away from you about three days. I think you should've looked for me when I showed up missing longer, don't you?"

"I'm sorry, I can't read your mind."

"What the devil kind of genius do you have to be to see when it's time to look for me?" she said.

He peered off at the horizon, not knowing what to say, realizing no amount of logic would communicate to her, which was a lesson he'd been slow to learn with Luana.

She meanwhile saw him as a different, unfeeling species who continually amazed her by his coldness and stupidity.

"'Should be a good season for cherries, don't you think?" he finally offered after a painful silence.

She tried holding back her feelings. "So, you got safely to California?" she said, trying to calm herself.

"Yeah."

"What did you do there?"

"Visiting," he said.

"Emily only?"

"One other."

"What other?" said Emily.

"Her husband."

"Why'd you leave me so long?" she said.

"Felt like it."

"Care to explain?"

"No."

"Miss her?"

"I Reckon."

Mary Ann could not shake the apparently un-ending envy she felt towards Emily.

That night they slept in separate quarters — she in her parents' cabin, he in the new structure. The next morning they argued over where they would live permanently. He demanded they live in his cabin.

She demanded they live in the new structure just a hundred yards from her parents.

He suggested a compromise.

So they moved a hundred yards from her parents.

"Do you call this a compromise?" he said.

"If you want to keep living with me, it's a compromise," she said.

Porter felt grateful she was taking him back, but frustrated at the whole situation. He would have to let his love for her smooth out his frustration, he realized. Without such feelings, he would only feel anger and resentment. Brother Brigham's church sermons on that issue had been clear. "She's a good woman," he told himself. "Deserving of better than me." He felt the resurgence of love towards her he had felt in their courtship. By the second night, she was finally melting towards him, and decided to move back to their ranch and let her father use the new cabin for other family members. Porter was relieved; he needed more each day the privacy of his own property. He also felt a certain satisfaction living in a cabin he'd constructed with his own hands, so was anxious to return for that reason as well. And they were finally home, together.

Porter decided again he would not take any assignments that would draw him away from the ranch for more than a week.

He was also waiting for the day a letter would come from Emily.

When Mary Ann learned that was a materiel factor in keeping him home, she was frustrated deeper than ever. "Why couldn't Porter stay home for me?" she thought. Porter practically lived for the day Emily would actually show up at the door.

To the extent he looked forward to it, Mary Ann feared it. She really feared, deep down, even more than that . . . the day Luana would show up at the door.

But then came a strike that drove the most painful spike yet into his relationship with Mary Ann . . .

One Friday evening Porter took her out for a play at the Social Hall. Upon the conclusion of *Hamlet,* as she spoke with her friends across the lobby, Brigham ambled up to Porter.

"Where's the Huntington boy?" said Brigham.

"What do you mean?"

"I heard he's taken a liking for you since you helped him — and I even thought you might bring him to the play."

"I thought of it," said Porter. "I know he likes plays a lot. I just never got around to it."

"He wasn't a bad performer in a couple plays when he was younger," said Brigham. "He just needs folks to look up to. Though I don't know how in tarnation he chose you," smiled Brigham.

"A big mistake if I've ever seen one."

Across the lobby watched Simon LeFevre, dressed fastidiously and unescorted. He was in town for a week, relieved to be out of Fillmore. Beside him strolled William Drummond, equally grateful to be in the big city and now arm and arm with his tall, laughing companion, Ada Carroll, whom many supposed to be his wife. His real wife, in the meantime, had threatened him through recent letters that if he would not drop Ada and send for her and the children immediately, she would begin writing letters to the newspapers. He laughed at her ludicrous threats. He appreciated the companionship of any good woman, so he was fundamentally pleased with this particular female with her striking red hair and piercing, green eyes. And he was especially glad he had brought her West with him. Above all, he was downright proud of his new-found boldness. Deeper, he hoped his wife would actually divorce him. Presently, he spotted Porter and Brigham, then nodded Simon LeFevre over to them to eavesdrop.

LeFevre glided unobtrusively across the lobby, then stopped to listen. He lit up a cigar. Numerous smoking "gentiles," the non-Mormons, filled the lobby, many sporting a cigar or pipe.

"'Reason I wanted to talk, Porter," said Brigham, "is about our problems. We need to get rid of the robbers and thieves at all costs. The outlying settlements are being plagued by them. Even the bank in town is a continuing target. They're bleeding us dry. But bring them in alive if you can."

"And if they fight back?"

Brigham sighed. "Do what you need to."

Outside, walking with Drummond and his escort down State Street, LeFevre relayed to Drummond what he had heard.

"We've got our fuel," said Drummond, coolly. "'Sounds like he's been appointed judge, jury, and executioner. "Now do what you can to burn him."

LeFevre smiled at Drummond's twisting of Brigham's words, but shrugged it off, knowing the assassin Slade would expeditiously take care of Porter anyway.

CHAPTER 30

In the middle of the night, through a deep sleep, Porter heard a loud knock. He jerked awake. The door flew open and dust whirled in. He squinted into the darkness and cocked his Colt. Fresh sage filled his nostrils and the breeze cooled his sweat. Quickly he made out the figures of two men in the darkness.

"You Port Rockwell?"

Porter was not sure what to do but finally answered, "I know where he's at."

"We need him right away, if you can direct us to him."

"Who are you?"

"I'm Nick Searle, this is Howe Chambers." Both men were medium, lean and middle-aged, and both hailed from New England, as did their dialects.

"What do you want?" said Porter.

"We're the new assistant bank managers."

"Good. You didn't answer my question."

Searle, the older, explained they had just been robbed for the second time in eight days and finally asked, "Where might we find Mr. Rockwell?"

"Follow me."

As they followed Porter outside they saw his long hair braided behind his head in a pony tail and falling half way down his back into view. They glanced at one another.

After saddling and mounting his favorite steed, then awakening Ugly in the barn, he muttered to Ugly, "Some guard dog you've turned out to be."

Ugly yawned.

"You're just getting old, boy. At least on the trail you're worth your weight in gold," he said, helping Ugly up to the saddle. "You're also getting heavier with age." He glanced back at Mary Ann coming outside to see him off. She noticed the two men riding ahead, waiting for Porter to catch up a quarter mile down the road.

"I'll be waiting here," she said, forcing herself to smile.

In the moonlight Porter studied her, and winked.

"I'll be back soon."

The confidence he radiated still did not alleviate the foreboding fear she felt, causing her to wonder, as always, if this might be the incident from which he doesn't return alive.

Out on the desert, Porter thought of young Lot. "If I get time when I get back, I'll take him hunting," he mumbled. "But only for critters that don't shoot back and taste good," he chuckled.

Three days later he found the tracks of the six bank robbers. Riding beside him were Searle and Chambers, exhausted. Presently Porter led them to a miner's hut where six horses were hitched outside. Ugly licked his neck while facing the hut, confirming that men were, inside.

"So this is their hide-out?" said Searle. "You don't think they'd still be in there, do you? It's almost noon."

"I know they're in there. My dog smells 'em."

"Your dog?"

"Yep."

"Your dog talks to you?"

"Sorta."

Searle and Chambers glanced at each other again, wondering what the devil they had gotten themselves into.

Porter noted their expressions and held back a smile. The mischievious side of him began to take over. "Let me check to see what they're doing." Porter put his ear down to Ugly's muzzle, and simultaneously tickled his dog's tummy. It made a noise.

Porter glanced over at the bank assistants. "He says there's six men inside."

Chambers was not wanting to be drawn into such a ludicrous conversation, but couldn't help himself. "How can he see through the walls? That's crazy."

"No it ain't," said Porter. "What's crazy is that you believe he can *talk*."

What'd you say?" said Porter to Chambers. "You need to see a doctor, Mr. Chambers. Very few lunatics even believe dogs are conspiring against them."

Searle broke in, "What about the outlaws?"

Porter squinted at the hut, "I reckon they played poker till dawn and are asleep."

"Let's get 'em."

"I don't care if they"re half dead!" said Searle. "They're criminals and they're dangerous! We'll head back to the city for a posse."

"They'll be gone by the time you get back," said Porter. "We'll take 'em now."

"We?"

Porter observed their horror. "All right," he clarified things somewhat:

"Me."

"It's suicide," said Chambers. "We'll get you a posse."

Porter ignored them and rode down the gully alone. The two bankers watched, amazed.

CHAPTER 31

Five of the outlaws played poker while the sixth stood guard.

Porter saw them through the window and muttered, "So much for my theory they're asleep."

Suddenly the outlaw guard shouted to the others. All six stared in amazement at a man whose shoulder-length pony-tail swished back and forth as he brazenly rode down the hill toward their hut on horseback, whistling a little tune.

"Whoever gets him in the chest gets his horse," said Rulon Thompson, their leader.

"Naw, he don't know nothin'," said another, "or he wouldn't be here."

Still another agreed: "And you ever seen a lawman looking like that? Let's invite him in for a meal."

The long-haired stranger lurched from his horse and jumped behind a boulder.

Thompson tensed. "I told you we should'a got him while we could."

"Don't matter," said the second. "We'll get him anyway."

The six outlaws loaded and cocked their weapons. They heard the long-haired one's voice echo down the canyon:

"You boys come out and surrender."

Thompson laughed. "Did I hear what I thought I heard?" All six broke out chuckling and began firing.

Gunfire suddenly shattered their chuckling. Two bodies jolted backwards and one spun on impact.

Porter reloaded.

The other four, still unhurt, aimed directly at the stranger and fired — but all they saw was a flashing weapon: Porter now bounded down the hill firing. One got off a second shot but seconds later fell back with a bullet hole through his forehead.

Porter dived into the door and fan-fired. Bodies jolted and jerked, and soon all six men soon lay completely, perfectly still.

Porter panted a moment and viewed the scene. Behind him presently appeared the two bankers and Ugly. They stepped into the doorway and stared. The stolen money lay in two sacks in a corner.

Searle's eyes were wide, incredulous. "I think it's time for lunch."

Lunch that day for Mary Ann was only a tamale. She had soon fallen asleep in a rocking chair on the porch. Hours passed, and it was dark. Suddenly she awakened to see, in the moonlight, a man packing a mule with six bags draped over it. The man stopped on the south range at the old dry well and dumped each one into it.

She then recognized him. She felt sickened as it dawned on her what the bags were.

When Porter arrived with Ugly at the cabin, Mary Ann shook her head in disgust, then entered the bedroom and slammed the door.

Porter and Ugly slept by the fire on the bear rug that night.

Across from Brigham's desk sat Porter.

"The reason I asked you to see me," said Brigham, "is for another assignment."

"Mary Ann will love it," responded Porter.

"Yeah, let's act how unexcited we are," said Brigham. "I know perfectly well how much you enjoy getting out on the range."

"I have promised her, though, I'd shy away from gunplay. Especially since my last little episode."

"Well then, this will fit your plans beautifully, because I need you to go to Fort Bridger and help James Brown bring down Indian goods to sell here. Just as you did a couple years ago. By the way, how's young Huntington doing?"

"Haven't seen him since he worked on my ranch. I reckon he's with his folks. But when I get around to it, I might talk to him about helping me with deputy work."

"Just so long as Judge Drummond doesn't get wind of it," laughed Brigham. "He'd probably find a law against former rowdies having a chance to repent and join law enforcement!"

"Prob'ly so," said Porter. "And that's the first law he'd use against me, I reckon. I feel the hairs on my neck raise when I even think of his court decisions. Mary Ann keeps up with the newspapers, and tells me he's a bandit in a black cloak."

"True," said Brigham. "I've never seen a legal demon hurt our people like he does."

"Maybe he needs a little warning," smiled Porter with squinted eyes.

Brigham sat up straighter and lost his smile. "Porter, you keep your nose clean and let me deal with the legal demons."

Mary Ann said nothing as she held baby Mary Amanda on the porch and watched Porter ride away. She had agreed to not put up a fuss over short trips for Brigham, but she was still nauseated over his last little episode, as short as it was. She bit her lower lip, watching him but trying to remain supportive.

"Where's he going?" said Lot Huntington to Mary Ann. Lot had ridden to their ranch to pick up his last payment.

"Wyoming."

Lot felt left out of Porter's life once more as well, as he watched Porter ride off in the distance, and muttered, simply:

"Oh."

As Porter rode northward with Ugly behind him, he glanced back and noticed Lot and Mary Ann waving. Mary Ann held up the baby's hand as if to wave also, and he felt a twinge as strongly as he ever had — to stop at a tavern for a drink. He had frequented one several times a week lately compared to the once-a-month occasions before coming West. He simultaneously felt torn, wanting to invite Lot along and even spend a few more days with Mary Ann and the baby before leaving, but he told himself he just wanted to get it over with, and, since he had to go anyway, to enjoy the coming days alone in the wilderness. So off he rode, shaking his hauntings to the wind.

CHAPTER 32

Drummond sat in his Fillmore chambers with LeFevre:

"I've heard of that man James S. Brown. Did Rockwell ever see him?"

"Yeah, in Wyoming."

"What happened?"

"The story goes there were nine white men and some Indians at Sutter's Mill when gold was discovered. Seven of the nine were young Mormon soldiers discharged from the Mormon Battalion at San Diego. James S. Brown was one of the seven."

"So what happened in Wyoming?"

"Porter helped Brown bring Indian goods here — several thousand dollars worth to sell to passing immigrants journeying to California. I guess Brigham needed cash for the territory. Just as he did in July of 1853. But that's not the big story. The real story is this: Remember when Rockwell rounded up the Pahvant braves for Colonel Steptoe?"

Drummond nodded.

"They did that because Pahvant braves had killed eight Pacific Railroad crewmen. Their crew boss was a Captain Gunnison who once wrote a book critical of the Mormons. Some people think the Indians didn't really ambush his crew — but Brigham had sent Rockwell to do it."

"Did anybody else have a motivation to kill Gunnison?" said Drummond.

"Two Pahvant braves had just been killed by Missouri emigrants. So a band of the braves may have killed Gunnison and his crew in retaliation. That's what Brigham claims, of course."

"But there's no proof?"

"None."

"Yet there's no proof Rockwell didn't kill them," said Drummond. "We might use that. Go on."

"That's all."

"I've got a plan," said Drummond. "But we need harder evidence. See me in three weeks from tonight at our Salt Lake tavern."

"Tell me what you've learned since I last saw you," said Drummond. Both men sat in a darkened corner. "Specifically, who has he killed recently?"

"Nobody knows," said LeFevre.

"What do you mean?"

"Most desperados make their way West and get killed with no identification," explained LeFevre. "Their associates aren't stupid enough to come into the cities to file reports — so a man like Rockwell has basically left a trail like any lawman has — with no names under the gravestones. Additionally, neighbors say the Indians respect him because they can't kill him. Anyway, Rockwell believes his legend that he can't die, and that makes him all the more ferocious."

"But if what you say is correct — that Rockwell doesn't bring outlaws back alive — he must be acting as judge, jury and executioner — just as Brigham mandated," said Drummond.

"That's not exactly what Brigham mandated. You know that."

"What then?"

"He just said to do what needs to be done."

"He doesn't need to bury every man he faces," argued Drummond.

"Outlaws will do anything to not face prison. You know the conditions there — they'll usually draw on the law rather than be taken."

"Then why can't anybody outgun him?"

"I'm just telling you what I know."

"Do you know how many bandits he's killed?"

LeFevre shook his head.

"You're certain he shoots only outlaws?"

"That's all I know so far."

"Do you know where he buries them?"

"No one knows."

Drummond perceived something in Simon LeFevre that bothered him. He discerned in his aide's eyes a growing admiration for the killer.

"They say he'll walk into any den of desperadoes and just cut them down," said LeFevre. "That's why there are no judges or juries."

"Then that's what we can stick him on," said Drummond, sitting up straighter. "You shouldn't be bothered with that."

"No court would indict him."

"My court will."

"Not unless you pack the jury. The folks here believe religiously in frontier justice."

"We'll see. He can be nailed one way or another."

"I think, with all due respect," said LeFevre, "you're dreaming. Just let Slade do his job and assassinate him."

"I don't want him killed just yet. You don't seem to understand that."

"You need something bigger if you want some kind of indictment against him," said LeFevre. "Something more fact-based." While deep down he did hold a growing admiration for the lawman, as Drummond suspected, he held it in check, knowing a promotion was in the wind and that it was based solely on his ability to perform; additionally it was based — as events were shaping up from Drummond's perspective — on his ability to actually get Rockwell nailed. As LeFevre understood it, though mistakenly, Drummond alone possessed the power to recommend him to a district office in San Francisco and away from this puritanical desert. And for that, LeFevre was itching to help Drummond any way he could, despite his inclinations otherwise.

Porter rode through downtown Salt Lake City at sunset. He noticed men coming and going from a tavern and suddenly experienced the strongest thirst he had ever felt. He tried riding past and turning his head, but as he passed the tavern, he halted his horse and turned his head slowly back, then stared inside.

Assessing the vicissitudes of life, he sat at a rear corner table, staring at his half-empty whiskey bottle, its contents sloshing about, having just been set down after another shot glass had been poured and killed.

His eyes swam to the other patrons and slowly focused on the area's esteemed federal judge, William W. Drummond, seated across the darkened corridor. He smiled and arose, casting all anxieties to the wind, leaving Ugly lapping whiskey from a wooden bowl at the table. He staggered forward and arrived at the judge's table.

"Evening, Judge," said Porter.

Drummond glanced up. When he saw the long-haired lawman staring down at him in the low light of the saloon, one could see the blood drain out of Drummond's face — his skin went white as a ghost.

"Yes?" said a completely disconcerted Drummond, eyes wide with terror.

CHAPTER 33

"**I** just want to congratulate you on your talents," said Porter, "of harassing my people so well in court."

Drummond looked about the crowded saloon and noticed all faces turning to him. It was a classic showdown, he told himself, of good versus evil, and he had to put on a good show for his many admirers to prove that right always prevailed.

"You're drunk, sir," he said with forced insolence.

"My friends have put up with your behavior as patiently as turtles laying eggs and waiting for them to hatch," hiccuped Porter, realizing the drink was helping him practically wax poetic, "but I'm a bird of a different color."

Drummond smiled at his mixed metaphors and obvious stupidity.

"Let's talk after you sober up," said Drummond impatiently.

"Let's not."

"Then what do you want?"

"Things to change," said Porter. "This stuff has gotta stop. I've also heard you're bringing some loose woman into the courtroom and having her sit on your lap during court sessions. Is that true?"

"I don't mind admitting that it is," said Drummond. "So what concern is that of yours?"

"Is that supposed to insult us?"

Drummond smiled. "On occasion."

"I've heard the newspaper articles," said Porter, "about your wife's letters to the *Deseret News*. Why would you break her heart?"

"And why would you break Luana's? And now Mary Ann's? And even Emily's?"

Porter almost became sober hearing that. "How'd you know all that?"

"You have some soul-searching to do before you start laying into me, Mr. Rockwell."

"So — answer me — how'd you know all that?"

"'Isn't it really true we're just birds of a feather, Mr. Rockwell? I have Miss Carrol; you have your adventures. I suppose we're both just traveling through life with our own mistresses, aren't we?"

Porter stared at him, stunned.

"If we weren't on opposite sides of Brigham's kingdom, I'd dare say we'd be drinking buddies," said Drummond. "Now come visit me sometime when you're sober if you want to complain about me."

"I'm warning you fair and square. You stop this stuff with my people."

"Your concern is noted," said Drummond with a sneer.

The crowded saloon cheered their esteemed judge as one who would boldly stand up to the local hierarchy.

Porter staggered away and out the door, haunted by his curiosity of Drummond's vast knowledge of his personal life. Ugly wobbled along behind him, somewhat inebriated.

Drummond meanwhile was now more anxious than ever to use Porter for his ends . . . until he could dispose of him.

At their cabin next early evening, Mary Ann fought a singular depression overtaking her. Her dominant emotions heretofore had been associated with neglect, but now the anxiety was taking a different course. She actually feared her husband's life was in immediate danger.

She turned to Porter. "You going to the big hoe-down at Oakley's barn tonight?"

"I'd just as soon rest," he said. "'Been a long day." He had worked hard on the ranch since sunrise, and it made him appreciate Lot's assistance all the more now that he was gone.

"'Been years since we danced," she continued.

Porter studied her. "If you want to go, yeah, let's go."

"Not unless you want to," she said.

"I want to," he said, not really wanting to.

"You really want to go?"

"Yeah, I really want to go," he said, definitely not wanting to the more he thought about it. "So what dance is it?"

"Folks are actually celebrating the hope Drummond might be ousted as federal judge. His wife is really burned over the Ada Carrol issue. And she's convinced his superiors in Washington to review his situation here. She told the Eastern press everything — and he just might be gone soon. So, are we going tonight?"

"Yeah," said Porter, sincerely. "I guess I really do feel like dancing."

Carriages and horses were tied in front of Oakley's barn at the south end of Salt Lake Valley. Arriving there, Porter glanced around to see if Lot and his horse were around. He quickly forgot about him. Ugly was meanwhile resting at the ranch, tempted to unearth a tunnel under the chicken coop for a midnight feast, but eventually was overcome by sleep. He did allow his tail to wag pondering the possibility as he drifted off, but realized he was just too old and tired.

Inside the dance, Porter twirled Mary Ann until she laughed with dizziness. But her laughter was not heartfelt — it was the laughter of souls trying to forget their pain. The music finally ended.

On the sidelines Brigham ambled up and placed his arm around Porter's shoulder. "This is not the best news you could hear."

Porter peered at him curiously.

CHAPTER 34

"**W**hy do you have to go?" said Mary Ann nearly in shock as they rode home from the dance in their buggy.

"I don't know." Porter didn't know. But he knew somebody had to lead Almon Babbitt eastward.

"I don't trust Babbitt," said Mary Ann. "He cheated on his wife and I don't think I like him."

Babbitt, despite his excommunication from the church for adultery, had been recently appointed by Brigham Young as Territorial Secretary, and now Babbitt seemed possessed with a burning desire to return to Washington, D.C. His mission: to obtain for the territorial capitol several wagon loads of supplies. Porter knew he was perhaps the most qualified scout to lead Babbitt eastward, despite the fact he never trusted Babbitt much after his turning his back on Joseph as a potential attorney at Carthage, and being the attorney that represented Luana when she divorced him. Nevertheless, despite the man's ego, Porter appreciated his legal competency, having freed him from Galena Jail just prior to their exodus West.

Furthermore, Babbitt seemed remorseful over his past mistakes, and Porter was the last man to hold judgement over someone else since he saw his own mistakes glaring him in the face; however, Babbitt's dealings with Joseph and Luana made it particularly painful for him.

Porter's feelings toward the trip were mollified by the fact Brigham wanted him to go. And since his own painful experiences from not heeding counsel regarding Emily and his hair, he was determined to not make the same mistake again, despite his prejudices towards Babbitt.

Furthermore, Porter recognized the fact he smelled salt in the air, much as a sailor does. He knew it was time to go back to sea.

"I know it'll be hard," he continued to Mary Ann, "but I'll be back soon."

"Yeah, real hard on you."

"You think not?" she said.

"I know not," she quipped. "You're lying through your teeth."

"I guess you're right."

She shook her head, taken back by his honesty so much that she almost smiled, but also felt chagrinned over their ongoing problem.

"You're prob'ly worrying that a few hundred enemies still might wanna lynch me across the Mississippi River," he said.

No reply.

"I guess you wonder if I plan to go there for a fight," he said. "Well, I'm only gonna lead the expedition. No gun play. I promise. And if it'll make you feel better, I won't go very far

East — I'll stop at Ft. Kearney, Nebraska and stay there while Babbitt goes on to Washington."

"It'll make me feel even better if you don't go, but Brigham wants you to, so I can support that."

He appreciated the unwavering faithfulness that Luana lacked.

"But when will you be back?" she said.

"As soon as Babbitt gets back to Ft. Kearney from Washington. So don't worry — I'll be safe at the fort."

She knew however he'd be crossing the plains where Cheyenne and U.S. Cavalry had been embroiled in a firestorm. While she supported Brigham, she was disappointed. Certainly someone other than him could perform the duty — particularly a danger-fraught task such as this — because, after all, he had given his whole life to assisting Joseph, and then Brigham, and now more? If any man deserved to settle down, she mused, it was him. She caught him studying her. Not only did she remain silent, she glared at the ground. But finally forced a small smile.

"Why're you smiling?" she said.

"I'm murmuring like Sarah," she muttered with another smile.

"Who's Sarah?"

"Lehi's wife."

"Oh yeah — that Sarah."

"What Sarah did you think?" she asked with a wink. "Did you have a girlfriend named Sarah or something?"

"Something," he mumbled.

"You must have had lots of women who liked you," she stated, hoping to learn more about him.

"Not as many admirers as you. Somehow I think long hair on women works better than on men. Not many females are interested in courting Samson, I learned."

"I think more women liked you than you realize."

He shrugged off the compliment.

"I'm just lucky I got you, Mr. Samson. You know I love you — even though you do drive me crazy."

"And I'm glad of that," he smiled. "Oh yeah," he added. "I guess I love you too."

"You guess?" she said.

"I reckon," he teased.

"You guess you reckon?"

"I'm *sure* I guess I reckon."

She studied his eyes a moment. "You're just a born poet."

He liked teasing her and kissed her. She kissed back, and the wagon rolled forward without anyone driving it.

They hit a big bump in the road. She flew off the buckboard, but he sprung forward and caught her.

"Did you have that one planned?" she muttered.

He smiled, sat down with her, and kissed her more.

"If you make it back alive," she said as they hit another, but smaller bump in the road, "you must not leave us again. Not for more than a week . . . not ever again."

He pulled back and saw the intensity in her eyes. He considered her words, and was certain he needed just this one last bit of adventure to clear himself of whatever it was still gnawing at him. He cleared his throat and made her a promise.

"On this trip, I will stay away from trouble. Now don't worry about me. What could possibly go wrong?"

A stiff wind flapped the shutter above Mary Ann's head. She dreamed strange dreams. She saw Porter shooting two outlaws, then standing on a cliff at midnight. She gazed close into his starlit eyes and watched him with curiosity. Rockslides and bonfires filled her head as she heard him laughing. She awakened. He was gone. She jerked up.

"Porter?"

No response. He was to leave in two days. Why was he gone now?

She darted to the front room and looked around. No sign of him. She noticed the door slightly ajar.

Outside, she came onto the porch.

"Honey?"

She heard nothing but the flapping of shutters. Then a faint laughter in the distance.

Her eyes scanned about. She heard in the brisk breeze a whistling sound. A person whistling.

Behind their small barn she arrived.

Porter was sitting on the ground with his back against the barn wall, laughing and whistling a tune, sipping from a near-empty whiskey bottle.

Mary Ann glared at him. "Again?"

He looked up at her and laughed. Then harder. But it evolved into a drunken sob. Both his frustration and his sense of the absurd tore at him from opposite directions. He alternately laughed and sobbed. He had never felt so frustrated with himself. Just days earlier he had promised her he would never touch it again.

Downtown Salt Lake City bustled every day of the week, except Sunday. On an unusually warm Monday morning, Almon Babbitt and 50 others loaded their carriages. Porter was the appointed head scout of the expedition. He and Ugly sat atop their buckboard waiting for the wagon train to roll out. It was April 22, 1856.

When Babbitt noticed him imbibing openly, he smiled. Through all his own troubles he had learned a bit of tolerance, and was actually now and always had been amused by Porter's antics. The street was full of people walking back and forth on the boardwalks and crossing the wide dusty Main Street. Porter watched them all as he downed the last of his bottle. He noticed several disapproving glances from nearby pedestrians, and gave each a little salute. One lady glared back. He smiled broader and tossed the empty bottle at her.

As the bottle sailed end-over-end toward her, Brigham stepped out of a store, saw the bottle coming straight toward his own face now, and at the last second whipped up one hand and caught it.

Porter's eyes widened.

Brigham stomped up to him and grabbed him by the lapels.

"I want you in my office immediately."

CHAPTER 35

In Brigham's office, Porter sat in a soft-cushioned chair facing the Prophet across his desk.

"You've got to, Porter. You've got to give it up."

Porter gazed sheepishly at him, petting Ugly beside him, who whined, overly anxious for a reason mysterious to Porter.

"It's a disgrace to you, to all of us, and especially to your wife."

"I'll think about it."

"Or it'll kill you."

"Something's gotta," said Porter.

"Take this as lightly as you want. But your wife is heartbroken over it."

Porter thought a second, stood and shouted:

"Don't you think I know that!"

"Then stop it!"

"I can't!"

"You've got to," said Brigham softly.

"I try every day of my life," said Porter, also softly. "Why am I afflicted with it?"

"By the Lord's tender mercies, you are," said Brigham. "You already know that."

"How do you know what I know?" said Porter.

"Were you surprised to hear Joseph tell you a time or two what was in your heart?"

"Not really."

"Why?"

"It was his calling. I guess."

"The mantle was passed on. You also know that. You witnessed the miracle of Joseph's speech and persona in me when I returned from Europe after Joseph was killed. What more do you want?"

Porter nodded.

Brigham continued, "I feel impressed to tell you what you, the Lord, and I already know. You lost not Joseph's promise of protection after all; instead, the Lord saw fit to keep you from harm's way while you protected his people, yet has afflicted you with this trial and punishment."

"My whole life I've had trouble heeding counsel."

Brigham nodded. "Nearly everyone's struggled that way."

Porter exclaimed, "Do you want to know why I cut it?"

Brigham studied him, then nodded ever so faintly.

After Porter told him of Agnus and her typhoid fever, Brigham reflected on his story and finally responded:

"I suppose it may have been worth it at the time to save the woman's pride, but I'm impressed by the lesson of a story in the Old Testament — that obedience is better than to sacrifice, and even of more value to the Lord than compassion, as hard as it is for us to understand that. I'm afraid it's a trial you'll have to live with. And maybe die with."

As Brigham and Porter walked outside, Brigham stopped.

"I want you to see who's here to visit you."

Porter stopped and looked to the side curiously, where Brigham nodded.

Standing on the porch of the building 20 feet from them and to the side . . . was the last person in the world Porter expected to see. He blinked and squinted, not believing what he was seeing.

"Want me to pinch you," said Brigham, "so you know you're not dreaming?"

Porter squinted again, then swore.

It was Emily.

CHAPTER 36

"**P**apa?" is all Emily could say.

Porter caught the anguish in her demeanor, and stepped towards her compassionately as she ran to him. They hugged. Ugly jumped about and yelped. Emily knelt and hugged him. It dawned on Porter why Ugly had been whining in the office — it had been Emily — and her scent outside.

Brigham noted with consternation that Porter was both joyful to see her yet was still reeling, hurt over her earlier rejections of him.

"What do you want?" said Porter gruffly, fighting the softness he felt towards her.

Emily stepped back, disappointed and surprised.

"Porter," said Brigham, "this is your daughter."

"Papa," said Emily shyly, "Henry is dead."

Porter stared at her.

"He died from disease," she added.

"Young lady," said Porter, aching for her but forcing a smile, "How come you never keep anything you catch?"

"I guess," she said, smiling through watery eyes, "I learned it all from you."

He chuckled. "So what're we going to do with us?"

"I suppose I'm back to stay," she said. "But I'll live in town. I can't stay on your ranch."

Brigham piped in, "We've arranged for a few brethren to build her a cabin. It's the least we can do for the little pay you've been getting. You've put in long hours, Porter."

Porter thought a moment, his mind still twirling a bit from the whiskey. He finally spoke up. "Mary Ann is staying at her parents while I'm in Nebraska. I reckon she's trying to sort out her feelings about my little problem with the bottle."

Emily's eyes widened with hope.

Porter read her eyes. "So you're welcome to stay awhile at my cabin. And we will keep our marriage, honey. I know Mary Ann deep down. Unlike some, she'll stay."

"I'll find somewhere else to stay while the cabin's built," said Emily, miffed at the reference to her mother's lack of commitment.

"I want you to stay with me till your cabin is built," said Porter, softer.

"I don't know if I can," she replied, melting. "Your new ranch won't be the same. It'll never be home. Mary Ann's touches, you know."

Porter nodded, "Honey, you've got to get over what's happened. Mary Ann and I are husband and wife, no matter what you think."

"I can't get over it."

"It's your choice."

She was torn, seeing her father's love for her.

"I'll move to your new property," said Emily, "but I'll stay in the barn till she moves back on the ranch. Then I'll move for good."

"Your cabin should be done in a few weeks," said Brigham. "All our men are busy with other assignments right now."

She smiled gratefully.

As Porter placed his arm across her shoulder, they walked towards his carriage under a canopy of rain sprinkles falling from a low, dark sky. Thunder clapped ominously in the distance. She smiled through her pain. "After you plant spring seeds," she said thoughtfully, "you usually get a different crop than expected, huh?"

Minutes earlier when she had arrived, Brigham had told her of Porter's assignment with Babbitt. She now waved to her father as he rode away atop the carriage, eastward.

When Porter looked back at her, he finally felt the impact of having her home. Yet his realization of her not accepting his new life, coupled with his discovery of her despondency from her husband's death, caused the entire reunion to be cast in a cloud of bittersweet rain.

PART IV

Storms

CHAPTER 37

William Drummond was about to learn the pivotal piece of information needed to take action against Porter Rockwell. He had laughed off his wife's reports to the press, figuring any review of his judgeship was a mere formality, knowing his superiors must be not only pleased, but impressed with him. With his aspirations still intact for the governor's chair, he saw the pieces falling into place one by one. After Porter was out of the way, Brigham could finally be removed.

In an adjacent room sat Frank Slade, impatient to get on with the assassination. He had left the territory at LeFevre's request and returned only occasionally to check in. He had for his own peace of mind followed Porter around a few times to learn his habits so he'd feel completely familiar with the lawman once he got the drop on him. And, when away from the territory, he had kept himself fresh by killing another lawman in California — just for the fun of it. He had also returned to the Mexican border bar and apprised them of

the delay. All the regular patrons there were anxiously awaiting the gunfight. But none more than Slade. It was therefore with some relief that, upon meeting with LeFevre this
day, he was told, "The time is all but here. Stay in town."

As LeFevre dismissed him with a nod, he watched Slade
disappear, then LeFevre entered Drummond's chambers. He
sat before the judge and talked of the opera they had attended
the previous weekend. It was an unseasonably warm February
in 1857.

Drummond was in anxious spirits, and cut the small-talk
short. As he poured shots of whiskey for himself and LeFevre,
he faced his hotel window over-looking the alley leading to Main
Street. It was a depressing sight as he could not see the street
itself with all its bustle — only a couple stray cats fighting in
the alley. While their hissing and screeching annoyed him, he
watched them with his back turned to LeFevre and declared,
"Tell me what happened to Babbitt — why didn't he return?"

"I think we've got what it takes to nail Rockwell in the cof-
fin. Nine lives or no nine lives."

Drummond did not care for LeFevre's use of "we" in the
sentence, as this whole operation was his own creation. Certainly no underling was going to take credit; nonetheless,
Drummond patronized him, turning around to face him:

"Excellent work, son. Now give me the details."

Simon LeFevre suggested they walk from Drummond's
hotel room to the tavern. The judge complied, wishing as well
to escape the bothersome noises of the alley cats fighting.

Both men found themselves seated at Drummond's favorite corner table, assiduously staring out the window at passing

wagons and horses. Drummond had always enjoyed this table most, and from it would learn that which he now knew would result in Porter's downfall:

"Rockwell led Almon W. Babbitt and 36 other Mormons Eastward on April 22nd. They went to obtain territorial supplies — while the other 36 headed to Europe."

"How far did Rockwell go?"

"Only to Fort Kearney in the Nebraska Territory. He stayed at the fort for some unknown reason, while Babbitt and company went farther East. But soon they were all involved in the middle of a plains war."

"What happened?"

"Before Rockwell got there, a Danish Mormon wagon train went through Miniconjou Indian country. As fate would have it, one of their cows wandered off. A brave found it and butchered it. The Mormons mentioned it to the Army at Fort Laramie, and their officer was a bit anxious to punish the Indians. They sent a platoon of 29 cavalrymen to arrest the brave that killed the cow. They found the brave with a group of others but he refused arrest. The soldiers got in a fight with them — and all the cavalrymen were massacred. That made General William Harney madder than a hornet. He rode to the Sioux camp and slaughtered 80 men, women, and children. It was from that battle he got the name, 'Squaw-killer Harney.' This all happened just before Rockwell and Babbitt arrived."

Drummond leaned forward, anxious to hear the remainder of the episode.

LeFevre paused as he regarded Drummond, then resumed:

"Babbitt finished his business in Washington and got his supplies. He started back to Fort Kearney to rejoin Rockwell, but on his way, his supply train was attacked. One teamster, a woman and her child were killed, but Babbitt made it through safely. He was in a buggy several miles back. When Babbitt made it to Fort Kearney, he tried to persuade Rockwell to take his supply wagons on to Salt Lake City. But Porter refused. So Babbitt announced he would go anyway, with only a driver and a guard. Rockwell and a Captain Wharton of the Army tried talking him out of it. Wharton promised he would even provide an armed patrol for Babbitt if he would just wait a few more days when soldiers would return to the fort, but Babbitt wouldn't listen and wanted to leave immediately. He took off in his buggy, never to be seen again."

"What happened to him?" said Drummond.

"Several days later the Indians came to the fort to sell his effects at the trading post. They praised Babbitt — 'said he had fought 'like a bear.' They also said he had run out of ammo and taken to swinging his rifle at them, but there were too many for him. One Cheyenne finally snuck up behind and tomahawked him. Apparently he had been just as fearless back in Nauvoo, riding back and forth from Nauvoo to Carthage through enemy territory when Joseph was about to be killed, strangely maintaining sides with his people, while agreeing to represent their enemies at Carthage. The man was fearless and loyal only to himself."

"Where was Rockwell when Babbitt was killed?"

LeFevre studied his mentor. He did not know what was going on in the judge's mind, but continued:

"East of the fort where the supply wagons had been attacked on the way back from Washington."

"What was he doing there?"

"He was getting Babbitt's supplies left on the plains. But by the time he arrived back at the fort, rumors were rampant: Some were claiming Rockwell had assassinated Babbitt west of the fort."

Drummond's mind was reeling. LeFevre was finally able to read it.

"And some emigrants passing through Salt Lake are now repeating the rumors," continued LeFevre. "But nobody — I repeat, nobody — back East knows the difference."

"And Rockwell's motive for the murder?" asked Drummond.

"According to the emigrants, Brigham simply wanted Babbitt 'out of the way.'"

"For what?"

"Babbitt had threatened to return territorial government money to Congress. But that's a whole different story. Nobody who knows Brigham well thinks he'd actually call for Babbitt's death, but then nobody back East knows him."

Drummond sat back and gazed on LeFevre thoughtfully. "We've got what we need."

LeFevre continued:

"I find the postscript to this story very interesting: On his way back to Utah, Rockwell went only so far as Fort Laramie with Babbitt's supply wagons. Then he stopped for the approaching bad weather. Several Mormon handcart companies wouldn't listen to him and decided to keep going. On the way to the valley they got caught in a blizzard. Hundreds were killed. But Rockwell waited till the worst weather passed, then came to Salt Lake November 4th."

"What happened to him then?" said Drummond.

"His wife had given birth three months earlier while he was gone, so when he arrived home he decided to settle down with his family. It had been a 6 ½ month trip. He's now home — been here awhile."

Drummond sighed, feeling victorious. He sat back casually. "Get word to Rockwell that I wish to see him."

LeFevre's eyes dilated. "You're certain?"

"And make that tonight at my hotel."

LeFevre merely stared at him.

"You heard me," smiled Drummond.

CHAPTER 38

T he warm winter afternoon invited Emily outdoors. She anticipated strolling among early-blooming wildflowers to pick a few, but first looked forward to finishing cooking breakfast. She did so at the cast-iron stove which neighbors had hauled into the barn. There, she also had her old bed placed in a tidy area of the structure. Tools were neatly arrayed at the other end. Porter had commissioned a group of builders to construct a new barn just for all the horses he was breeding, but while she lived in the barn, they would live in a large shed. She was also invited to stay at Porter's mother's home, but his siblings still launched veiled innuendos about Luana, which pained Emily deeply. She therefore only visited Porter's family once a year since her arrival in the West, and completely dismissed any notion of living with his side of the family.

As Emily finished eating bread and butter with fried eggs and potatoes for herself, she realized how lonely it felt to cook for a family of one. After several days living in this situation, she could not get used to it. She heard a door knock. She opened the wide door and discovered in the framework . . . Mary Ann. She practically gasped.

"May I visit you a moment?" said Porter's young wife.

Emily nodded her silently inside.

"I want you to know," said Mary Ann, "that I'll be staying with my parents awhile longer."

"Is something wrong?" said Emily, at once hopeful she could stay on the property with Mary Ann gone yet hopeful something had indeed gone wrong — between Mary Ann and her father — as the distant hope still lingered of reuniting her parents.

"To the contrary. I've done a lot of soul-searching," said Mary Ann. She noticed Emily gazing at her curiously. "I've concluded your father is a remarkable man, despite my problems with him, and I'll stay with him through thick and thin."

Emily was both disappointed for herself and relieved for her father's sake.

"But I wish you to be comfortable," said Mary Ann, "and to not feel awkward, so I'll stay at my parents till your cabin is built or whenever you feel like leaving. Porter will stay here, I believe, in the cabin. Actually, I wish you'd move back into the cabin with your father. He's lonely after his long trip to Nebraska."

"That's your responsibility, don't you think?" said Emily.

"Look, I know you have a lot to be defensive over."

"Who's defensive?" said Emily. "Some of us have sugar-coated lives, and others — "

"What's this all about?" said Mary Ann.

"What is what about?" sneered Emily.

"This attack?"

"Must we state the obvious?" said Emily.

"Look, he's told me you're still hoping he and your mother will get back together someday," said Porter's young wife.

"That's pretty much my business," said Emily, "and his."

"Well it's not going to happen," said Mary Ann. "He and I have a life-long commitment."

"We'd never know it by our leaving him all the time, would we?" said Emily.

Mary Ann sighed. "Twice I've taken a short reprieve . . . "

"I'd call it a separation."

"Why would you be so concerned we're apart if you don't even approve of us being together in the first place?" said Mary Ann. "It seems you should actually want us apart."

"I just want him happy." She actually wanted Mary Ann to see she wasn't suitable as his wife.

"Then let him be happy, and leave us alone," smiled Mary Ann icily. At that she turned and strutted out the wide, open door. Mary Ann was not happy with her own behavior, and once outside alone, she swore.

Emily watched her disappear, grabbed her breakfast plate, and threw it against the wall, watching it smash into a thousand pieces.

At the Neff cabin, Porter visited Mary Ann and their two children each day. Ugly was gentle with the little ones and they loved playing with him. Baby Sarah was now six months old, and Mary Amanda was almost two years.

"Thank heavens," chuckled Porter, holding one in each arm as he sat on his porch, "they look like their ma and not me."

"Thank heavens," smiled Mary Ann.

Gratefully, Porter noticed his relationship with Mary Ann improving. Neither she nor Emily told him of their confrontation — and it would be a well-kept secret for many years. Meanwhile, Emily's new cabin, barn and fences were close to being finished by Brigham's assigned crew, as they could work on it only a few hours a week. Porter considered taking things into his own hands, but used the slow progress on the cabin as an excuse to keep Emily home, even though she still insisted on living in his barn, wanting her privacy.

Porter spent his days scouting new horses to purchase in Riverton, several miles southwest, always taking Ugly on the saddle behind him. He thought of Lot often. Finally he decided to do something about it. He dropped by the Huntington residence for a visit, but Lot was not home. Since it was late evening, he surmised the boy was out with friends. He still called him a "boy," though he was closing in on 23.

On his return home that night, Porter bought two young horses, then felt very tired and decided to sleep in the open air and ride the last couple miles home at dawn. Suddenly he sensed he was being followed. He built a campfire and felt something in the air not quite right. He then felt Ugly's warm wet tongue on his neck. Silently, he arose and placed his sleeping blankets beside his saddle, then snuck away into the dark. When he returned, three strangers were cocking their weapons, standing over his blankets.

One bellowed, "So that hair protects you, eh, Mr. Rockwell? Well, Goodbye." They blazed their rifles into the blankets.

Suddenly they heard a voice behind them piercing the quiet darkness, though it was a soft voice. "Hello, gentlemen."

They gasped. They turned and beheld Porter with his white teeth reflecting off the campfire, smiling.

And a big grey dog beside him with his tail slowly wagging. Waiting for the action.

CHAPTER 39

One man whirled his weapon around, but Porter fired and the fellow flew into the campfire. Another pulled his pistol up and Porter shot him in the chest. The third assassin whipped up his rifle, only to find Porter's revolver firing repeatedly at him.

Ugly just kept wagging his tail.

The next morning, Porter ambled eastward to his ranch, hauling three corpses over the back of the two horses he'd procured.

Emily raked the leaves in the little yard between the cabin and the barn. She spotted a horseman approached from the north and she smiled. She recognized him as Josh. He smiled back as he reigned in.

"It's been awhile," said Emily.

"A long while."

"'Heard you still work at the store," she said.

"'Heard you went and got married again," he smiled.

"Count your lucky stars you never got mixed up with me," she grinned. "Or you'd be dead as a coyote by now."

"I thank my lucky stars every night," he muttered.

She laughed.

"I'd still like to ask you out again," he offered.

"O.K. that wouldn't hurt."

"So you'd go out with me?" he said, trying to hide his nervousness.

"No, I didn't say that. I said it wouldn't hurt if you asked."

"It might hurt me, he smiled. "Cause you might turn me down."

"I might, but I might not."

He smiled bigger.

"How about the dance this Saturday?"

She smiled.

He looked down. "Just promise not to marry me."

She giggled.

"Well?" he said. "What about the dance?"

"Maybe so. Come see me in a couple days."

"That means you really aren't sure?" he said. "Or you are just plain lonely and want to see me again between now and Saturday, or you just like to work the daylights out of me, forcing me to ride all the way out here again?"

"All three," she flirted.

He tipped his hat and galloped away, excited. She chuckled at his excitement.

Emily had thought just as often about Josh as he had about her. They had seen each other in crossing on Salt Lake's Main Street when riding with their fathers, but had only waved. His family had kept him too busy to see her — somewhat on purpose — afraid of her for their son's sake.

Her self concept was so low that she figured something really would go wrong with anyone who married her. She looked upon Josh as a vulnerable lad, such had been her experiences in life. And she would not allow herself to hurt him. So she had, since returning from California, kept her emotional distance. She was not certain what to do with him, and decided she would think about it between now and Saturday.

From the southern range she noticed a rider approaching. She smiled when she recognized her father. She instinctively wished to run to him — like the little girl inside her dictated — but she held back, and carefully, clinically watched him. Then, curiously, he stopped and dismounted a half mile away.

From two horses he cut down a large bag, then two others. One by one he dumped them into the dry well. She did not want to know what she suspected. She shook off her morose suspicions and decided to make him dinner. But she again glanced at the well. The mere sight of it wrenched her insides. When he remounted and arrived at the ranch, she perceived he had been drinking heavily. Ugly jumped from the horse first, brushing against her and nearly knocking her over.

"You're both drunk," she said.

"I was hoping you were still here," he said, "and not out looking to marry the first fella to come along."

Emily broiled inside. "What were you doing at the well, Papa?"

"Dumping garbage."

"What kind of garbage?"

He noticed her scornful expression, and sighed.

"What are you now?" she said louder.

"There's no other way for justice here."

"How often do you get drunk?"

"As often as it takes."

"You reek with it! Completely!"

"Thank you — I hate doing things half way."

"Is this the only time it's happened?"

"Oh, it started with a little mishap on one of my trips to California," he said, smiling.

"Does Mary Ann know anything about it?"

"Enough."

"You'll always be mad," she said, "and taking it out on the lawless, won't you?"

He looked at her, surprised she saw what Boggs had seen. "You don't know what you're talking about," she said.

"How could you do this?" she bellowed. "Right when we're trying to mend the fences between us."

Although angry at himself, he directed it at her:

"Who do you think you are, to judge your own pa!"

"It's sickening," she seethed, staring out at the dry well again.

"If you don't like what you see here," he retorted, "then you can change the scenery."

"It's not just what I see — it's what I feel," she mumbled.

"No one's forcing you to feel anything you don't want," he muttered, his eyes now fiery red. "So get out."

Were it not for the hurt she felt, she would have been frightened by the look possessing him, his anger shining through his drunkenness and forming an amber glow to his entire face. So disgusted and surprised was Emily that she could only shake her head, then she turned and disappeared into the barn and locked it, taking Ugly with her.

The animal staggered and tripped over his own feet and crashed into the hay, snoring within two seconds.

The next morning Ugly awakened, and would not eat the breakfast she offered him. He was unhappy with the conflict between the two and, though soused the night before, he could remember their argument, sensing some sort of problems, but he enjoyed Emily's company when he could visit her, so he stayed the afternoon in the barn, where Porter wished deep in his heart he could also be.

Josh Anderson, the store proprietor's son, arrived on his wagon Saturday afternoon. Emily noticed him out the window, sighed and came out and greeted him, distant and distraught. Ugly lay lazily in the sun, swatting flies with his tail, having picked up the idea watching cows.

"Where's your pa?" said Josh.

"Packed his gear and headed to Arizona this morning."

"What for?"

"To track horse thieves. But I'm afraid for him."

"You look mad at him."

"Both."

He helped her onto the buckboard. They rode in silence to a new play at the nearest large chapel sporting a cultural hall.

She spoke little during the play, and laughed not once at the comedy, so on the road home Josh was concerned and began to probe:

"I reckon I've been through tough times with my folks, too."

"I thought you came from a perfect family," she said surprised, turning to him. "I thought everybody's family around here was perfect compared to my messed-up clan."

He shook his head. "It's hard for parents to live up to what they oughta do, huh?"

"I haven't seen a whole lot of it," she said.

"I don't know. Your pa is kind of a hero of mine. He still plugs along even when times are tough, which has been nearly always, huh?"

She nodded. "I just wish I could've been from another home."

"Your pa is famous."

"Who cares unless things under your roof are smooth? I wonder if homes like that even exist."

"I've seen some," he said. "A lot of my neighbors have them. You can walk into their cabins and feel the Spirit of the Lord like what the Nauvoo Temple musta felt like inside. They must have real happy homes."

"I've always wanted a family like that," she said. "I just don't think it's ever gonna happen. My ma always had problems, and we always felt storms under the roof back in Missouri and Illinois. Mainly 'cause she always had a storm in her heart. I'm going down the same path I figure."

"Well I've been through the same with my parents, but I'm determined to make my home as calm as I can."

"We have something in common," she said.

"I'm glad we have," he smiled.

"But I fear our compass is for different paths."

His smile faded. "I gotta confess, Emily. You are the most beautiful soul I have ever met."

She smiled. "I feel like an old hag, Josh, like I've lived two lifetimes in one, and I'm already starting my third as a single 19 year old."

"I wish you'd look at someday considering a fourth."

She studied him, surprised.

He realized he had said too much. "Pretend I didn't say that. What I mean is — just think in terms of the fact you can just keep going."

She nodded and smiled, but saw in him too much interest in her, given their differences.

"You," she said, "are the most handsome boy I have ever laid eyes on, and could charm the shell off a tortoise. But I don't know what to do."

"I guess I have said too much," he muttered.

"I'm also seeing Tommy Clayton, my neighbor."

Josh looked surprised.

"We went to a stake dance last night."

"I guess he has a lot to offer compared to me."

Emily took his hand and looked in his eyes, surprised to see what she had thought was the most confident young man alive now laying open such vulnerability. She could see in him a hurt young boy who never recovered from problems suffered in an imperfect family.

"He has an honest soul, just like you," she said. She reached over and kissed him.

He pulled the wagon up to her cabin and walked with her to the door.

"I guess," he said, "you're going to want to see him for awhile?"

"I think so. He's not as deep and messed up as me — and maybe you," she smiled. "He's lost in his farm chores and fishing. I like that simpleness. We're going fishing again tomorrow. We probably won't talk. Or say anything worth remembering like you and me. But maybe that's what I need."

"You're getting serious with him already."

"I don't know if I want or can be serious with anyone here. I've got other things to deal with."

He forced a smile. "I'll see you at the store then, and I'll take great pride walking you out to your wagon to carry your goods."

She gave him a long, poignant hug goodnight.

As he walked away, he realized he had just been dropped by a girl for the first time in his life.

CHAPTER 40

As Emily cooked for herself and fed the horses over the next several days, her mind remained riveted to her father. She wondered what made him treat Luana as he had. She knew deep down his attitude had impacted her own motives for having marrying the two men she'd chosen, despite the fact she had developed feelings for the fellows. She nevertheless hated herself for wanting to retaliate against the man she loved most in her life.

She had earlier that week gone fishing with Tommy Clayton, had enjoyed the quiet afternoon together, and had even felt comfortable with his visits the next three days as, like a puppy dog, he had dropped by faithfully every sunset after chores and had helped her feed the horses. He still did not say much, and she liked that, wanting to just think. By the end of his third visit however, he was beginning to annoy her.

"I reckon you're not in the mood to visit much awhile, huh?" is all he had said.

She had nodded, relieved he was going, so she could more deeply concentrate on her thoughts, and that was the last she had seen of him.

A week had passed since, and it had been two weeks since her father's most recent departure on a new adventure. She was lonely without having even Ugly to keep her company.

Porter returned late that night. He dumped two bags in his dry well. Emily was asleep when he and Ugly arrived at the barn and entered. She arose and began cooking an early, pre-dawn breakfast of grilled steak, fresh eggs, garlic-spiced range potatoes, and hot peach cobbler. His appetite was ferocious and he ate heartily, smiling all through the feast.

Ugly was especially pleased he had possessed the foresight — as dogs naturally do — to keep a large portion of meat on the bone Porter had tossed him. Upon being served dessert, Porter also shared half his cobbler.

"His appetite reminds me of you," said Emily. "He eats twice his weight at every meal."

Porter smiled but his mind was distracted. He could not get the gunfight he'd just experienced out of his mind.

In Illinois he had not dreamed about fights, but here, something beyond adventurous caught his imagination, induced perhaps by the wind and the mountains and the stars coupled with the badge he was fondling in his hand and the smell of sage in the air. Emily watched him and trembled faintly, sensing the violent nature of his recent trip.

"So how do you feel," she said, "about what you did?"

"It had to be done. But I wasn't angry at the victims like I used to be." But what he did not tell her was the strange sense of satisfaction he had felt. He turned to her. "Tell me what you've been doing."

"'Same thing Ma did when you were gone. 'Kept up the place. And stewed."

"As in making stew?"

"No, as in stewed."

Porter winced at the comparison between her and her ma.

"What's wrong?" she said.

"Nothing."

She felt victorious in the moment.

But another concern clouded her. "Tell me, how's your new family?"

Porter saw the anguish in her face, and neither said another word that night.

The next morning, Porter sat on a chair in front of his cabin. He felt pricked in his conscience for having enjoyed the hunt and kill of the horsethieves he'd tracked down in Arizona, despite the fact he had felt victorious in conquering the last remnants of his anger. "If it wasn't one problem you're fighting in your soul, it's another," he confided to Ugly.

He had felt a rush of excitement during and after the event — and *each* killing lately — but figured it only a natural reaction, so he knew he had to reestablish his course to prove himself to his deceased father, and even in some way to Boggs, as having the ability to fight civilization's harshest enemies without any sort of carnal satisfaction, and to engage in combat only as duty dictates.

After lunch with Emily in which she remained pleasant but concerned over her father, Porter rode off to stay with Mary Ann and his children. As he sat on her cabin porch, with Ugly at his feet and holding both little girls on his lap, he silently prayed for help in returning to the compass. Afterwards, he hugged little Sarah tighter. Since his youngest daughter he had with Luana — Sarah Jane, now living in Minnesota — would not return the letters he had dictated for her, and had evidently been poisoned against him by Luana, he decided to start over with another Sarah in his life, named after his mother. He was somewhat shocked therefore when he suddenly realized, gazing upon her, that her looks were changing and she was now beginning to look exactly like him.

"Poor critter," he chuckled.

Mary Ann came outside and informed him dinner was ready. He confided in her of his repentance, and she felt relieved, sensing his sincerity. She smiled at him, feeling a sense of security she had never felt. The lust for adventure was out of his system, he informed her. She took cautious comfort in the security that he would never again leave her for an assignment lasting more than a few days and certainly for none that would involve danger. He also felt a peace, security and happiness he had not experienced in his lifetime. His beloved Emily was back, and she seemed to be working out problems within herself, and here he had his own family, coupled with a strong desire to actually stay with them.

As he arose from his chair with his infant daughter, a rider reigned in at the porch. He was quite curious to note it was Judge Drummond's over-educated, snobbish assistant, Simon W. LeFevre.

"I've got a message for you from Judge Drummond," said LeFevre. "It's urgent."

Porter and Mary Ann looked at him curiously.

"He wants you at the Empire Hotel tomorrow at noon."

Little did Porter know, but LeFevre actually considered owning up to his conscience and spilling the whole of Drummond's scheme to him, but at the last minute shook away the feelings and merely presented Drummond's message. Porter thanked him, looked at Mary Ann, and immediately disregarded LeFevre's request, figuring Drummond a complete waste of his time, and indicated such with a certain expression on his face.

LeFevre could not hold back a faint smile. He liked this lawless Mormon lawman. And rode away, wondering what was going to happen next.

CHAPTER 41

It was nearly 2 o'clock in the morning. Brigham rarely re-mained awake that late but just had to enjoy the festivities of another community barn dance.

Porter arrived later than he had planned, leaving Ugly on Mary Ann's porch where she had made a bed of blankets for the animal. He soon got bored and went to see Emily. Mary Ann had retired early with the children and told Porter to have fun at the party. He hoped again to see Lot Huntington at the dance, but once again was both bothered and bewildered to not find him. He would have to ride by the Huntington's again and pay a visit, he figured. Perhaps even tomorrow. Perhaps even to go fishing for a weekend. But once again, deep down, he wondered when he'd ever actually get to an actual fishing trip with the boy.

Brigham approached Porter, put his arm over his shoul-der and led him firmly to a private corner. Porter sensed the seriousness in his face.

"What's the matter?" said Porter.

"William Drummond. He has written a note to me, saying you are trying to steal Ada Carrol away from him."

"So?"

"What do you mean — so?" said Brigham aghast.

Porter broke out laughing. Not only was it the most ludicrous accusation he had ever heard, but Brigham's serious countenance added to it an alarmingly amusing exclamation point. Porter could not help himself and began laughing. People from the dance floor gathered about, wondering what was the matter, until they saw Brigham also breaking out laughing. Then they all began chuckling at Porter's turning red from laughter. Brigham walked away looking down and shaking his head.

When Porter left the party and returned to his buckboard close to dawn, he was shocked to find a note on the seat. He shoved it to the nearest person, who happened to be an old acquaintance from Nauvoo, Lot Smith.

"Could you read it for me, Lot?"

Smith, a burly, sandy-haired fellow of Porter's age and known for being every bit as opinionated, unfolded the note and read aloud:

"'Dear Pa, I had to get away for awhile — maybe a long while. I want a new life in California — where it's not so hard — no new families, no dry wells, no pain. Love, Emily.'"

———————

Meanwhile across town in the early morning hours, Frank Slade entered William Drummond's Salt Lake City office.

"Your aide said you wanted me, Judge."

"I want you to appear tomorrow evening in front of the courthouse," said Drummond.

"What for?"

"A little errand."

"Errand?"

"Make it six sharp. Set your pocket watch to that clock on the wall. When you arrive, bring these papers with you to hand my assistant, Mr. LeFevre. I'll . . . be at another appointment." He handed Slade a file of papers. "Just before six I want you to ride to the surveyor's office and there have them signed, then deliver them right at the appointed hour."

Slade looked at him curiously and left. Then he stopped at the door. "And Rockwell?"

"Stay off his trail the next two days. After that, when you find your best shot, take it. And he doesn't need to see it coming."

"I don't know what you're expecting," said Slade, "but not from the back — I don't play by those rules."

"Then play by whatever rules you like. It is refreshing, I have to admit, seeing an assassin with such ethics," mused Drummond. "But he shouldn't have a chance to kill you first."

"Don't worry," said Slade. "If I don't worry, you don't worry."

Drummond sat confidently in his Salt Lake City courtroom between cases. He stared at the empty benches and sipped coffee, pleased with his scenario of warning Rockwell in order to double-cross Slade. He had orchestrated the scene well, complete with several witnesses who could testify of Rockwell performing the assassination in broad daylight. The carefully planned machinations would lead directly to Rockwell's demise at last — in a manner that would take down the entire desert kingdom.

CHAPTER 42

Porter had gone a week without a drink. But leaving the barn dance, he had turned toward downtown Salt Lake City.

There, he rode about all day, thinking, when he finally noticed through a window a large wooden bar with liquor bottles set neatly on it. His mouth watered. He stopped his horse. It was now early evening.

Sitting at the bar two hours later, his heart agonizing over Emily, he was torn about tracking her down or simply letting her go. Once again. He then half-consciously caught the words of one cowhand telling another, "Old Port took care of Babbitt on the plains, and made it look like Cheyennes by using their arrows." Suddenly Porter, who had his back turned to the man, rotated slowly on his bar stool and faced the man.

"Could you repeat that?" snarled Porter.

The man's eyes completely dilated. Porter grabbed him by the lapels. He was taking out his anguish over Emily on this poor stranger, and was infuriated over the rumor and frustrated with himself for even retaliating — all simultaneously. "Where'd you hear that?" he said, softer.

Half-soused himself, the fellow spilled all:

"Here, the other night."

"Who from?"

"Judge Drummond."

Porter seethed, then let him go.

Bursting through the dual-swinging doors, he tromped outside onto the wooden boardwalk. He peered up and down both ends of the street. He would have to pay Judge William Drummond a little visit after all.

CHAPTER 43

William W. Drummond lay asleep beside Ada Carroll when the door crashed open.

Moonlight beams shot onto his face and he squinted. A darkened figure shuffled to the foot of his bed.

Drummond flushed and shouted at the man. "Who are you and what do you want?"

"I'm Porter Rockwell and what do you want?"

Drummond stared at him, baffled. "What time is it?"

"Full moon — what time did you think it was?"

Drummond cleared his throat and felt his heart racing. "I'm not armed."

"I didn't say you was," said Porter. "Though you should be after them rumors you spread in the tavern. I got word from LeFevre you wanted to see me."

"Only to warn you. Since you wouldn't bother to see me, I got your dandruff riled up a bit. That way I knew you'd come here. As you may know, immigrants are already passing the story around about you and Babbitt."

"I didn't know, and I don't care."

"Anyway, I'm glad you came."

"You said something about warning me?"

"Your life is in danger and I had to get you here."

"That's awful nice of you . . . " Porter began walking back to the door, disgusted with the man's methods more than ever, "but I'll pass."

"You don't wish to hear what your life is in danger over?" said Drummond.

"I can take care of myself."

"I can keep you from getting in real trouble if you merely dictate something to me," said Drummond.

Porter stopped at the door and glanced back curiously.

"Dictate?"

"Your life's story."

"It'd never sell," he mumbled, heading out the door.

"Wait a minute."

Porter stopped again.

"You only need to confess your killings to me. And if you would, you'd save yourself and your people a great deal of grief."

"That's real thoughtful of you — being concerned about my grief and all but, well, I've gotten used to dodging trouble; now if you'll excuse me. . . ."

Drummond realized his first strategy failed, so he went to his next ploy. "I've got paper and quill pens on that desk. You stay here and dictate to me, shall we say, what you have done in the name of law enforcement. Especially, shall we further say, what you feel I would need, and then you could be a man well taken care of . . . for life."

"Judge, I reckon I read what you're saying . . . "

"That's quite a feat for an illiterate man."

"But I don't think so." Porter tipped his hat to the woman. "Mrs. Drummond."

Ada replied, "She's not in town." To Drummond she asked softly, "Honey, do you know when she'll be out here?"

Drummond winced at her remarkable stupidity. He quickly turned to Porter with still another ploy:

"Mr. Rockwell, I just happen to be aware of a particular plan against your life. An assassination-in-waiting, as it were. If you want the drop on the trigger-man, you need only to follow my instructions and meet him at the courthouse at six tomorrow night. That's when he's not expecting you, and you can eliminate him and the threat he poses on your life . . . if you're interested." Drummond knew of course he would be interested.

"No thanks."

"What do you mean, 'No thanks?'"

"I'd have to think about it."

"What's there to think about? I'm offering you fair warning about a vicious killer out for your blood, for heaven's sake."

"So what do you want?" said Porter.

"Your assurances you'll be there . . . "

"That means you want an answer now?"

"And perhaps a 'thank you.'"

"No thank you."

The lawman walked away, leaving the door swinging in the breeze. Drummond stared at the open door . . .

He was shocked Porter would turn him down. On all three levels. Nevertheless, Drummond had vaguely considered the possibility, and therefore had a contingency plan . . . for his fourth and final play. And it was time to turn to it. The one most foolproof of all.

CHAPTER 44

A knock sounded at Porter's door. It was two days later. Mary Ann was the first to awaken. She had moved back on their property the day following Emily's departure for California.

"What're you going to do about Emily?" she said.

"I don't know," growled Porter.

Suddenly she saw outside the door, silhouetted against the dawn, Brigham Young.

"May I come in?" said Brigham.

Porter rolled over and opened his eyes to the bearded territorial leader standing at the foot of his bed.

"That was a plain, stupid move, Port."

"What plain, stupid move was that?"

"Threatening Judge Drummond."

"Is that what he told you?"

"You should not have seen him."

"He baited me to see him."

"Next time, clear it with me."

"'Won't be a next time," said Porter. "He bores me. I don't bother re-visiting people who bored me the first."

"You're right about one thing," said Brigham, "there won't be a next time. You're staying away from that crazy judge for good — and to help you do that at least for awhile, I'm sending you on another assignment."

Porter shot a glance at Mary Ann, who looked away, distraught.

"Brother Brigham," said Mary Ann, "Porter's daughter took off again. I don't think he's the same without her around. And I think that's why he saw the judge. But I don't think he'll do that again, will you, dear? In fact I know you won't," she said, glaring at him. "Brother Brigham, I'm sorry this happened.

"I'm sorry, too. I am. But Porter you're not holding yourself together as we need right now. It'd be best if you went on this assignment simply to give your head a chance to clear itself. We've got too much at stake."

Porter nodded, though in anguish over Emily, and also distraught for Mary Ann's sake. But deep down, the desire to get out in the wild was pulling at him again, and the assignment sounded downright delicious.

He almost smiled, but realized he didn't particularly feel like getting slapped, and that thought alone tugged at his smile muscles, so he turned his face from Mary Ann so she wouldn't see it.

"Darn shame," he muttered.

But Brigham saw his expression — and at once was torn over being amused by him and concerned for his *wanting* to be away.

———————

They had no idea William Drummond's plan of last resort was at that moment being implemented at Drummond's hotel. Frank Slade and Simon LeFevre faced Drummond across a small table inside his room. Drummond wore his black judge's cloak, "Symbolic of the plagues I hope to reign down on these people," he told them, "beginning with the first angel to be unleashed."

"That's fine, judge, but where was LeFevre and the papers when I showed up at six last night?"

"Plans changed. Now we have better plans." He turned his eyes to Frank Slade as the corners of his mouth cracked a faint smile.

"Now?" said Slade.

Drummond nodded thoughtfully, to the affirmative.

"My way?" asked Slade.

"Any way."

"I can do what I want with him?"

"All I want is proof of your work."

"You'll have proof," smirked Slade, standing and walking away. "Yes sir, you'll have your proof," he added, now laughing harder. He closed the door behind him.

Drummond then heard a boisterous belly-laugh from Slade out in the hall. "The pressure," mused Drummond to LeFevre, "of all this time waiting for his orders, must have somehow gotten to the pathetic slime."

As Slade cleaned his revolver in his hotel room the next morning, Brigham was at Porter's doorstep. "I want you taking the mail from here to Laramie. It's my new mail service. Not only is this trip for your own good, but few can handle the terrain or negotiate as fearlessly as you can with Indians," said Brigham. "John Murdock is to man the second leg — from Laramie to Independence, Missouri."

Porter hugged Mary Ann goodbye, despite feeling her coolness and fear, and he loaded up his wagon.

"Come in town for provisions and the load of mail," said Brigham.

Immediately afterwards, Porter set forth with Ugly and a loaded shotgun as his only companions. It was March 1847.

As he headed down the road whistling atop his buckboard, Drummond was meanwhile waiting in the wings, confident his plan would work.

When Frank Slade went to Porter's ranch and found his buckboard gone, he swore. Then when he learned from a neighbor of the mail trip, he was furious. Here he had waited all this time and now he would have to wait longer. He would just have to nail Porter immediately upon his return.

Mary Ann took some consolation in the fact her husband was to be gone much shorter than the Babbitt trip, but the idea he would be riding deep into Indian-infested wilderness, coming just off the plains war, did not digest well with her.

She worried incessantly during his absence.

When Porter returned from Laramie with a wagon full of mail he was cheered in the streets of Salt Lake City. Ugly stood on the buckboard beside him with his tail proudly wagging, possibly waving to the crowd, Porter figured.

He had no idea of the celebration he was riding into, but the *Deseret News* made such an event over it that he was embarrassed. At least, he figured, when he had built his legend as a killer of outlaws they didn't throw parades for him. His life seemed fairly safe, yet the distress he felt over Emily still tore at him every hour of the day.

He had no idea that one Frank Slade was now waiting in the wings to end his distress.

CHAPTER 45

Because of the new mail service, Porter's neighbors threw another dance, and hundreds once again poured into Charles Oakley's huge barn. This time Porter brought Ugly, figuring him equally worthy of the attention. He shared with Ugly a bit of his non-alcoholic Mormon punch, but Ugly was disappointed.

Waiting to greet Porter — and more cheerfully this time — was Brigham. When they had a moment together at the refreshment table, Porter divulged Drummond's offer to dictate his "confessions" that would, with some creative additions, obviously have sunk them both.

"Forget Drummond," said Brigham. "Despite his power, and our need to respect that, he's really just another hound barking at the caravan."

"Have you heard anything about Emily?" said Porter. "Have any of our people seen her in California?"

Brigham nodded. "She's been seen in Sacramento, seeing one of our young men there named David Tyrrell. I'm so sorry at what's happened, Porter. Do you want to go see her?"

"More than anything. But I don't dare. We'd prob'ly strangle each other."

Brigham sighed. "Well we could use your help with the mail service again. I've given complete autonomy to Hiram Kimball over it, and he wants you to take a second trip to Laramie."

Porter rolled his eyes. "Hiram Kimball?" he muttered.

"Something wrong?" said Brigham.

"Nothing I can't live with." He debated in his mind whether or not to tell Brigham. As he pondered it, his thoughts were interrupted by seeing Mary Ann dancing with Lot Smith, which made him uneasy. Lot was clever with words. Porter's wife and most women would laugh at Lot — more so in fact than at Porter's humor, which men seemed more inclined to take to than women.

Women seemed to take to Lot Smith in every way, in fact. Like most Mormon men, Lot was not a polygamist, although he could have afforded a second wife. Polygamy was an issue which had no interest to Porter. As writers had done with his own name, they had made fortunes off books about polygamy, writing on a topic about which they knew nothing. Porter was amazed by all the criticism his people received, even though less than five percent of the Mormon population practiced it. It had possibly been instituted for the sake of the numerous widows and "fatherless orphans," he believed, who needed support, and it was a resurrection of a Biblical practice.

He wondered if, with the increasing distance Mary Ann seemed to be displaying towards him, she would ever take to Lot Smith emotionally . . .

Porter had always found it a compliment of sorts that men would take a second glance at Mary Ann, but something about Lot Smith bothered him. He realized it was because she liked him back. Porter discerned that fact by the expression on her face as she danced with Lot. Then he caught himself smiling at his own jealousy. He eyed Lot again and found himself admiring a man who could charm the women. It reminded him of himself in earlier years.

Unknown to Porter, three-quarters of the women in the barn were intrigued by Porter. And Mary Ann was simply momentarily enjoying other male attention — she was hopelessly addicted to Porter's charm and often hated herself for it; Porter had always been able to manipulate her with it, yet it was a trait to which he was strangely unaware.

"Brother Brigham," said Porter, "The Laramie trip tired me out some. But if I know Hiram Kimball, he will probably want me leaving immediately — just to get back at me."

"Get back at you?"

"Yeah."

"What for?" said Brigham.

"A little fist fight."

"Fist fight?"

"About 12-13 years ago in Nauvoo," quipped Porter. "I can't even remember what it was about, but I whipped him in the dust." Porter smiled at the memory.

Suddenly he felt a tap on the shoulder. He turned and saw Kimball delivering a mouth full of fist into him. Porter went crashing to the wall and women screamed. The music stopped and all eyes turned. Porter flushed with embarrassment, lying on the floor.

Kimball stared down at him and smiled as big as a frog. "Now I reckon we're even." Kimball extended his hand to help him up.

Porter arose from the floor, staggered slowly towards him, and stopped. He clenched his fist and the crowd silently gasped. He glanced at Mary Ann, who scowled at him, then studied Brigham, who glared at him. Suddenly, he extended his right hand to Kimball and shook hands, then muttered, "I reckon we are even."

The crowd applauded, and Ugly barked approvingly.

Outside, Porter rode out the barnyard with Mary Ann on the buckboard to one side of him and Ugly on the other. He glanced up at the moon, rubbed his jaw and mumbled, "I like him. He's got a good fist."

On the ride home from the dance, Ugly licked his neck. Porter glanced to the side and thought he saw something move in the shadows. He called out to it, wondering if it were human or horse, the only creatures of which Ugly was trained to alert him. Wild horses occasionally roamed the area, so Porter could not always assume there were human riders.

"Anybody there?" he said.

No response from the shadows.

He kept riding and heard only crickets in the cool summer air. After a long silence he informed Mary Ann of his newest assignment — the mail load back to Laramie.

"When are you going? she said.

"Two days."

"I cannot handle this, Porter. You promised before, you wouldn't be gone more than a week for assignments. Can't Brother Brigham find single men for this job? You've got to ask him."

Porter figured Brigham knew what he was doing, and said nothing. At that moment he mumbled an idea . . . "I wonder if Drummond's got more up his sleeve . . . ?"

She stared off. If her husband only had not earned such a violent reputation for men like Drummond to exploit . . . But her comment went unsaid; she had long ago learned she could not win an argument. Despite his general kindness to her he was a man that could not be crossed, not after the battle he had apparently lost with Luana. On important matters, however, she spoke her mind, and generally he acquiesced, having cultivated a sensitivity to issues and ideas really important to her.

"All I want to know," said Porter, reading most of her thoughts, "is what the harvest will be like this fall." He was afraid to say what he actually felt. He wondered if he were driving her away . . .

The next day he left Ugly at the ranch to watch the cows, since the animal had proven himself an effective protector of the herd. He further helped them by stopping them from leaning against and breaking down fences, keeping them calm, checking them when they got excited, leading them into a circle when they stampeded, and warning Mary Ann of predators such as coyotes, whereupon the shotgun would pick up where Ugly left off.

Meanwhile, Porter headed south to Lehi for fencing supplies. At the south end of Salt Lake Valley a strange incident occurred. He rode his wagon through the pass at Point of the Mountain, and saw coming the opposite direction a stranger on horseback.

"Excuse me, sir," said the stranger.

Porter glanced at him curiously.

"I mean to talk to you."

"Yeah?" said Porter.

"I need help with directions."

Porter realized he had seen him briefly around town.

Frank Slade was immensely grateful the moment had come at last.

CHAPTER 46

The agonizing years of laboring at meaningless jobs before finding his niche at killing marshals was now a memory of Slade's about which he'd just as soon forget. Now — in the next few moments — he was about to experience his greatest satisfaction of his career, via the most significant confrontation of his life. While he had spent considerable time studying his prey and waiting for Drummond to give him the word, like a rattlesnake, to make his strike, his kitty had dramatically increased through visits to numerous territorial taverns, convincing its participants to float him credit on the bet. He had in fact made a comfortable living at similar bets before bagging other marshals, only this was the only lawman he had ever faced who had inspired ballads to be sung about him at literally dozens of campfires throughout the territory, the lyrics of which were becoming memorized by more than a few:

"They say that Porter Rockwell
Is a scout for Brigham Young—

He's hunting up the unsuspects
That haven't yet been hung.
So if you steal one Mormon girl
I'll tell you what to do.
Get the drop on Porter Rockwell
Or he'll get the drop on you."

Slade smiled as he thought of the lyrics. A Mormon girl from the nearest homestead would be his reward, he figured, within minutes, even. It was the only kind of girl he had not had, he mused, but that would soon be history.

"What can I do for you?" said Porter atop his buckboard.

"I've come clear from a bar on the Mexican border to settle something with you. And I've been following you longer, off and on, than I care to admit."

"Oh?"

Slade pulled a revolver from behind his hat on the saddle horn.

Porter held back his surprise and kept his voice casual. "What's that for?"

"A lot of people want to see you dead," said Slade.

"Is that a fact?"

"A well known fact."

"I'm flattered."

"You should be, so I reckon it's been worth my while to follow you around."

"Well this is kinda interesting," said Porter. "Where'd you get this idea?"

"It all started at a bar on the Mexican border. There was

some wealthy miners that pitched in. And that's where the biggest kitty lies."

"Thank goodness for that," said Porter. "I'd hate for you to have been following me around for free."

Slade chuckled.

Porter continued, "And worse yet, I'd hate to see you die for free." Both men laughed. Porter read him like a painting and at first hoped to dissuade him as he had young Lot Huntington with his ambush attempt, but quickly sized up this fellow as a different species than Lot. This was a cold-blooded scorpion. Porter's mind was racing for a solution, realizing within moments that only one of them would be leaving this encounter alive.

"You see," continued Slade, "I reckon a dozen saloons have a kitty riding on the outcome of this here encounter between us."

"I'd sure like a shot at some of those winnings," said Porter.

"How do you reckon that?" said Slade.

"By a fair contest. That way the winner takes all."

Slade smiled, "I think you'll be the one dying, Mr. Rockwell."

"Is that a fact?"

"Soon to be a well known fact."

"Well, now that we have our facts straight," said Porter, "I just need one thing."

"What's that?"

"The address of that Mexican border bar," said Porter.

"I ain't giving you the address to no bar. What do you want with that?" said Slade. "I told you there's no way you're coming out of this alive."

"That's fine with me. I don't want no bettin' money. It's against my religion. I need the address for another reason."

"What reason is that?" chuckled Slade.

"Just hypothetically speaking," said Porter, "what if you died?"

Slade laughed back. "First of all I won't die."

"Hypothetically," said Porter.

"All right, hypothetically. So, hypothetically if I die, what do you want the address for?"

"To send your remains," said Porter.

"Mr. Rockwell," laughed Slade. "That ain't happening. What is happening is this: After our encounter here, I will be showing the whole world of your demise."

"Very good," said Porter. "Now what do you plan to do to show you got me?"

Slade smiled as his eyes widened. "Cut off your head and take it off in a bag."

Porter smiled. "Who-ee! Griss-ley!"

Slade chuckled, taken back by Porter's reaction.

"But," said Porter, let's just pretend for a moment that you don't pull that off."

Slade lost his laughter a moment.

Porter continued smiling. "So what's that address?"

The thought suddenly crossed Slade's mind of what an interesting — and humiliating — surprise it would be for the bartender and all his friends at the Mexican border bar to open up a parcel only to find Slade's three week old, very ripe remains to both surprise and inform them Slade had lost.

"I don't think so," said Slade. "You don't need their address."

"Wait a second," said Porter, playing out his hand. "How're those fine folks at that border bar ever going to ever know if — heaven forbid — you lost?" said Porter. "They would be out of their winnings if you didn't return."

"If I lost," said Slade, "they'd hear about it."

"How?"

"You'd tell the newspapers."

"I don't tell the newspapers nothin'," said Porter. "Most make up what they print."

"Well I don't really care about that," said Slade, displaying a faint discomfort. "So let's get on with it."

"Don't you care about what happens to them folks' back at the bar?"

"Not really."

"You struck me as an upright fellow," said Porter. "Them folks at the bar deserve some kind of accounting of what happens to you."

"All right, all right!" said Slade animatedly. "If I lose, I lose. But I still don't want you sending my corpse to them. So let's get on with it."

"Wait a minute. Wait a minute," said Porter. "Don't you wanna know the alternative to you being shipped back in a crate?"

"No."

"Well I sure would wanna know what would happen to me if I was you."

"All right, what would happen to me if I don't get shipped back in a crate?" he said, rolling his eyes.

"The dry well," said Porter.

"What?"

"The dry well."

"Dry well?"

"Dry well."

"What the devil's the dry well?" said Slade.

"Well, it's a secret, basically," said Porter. "But since you're about to end up there, I reckon it won't do no harm to tell you about my secret. Better yet, I could show you."

"No thanks," said Slade.

"Well have it your way."

"I definitely don't care about your dry — "

"Don't you want to even see it from a distance?"

"No."

"Okay," said Porter.

"Definitely not."

"You don't know what you're missing. But have it your way."

"Where were we?" said Slade.

"It's over there." Porter pointed to the dry well downhill and northwest of them, out in a field. "I knew you were dying to know deep inside. Especially . . . what's in it. Now, were we?" said Porter with a smile.

Slade glanced back at the well, beginning to get a little curious. "All right . . . what's in it?"

"'Couple dozen corpses of outlaws, I reckon."

"You reckon? You don't know? Who put them there?"

"I suppose it was me," said Porter modestly.

Slade thought a second and tried to conceal his minuscule gulp.

Porter continued, "The flies in that thing have a field day. I reckon the maggots, too. The activity in that well is something ferocious, I'd imagine. Can you imagine it?"

Slade just looked at him, thinking.

"Now the bottom of a dry well is an interesting place," added Porter. "Do you like small, deep, deep holes to sit in a few hundred years?"

Slade was terrified of small places, and the idea completely disconcerted him.

"So," said Porter, "it's your choice. The well or the parcel post to the bar."

"Well I suppose anything's better than that well," Slade mumbled, daydreaming.

"Now what's that address?" said Porter.

"Miguel's Cantina, in Tijuana." Slade suddenly caught himself and jerked out of his reverie, realizing he had been suckered into Porter's mind game, and he smiled.

"You find it funny?" said Porter.

"Yeah, I find you funny."

"Well I reckon you can get on with your business then," said Porter. "Cause I'd hate for one of us to leave this earth without a smile on his face."

"I reckon so," said Slade smiling.

"At least in a minute or two."

"A minute or two?"

"Yeah," said Porter. "But only when you're ready."

"I'm not ready?" said Slade with a sardonic chuckle.

Porter snorted softly.

"What're you laughin' at?" said Slade.

Porter didn't answer. He just snorted.

Slade's laughter suddenly became laced with a tint of seriousness. "Have you ever seen a snake that's been gut-shot, Mr.

Rockwell? It squirms in the dust for hours before it dies. I reckon I've done that to a few snakes in my day."

"How many's a few?" said Porter.

"Maybe a half-dozen."

"Well now," said Porter, "you oughta be real proud of yourself. If you've gut-shot half a dozen snakes, I guess I would make an even seven, ain't that right?"

"An even seven?" Slade laughed. "I like you, Marshal. An even seven. Yeah, that's good. That's real good. I do like you."

"Well, I kinda like you too, Slade."

"Yes sir, you got a sense of humor as loco as mine."

"Maybe I am as loco as you," said Porter with a twinkle in his voice.

Slade suddenly lost his smile and trembled a moment, then broke into loud guffaws. "Maybe I oughta just shoot you in the head right now for sayin' that and be done with it. Nobody ever gets away with calling me loco."

"Naw, that'd spoil your fun," said Porter. "You wanna gut-shoot me like them snakes." Porter sensed Slade trembling again with anticipation.

Slade smiled. "I reckon you're right. But all it really matters is to get your head in this bag," he said.

"You could even mount it," said Porter.

Slade broke into laughter again. "That's right! That's it!" He gasped and panted.

"But what if I get lazy and don't parcel post you back to that bar in Tijuana? It'd be real convenient just to dump you with your new acquaintances in that well over there . . . All them thousands of maggots and flies and worms and bugs. Millions of bugs. Can you see the well all right from here, Slade?"

Slade nodded.

"On a clear day you can see it 30 miles away. On those days I reckon you can even see the odor rising out of it."

Slade was contemplative. It hadn't occurred to him anyone had seen odor before.

"Then again," added Porter, let's hope you're completely dead when I dump you in there. That'd be one horrible place to spend your last few hours if you was only wounded. Or to spend days — especially days, huh Slade? Now wouldn't it?"

Porter could see beads of sweat on Slade's forehead appearing. He observed Slade imagining many, many things as he glanced at the dry well in the distance again. Porter continued, "A hundred feet down — two hundred maybe, maybe even three hundred feet — cold, dark, moist, a million flies, and a billion maggots crawling over you, waiting for you to die, waiting to dig in."

"Dig in?"

"That's awful, huh, Slade?" said Porter.

"Yeah."

"I don't know that much about maggots, do you?"

"No."

"But I reckon that'd be an awful way to go — in that cold ... dark ... deep, deep hole. Where it's a real small room at the bottom. And real disgusting."

Slade felt a sudden nausea in the pit of his stomach.

"So, Slade, when you're ready to shoot it out, just let me know."

Slade said reticently, "I am ready."

Porter smiled, "No you're not."

Slade fought his emotions: He turned his uncertainty into anger. He spat out his words: "Nobody believes God protects you — hair or no hair."

"I never said the hair protects me — though I reckon it's true I won't die because of it."

"How can you say you don't say it when you just said it?"

"Did I?" said Porter.

"What are you — crazy? I heard you just said it!"

"Son of a gun."

"You don't really believe it, though, do you, Rockwell?" smiled Slade, trying to regain control.

"Maybe I do, maybe I don't. But the important thing," said Porter, reading Slade's slightly dilated eyes, "is that you do."

"That is loco!"

"I suppose it does sound that way, don't it? There you sit, looking at me, wondering if I am going to live through this fight because of my hair. Now being a good, Bible-reading Christian such as yourself, Slade, I'm sure you've heard of Samson."

"That's Bible story stuff and it's double loco."

"May be, Slade, but you believed it when your mama read you the Good Book as a boy. So now, here you are, face to face with some creature — namely me — who the little kid in you is probably saying, "Goodness gracious, this fellow looks like that creature who took apart the Philistines . . . and there's only one of me. Ain't that right, Slade?"

"Looks mean nothing," shot back Slade. "You and Brigham believing that trash proves you're both loco."

"I ain't convinced you're convinced of that, Slade."

"Well no matter, 'cause I'm gonna kill you anyway."

"Oh, Slade . . . there's one other reason you can't kill me."

Slade blurted out impatiently, "What's that?"

Porter stared at Slade's pistol. "You can't shoot that thing without a firing pin."

Slade thought a long, tense moment . . . There was no way on earth this conniving marshal was going to trick him into looking down where he could get the drop on him. Then again, Marshal Rockwell seemed awfully sure of himself, and pretty much like he believed what he was saying, too; furthermore, Slade had learned from many a poker game how to read faces, and he began wondering if Porter was telling the truth — if he really had left off his firing pin. He completely lost his confidence. He squinted and gazed closer at Porter's laughing eyes. He felt his own face flush. He glanced at his pistol. Porter was wrong! There was the firing pin! Satisfied and relieved, he looked up again and found himself staring straight into Porter's revolver.

A split second later, he found himself staring at a flash coming from Porter's revolver. Simultaneously, he heard an ear-piercing crack of a gunshot.

Presently, he saw nothing but barren desert dirt at close range . . . He was lying face down, sprawled across the road, staring now also into his own blood soaking into the sand. He then looked up and saw fluffy white clouds in the clear blue sky.

"Good," he groaned, "shot."

He then saw Porter descending from his buckboard.

Porter noticed Slade staring up at him, then at the clouds again. "It's a beautiful day," added Slade, "to die."

"I reckon."

One cloud in particular mesmerized Slade. He had never seen such:

A. an interesting cloud, and,

B. such whiteness, as the cloud or whatever it was in its intricate and interesting form drifted closer in from the distance.

"Are we headed to heaven?" said Slade.

"Not exactly," said Porter. "Naw, I don't think so."

That cloud was the last thing he ever saw. Slade died with his eyes open.

Porter tipped up his hat with his Colt Navy pistol, and sighed. He just couldn't even take a peaceful ride in the country anymore, he mused, without some disgusting idiot bothering him.

CHAPTER 47

Porter had sensed clearly that Slade was terrified of small places, so he just could not bring himself to dump his corpse into the well. Out of general respect for the fellow, he rode home with Slade's body to prepare a parcel post package for Tijuana. Stopping, he decided to offer one final thought, a moment of respect for the dead outlaw. He stood over the corpse and mumbled a soft prayer:

"God created man . . . but Colonel Colt made them equal." He chuckled to himself, and decided to take the body to a crate shop. This way he could make an indelible impression on someone specifically residing in downtown Salt Lake City.

The next day in Salt Lake City William Drummond pounded his gavel to end the day in court. He wondered where Frank Slade was. His eyes had been turned to the door all day, waiting for his return. The assassin was supposed to have eliminated Rockwell by now.

Drummond ambled into his chamber and poured his favorite whiskey into a shot glass. The bottle rattled against it. He was surprised at himself for his nervousness, particularly in light of the fact Slade had both a record and a passion for successfully dispatching death on whomever he wished — especially skilled gunslingers and lawmen. Then an odd thought skipped into his mind: What if Rockwell and Slade were off somewhere sharing a drink or two? And if Slade had been somehow charmed by the desperado as LeFevre had been? He pushed the thought from his consciousness and swore, quickly tossing the whiskey down his throat.

Outside, Drummond was about to cross Main Street to attend his favorite tavern for more drinks. Suddenly he saw Porter on horseback riding through town leading a pack mule. He broke into a cold sweat when he noticed a corpse draped over its back.

From atop his horse, Porter spotted Drummond and halted. He merely glanced at the judge, giving him a steely-eyed glint. Dozens of curious pedestrians stopped and stared at the sight.

Drummond, in horror, stared at the body's face. Frank Slade had a blood-stained streak running from his mouth across his face, having been mule back for hours. Drummond's eyes focused closer. Slade's green eyes were still open and glazed over. Beginning to tremble, and with eyes dilated, Drummond tore himself away and quickly changed direction.

Porter smiled to himself. After letting Drummond get a good look, he resumed riding northward. He had made his statement. He then turned west to a lumber yard where he'd hire the company to construct an air-tight crate to prepare the body for postage. Ironically he had no idea Drummond had knowledge of the ambush.

The judge was certain Porter knew of the scheme, and was convinced now his own life was in danger. He by-passed the tavern and went straight to the stage station and, with footsteps clomping faster with every step, he glanced over his shoulder out the glass pane door. Seeing no one outside, he hastened to the ticket window to book passage for him and Ada Carrol directly to New York City.

He rushed to his hotel room, packed hastily, and practically ran with Ada back to the stage depot. There, he decided he would launch his last attack against Porter Rockwell, an attack he knew would start an official all-out war against both Porter and Brigham, the likes of which the saints had never seen. Ever.

CHAPTER 48

At the Neff cabin Mary Ann greeted Porter with a hug, but in her kiss was the shadow of uncertainty. Rather than from frustration of his being gone too long, a new layer had evolved — the fear of losing him. She tried driving images of assassination from her mind, but was unsuccessful. She fought an ever-present depression. She knew he would eventually be killed.

Porter told her he was leaving next month for Wyoming.

"Again?" she said.

"Another assignment for Brigham." He then told her of Ugly leaving for California tomorrow — one of Brigham's assistants was taking him on a business trip to Sacramento. He wanted Emily to receive Ugly as a peace offering.

She nodded, frustrated.

"So do you think that's a good idea?" he said.

"Does it matter what I think?"

"It does. Yeah. If you'd rather keep him here to watch the cows . . ."

"I thought he was your inseparable companion," she said.

"Emily loves him too. And maybe she could use his protection in California."

Mary Ann smiled, "You have come aways, Porter. When I first married you, there was no way on earth you would've consulted me first on something like this. Well, it's my turn to consult with you. I've been thinking we should sell all the cows but one. We need the cash, and I need just one cow for milk and butter. The few chickens we've got are fine, but they'll be safer with Ugly away, 'cause I know he's tempted to attack their pen. And maybe we could raise a few more and sell the eggs. Sister Huntington said she'd buy more from me. She and her neighbors need a lot more. As for the horses . . . "

"Whoa," said Porter. "I only wanted to know if it's all right with you if I sent Ugly to Emily. What do you want to do with my horses?"

"I want," she smiled, "for you to get more. I've been thinking — raising the best horses in the territory is your dream. I want you to have your dreams come true." Her lips quivered as she said that.

He smiled, touched. "Here I've been all racked up over my dreams. What about yours?"

"You know them."

He stared at her, reading her thoughts. "I don't know if I can ever be on the ranch full-time."

"Isn't it your choice?"

"The territory needs me."

"You could tell Brigham to limit your assignments to overnight only."

"I guess so."

"You asked me my dreams."

He studied her, disappointed he was not what she deserved, but soon his thoughts degenerated, as before, into a posture of self-defense. 'Why couldn't she accept me the way I am?' he thought. At the same time, he did enjoy the ranch — and working with horses and especially the business end of breeding and selling the best animals in the western U.S. — far more than farm life which he had so despised in earlier years. Ranching and farming were quite similar in that they kept him tied to the property, yet he enjoyed the differences; more significantly, he realized he had changed — he had with more effort and even prayer become increasingly less lustful of danger and adventure. The irony he felt now was that while he truly wished to stay home more, his duty to the community dictated that he could not — he had to spend a realistic amount of time on the trail, and he wished she could see that. Yet he still wanted to be in the wild more than he should want, and for that was supremely frustrated with himself.

She read his mind and blew out a silent sigh of exasperation.

"Have you heard the news?" she offered, changing the subject before she cried.

"What news?"

"Drummond," she said. "He's left the territory — he's headed back East."

"'Good place for him."

She glanced at him curiously.

"He'll fit well there," he explained.

"Some say he left because of the upheaval over Ada Carroll on his bench. The non-Mormons got as fed up with him as we did, and I reckon he felt the pressure and left. Others say it was because of you."

"I'm flattered."

She was pensive. "I suppose we'll learn sooner or later what becomes of it."

"What do you mean by that?" he said. "He's gone. Period."

"You think a man like Drummond is going to just let something like this go — getting booted out? Period?"

"He left scared out of his wits," said Porter. "Don't worry about him."

She stared at him curiously. "And how would you know that?"

Porter forced a small smile.

"How dare you throw a rock in a lion's den like that!" she said. "Do you know the repercussions you could've caused?"

"Like what? He's last month's buttermilk. He stinks and he's been poured out."

"I don't know what — but something will come of it."

"Nothing on earth will."

"How could you act this way to people?" she said.

"'Comes natural," he muttered defensively.

He closed the door behind him, miffed at her criticism. He actually felt proud he had assisted Drummond out of the territory.

The next morning, his friend Elias Taylor came by to get Ugly, on his way to Sacramento. Porter petted the animal and kissed his back.

"You take care, Ugly. And when you get to California, give Emily a little kiss on the chin for me. Keep her safe, would you? I hope I see you soon. I'm gonna miss you, old friend. Now go with Brother Taylor."

Ugly looked at him sadly, and as Elias rode away on his wagon with him on the buckboard, Porter felt anguish in his heart. Ugly stared poignantly at him, and uttered a few whimpers dogs make when they cry.

Porter turned away sadly, and entered the cabin. He looked out the door and saw Ugly still looking back, now a quarter mile down the road, and he hoped — yet doubted — the future would bring them together again.

A month later, Porter hugged Mary Ann goodbye. On his way to town to obtain mail for his trip to Laramie, he detoured a few miles to the Huntington ranch. There, he found Lot's mother home.

"My husband's getting supplies in town."

"Well I'm actually here to see Lot."

"Lot?"

"Yeah, is he around?"

She struggled for composure. "I guess he's been busy."

"Doing what?"

She gazed off, thinking.

"Where is he?" said Porter.

"Come inside."

There, she fetched him a drink of water and some cookies she'd baked that morning.

"These are wonderful cookies, ma'am," he said, chewing and facing her.

She sat and regarded him a moment, then began.

"Shortly after he came back here to live, he talked of you all the time, but I reckon finally felt kinda distant from you. Don't get me wrong. You were his hero. But I know you have your life, and he respected that. He's a good boy. He worked hard here for several months, then I guess felt a longing to be with others. You know how boys are at that age. Anyway, we tried getting him to church, and he went a few times — I figure you and your wife had gotten him in the habit a little bit and I thank you for that; but finally the loneliness got to him and he went to see some of his old friends — the ones he'd gotten in trouble with before — and in a few weeks he moved out of here. I think he rooms with one of them in the city. I heard from a neighbor that he's drinking with them and getting in a little trouble. A couple of those boys were caught stealing at the hardware store last week, but fortunately Lot wasn't with them. I don't think he'd go back to doing that."

Porter stared at her.

CHAPTER 49

Porter rode fast into town. He asked around and found where Lot Huntington and his friend lived. He hitched his roan to a hitshing post and climbed the back, outside stairway into a fleabag hotel. He knocked at door #4. It was noon. No answer. Finally a foppish-looking lad opened the door and, half asleep, squinted at Porter. After a moment he smiled.

"Come on in," said the lad.

Porter strode in and, although it was no longer morning, found Lot on his mattress, awakening.

"Up early these days, Lot?" smiled Porter.

Upon seeing him, Lot startled and sat up.

"Good to see you, Lot," he said more seriously.

"Yeah, same," he said sluggishly.

"You know," said Porter clearing his throat and sensing how awkward both of them felt, "I'm thinking of going fishing and uh . . . "

"I haven't done that in years," piped up Lot with eyes slightly dilated. In his state of semi-consciousness, his old admiration for Porter was momentarily manifest.

"Well I'm headed to Laramie right now," continued Porter. "But maybe when I get back . . ." He noticed Lot's countenance suddenly sink.

"Yeah, maybe."

"Well, you take care of yourself," said Porter. He noticed a smirk on Lot's roommate's face.

Lot quickly looked down and walked him to the door.

Porter stopped at the doorway and turned:

"I got a better idea. Let's go right now."

"What?"

"This minute. Get your boots on."

The boy said nothing, staring at his feet.

"Come on, I'll wait for you."

"I don't know," said Lot. "You've got Laramie waiting for you and I got a lot to do here."

Porter was angry at himself for even mentioning Laramie. "Nothing's more important than fishing," said Porter. "Not your stuff to do or my Laramie. None of it's as important."

Lot glanced back at his roommate who was out of Porter's sight. He obviously rolled his eyes because Lot then returned a look toward Porter with a smirk.

"Lot, can you come out in the hall a minute?" said Porter.

Lot looked back at his roommate again and finally shuffled out the door with a small smile.

"Can I level with you, son?"

Lot's face could not be read.

"I miss seeing you," said Porter.

"Well, we've all gotten kinda busy, huh?"

"I'm sorry about that," said Porter. I liked our working to-gether and laughing over the campfires. Those were good days, huh?"

"It was a long time ago," said Lot.

"Why don't you come work for me again? We need you out there."

"I donno, I'm gettin' a lot of things done in town I need," said Lot.

"I'll pay you double."

Lot knew Porter could not afford that much, and did not even address it. "I've gotten a little out of shape for all that," said Lot. "I don't think so."

"Triple."

"Naw, you got bills to pay and new mouths to feed," said Lot.

"Tell you what. You come with me to Laramie right now. I need someone to ride shotgun — I'm taking the mail."

Lot for a moment revealed a veiled enthusiasm, but from behind the door Porter could hear his roommate's mocking voice:

"Oooh, shot-gun!"

"Naw," finally said Lot, holding back a smile. "I'm just too busy this summer."

"Well," said Porter, exasperated. "I reckon maybe when you're not so busy we can spend time together again."

Lot caught the irony and slightly smiled. "Yeah, when I'm not so busy."

Porter ambled away and stopped. When he glanced back, Lot looked away.

"You might wanna go by and see your ma," said Porter. "I know she cares a lot how you're doing. I reckon your pa does too but I saw your ma myself. She's worried, son."

"Thanks," is all Lot offered, then disappeared into his room and closed the door, where from behind it Porter could hear snickering from the boys. Porter stared at the door a moment, then walked away.

He drove the mail wagon post haste towards Laramie.

Mary Ann back home stewed. She had predicted Drummond would make more trouble for them — perhaps even take his story to the Eastern press. It was a deep feeling inside she could not shake. If he did, she figured, the press could be 20 times worse against Porter than it had been in Illinois: This could be national news.

Porter had a knack for bringing on himself half of what happened, she noted, but she blamed herself: She wondered why she could not have kept him home the night he insisted visiting Drummond at 3 A.M. She pushed the thought from her mind, glanced at his picture, and forced her eyes from it, angry at herself and at him.

She gazed out the window, wondering if she should even be home when he returned . . .

Not forty miles from Fort Laramie, Porter noted two horsemen coming his way. He cocked his shotgun.

He heard his name called. He set down his weapon. The men were Abraham Smoot and Judson Stoddard, two Salt Lake City officials returning from the East. They were tall, deeply tanned, middle-aged, and dignified-looking. They galloped up to him and reined to a halt.

"Port, turn the wagon!"

"What's wrong?"

"Drummond's written a letter to the *New York Times,*" shouted Smoot.

"So?"

"It's made its way to President James Buchanan himself," said Stoddard. "And he's sending the U.S. Army to invade the Saints!"

CHAPTER 50

The *New York Times* serviced hundreds of state and territorial newspapers with national news. With William Drummond back East now, bitter over his Utah experience, he was having a field day feeding letters to editors hungry for stories. One of Drummond's primary accusations was that Porter had murdered Almon Babbitt on the plains — at Brigham's command. As Porter, Smoot, and Stoddard rode back to Utah, Smoot explained to Porter details of what had been published.

With the two mens' horses added to his team, Porter galloped towards Salt Lake City. Smoot and Stoddard were seated beside him.

Within days they arrived at Salt Lake City.
It was deserted.

They drove to the Post Office. The Postmaster informed them everyone was celebrating the city's ten-year anniversary 25 miles east, up Big Cottonwood Canyon.

They turned their wagon southeast and rode to the party.

American flags snapped from a dozen peaks. The valley was filled with six brass bands, a company of infantry, and 2,600 applauding pioneers. The smell of barbecued beef filled the air. Brigham was about to address the huge outdoor assembly when he spotted the three racing a wagon into the canyon and up to the speaker's platform. All eyes turned to Porter as, being the most athletic of the three, he jumped from the wagon and bounded to the platform. Porter wondered if Mary Ann were among the celebrants; he knew her well enough to realize she was probably at home, but wondered if by chance she had attended and had her eyes on him that moment.

Brigham was curious at the sudden sight:

"You can sit up here, Port."

"I've got to see you privately."

"After the speech."

"Now."

As Brigham noticed the anxiousness in his face he lost his smile.

Smoot and Stoddard joined Porter moments later. "Can we see you in your tent?" said Smoot.

Brigham gazed at all three, and escorted them off the platform. As they waked into a tent the bands struck up a tune. The people waited anxiously for Brigham to return and begin the festivities. They began clapping in unison, anxious to begin the giant party and hungry for the barbecue. But when Brigham emerged from the tent, the music stopped. His heavy countenance concerned the crowd. He shuffled to the podium. His stocky frame stood erect.

Porter, Smoot, and Stoddard strode behind him and stopped. Brigham hesitated, thinking, then decisively folded his 20 page talk and stuffed it into his coat pocket. He cleared his throat and faced the crowd.

"When we arrived in these valleys 10 years ago, I said, 'Give us 10 years of peace and we will ask no odds of Uncle Sam or the Devil.' Now, God is with us and the Devil has taken me at my word."

That was his speech.

CHAPTER 51

After catching his breath, Brigham made an announcement, changing his tone to one of merriment and confidence. He told the crowd that U.S. troops were on their way to invade them, then he commanded them to take no thought of it and to continue the celebration. It lasted hours, and the numerous celebrants feasted, including Porter, who sat alone and searched the crowd through squinted eyes. They took obvious comfort in Brigham's confidence, and his assistants relayed that confidence, telling many not to worry, as the troops had no chance against them in *their* mountains.

While leaving the canyon, Porter finally caught sight of Mary Ann with their two children. It was dark now and the party was over.

Porter rode up next to their buggy, but she kept driving.

"Will you be home when I get back?" he said.

Her moonlit face was stone, revealing nothing. He knew it would be a mistake to press further, so he halted his horse and followed her with his eyes as the buggy disappeared around the canyon bend. His gaze then shifted to the moon.

At the war council in Brigham's home later that night, Porter sat with an ache in his heart. Brigham stood and faced the officers:

"Colonel Alexander of the U.S. Army wrote this letter to us and I quote it: 'Never have a people had so many odds placed against them as you have. We have the flower of the American Army — 2,500 cavalry and infantry plus artillery." Brigham added, "That's the end of his letter. So I replied to the colonel:

"'We have perhaps a hundred men to fight you at any one time from these formidable mountains. I see a predicament. So I plead for terms of surrender.'"

Brigham glanced up at his surprised officers. "Unfortunately, gentlemen," he continued, "when I asked him to surrender, he refused."

The men laughed.

Brigham became somber:

"The Army seeks to drive us into submission. They plan to make us an example of rebellion. Leading their force is General 'Squaw-killer Harney.' Brethren, for 25 years now we have been scorned, insulted, and condemned unheard. But this time, gentlemen, we shall resort to the great first law of self-preservation and stand in our own defense!"

Porter felt his blood rush, and at the back of the room he arose and listened.

"I wish to read you another letter," continued Brigham, "which I just penned to Colonel Alexander of the infantry forces:"

"'In the name of Israel's God, we will have peace, even though we be compelled by our enemies to fight for it. We have, as yet in our persecutions, studiously avoided the shedding of blood. But you can easily perceive that you and your troops are now at the mercy of the elements, and that we live in the mountains and that our men are all mountaineers. You should give us our rights and then let us alone. Both we and the Kingdom of God will be free from all hellish oppressors, the Lord being our helper. But if you persist in your attempt, you will have to meet a mode of warfare against which your tactics furnish you no information. We, for the first time, possess the power to have a voice in the treatment we will receive.'" (Author's note: This was the actual text of Brigham's discourse to his men.)

He lifted his grey eyes from the letter and gazed across the room. His officers were sober. His eyes rested upon Porter, who suddenly winked at him.

In that, Brigham found a certain spark of courage to arouse his soldiers. He broke into a broad smile and said, "Let's save the Saints!"

Porter was the first to raise his voice, then all the officers broke into a cheer.

Porter shouted, "We'll beat these fellows! We had our chance at Far West, but Joseph was talked into surrendering. Now we have no place to go!"

Brigham piped up, "Brethren, the mountains will be ours!"

Porter exclaimed louder, "The Army will be ours!"

The officers cheered even louder.

CHAPTER 52

Three days east of Salt Lake City Porter sat horseback atop a mountain. He and his dozen volunteers were watching a wagon camp below — an advance camp of 300 U.S. soldiers.

He perceived in the moonlit mist several infantry officers parting from a campfire and disappearing into tents. As the soldiers drifted asleep, Porter and six of his guerrillas snuck forward. They silently made their way to the Army's horses, smacked them, and yelled. The horses stampeded.

An Army officer ran from his tent, saw the guerrillas, and shouted, "Commence firing!"

Porter's aide, a trustworthy neighbor and worthy scout in his own right named Henry Ballard, ran beside Porter and disappeared into thick woods. Both men broke out laughing.

"I reckon the fun ain't even started," said Porter.

———

Porter and his men then herded the Army's stolen horses to camp headquarters. There, he sat on a boulder and rested. He was soon approached by his assistant again, Corporal Henry Ballard, who happened to possess beady eyes and stiff, protruding lips that reminded one of a talking oyster.

"Are the trenches dug yet, Henry?" said Porter.

"Yes, sir, our men are rolling boulders to the edge of those cliffs," said Ballard, nodding towards them. "And the canyon road passes directly beneath the cliffs."

Porter reminded him of Brigham's mandate to "shed no blood" . . . but they could harass and terrorize the Army all they wish.

"Are you sure the enemy will stay on the road?" said Porter.

"Yes, sir," said Ballard. "We've dammed the river and the water goes all the way up to the road. They have to stay on the road."

"Is the water deep enough?" said Porter.

"It's not the depth that matters — it's the quicksand we've created, sir." Ballard smiled, "It's beautiful quicksand."

Porter also smiled. "By the way, we're still neighbors and friends, so call me Porter."

Ballard winked and continued, "Once we keep them on that road, we can smash their wagons to splinters with those rocks up there."

Porter looked up and saw boulders lined atop the cliffs.

Ballard continued, "The trails to our cliffs are secret — only we know where they are."

Porter thanked him and ordered him to sleep first. Porter volunteered to keep first watch. This followed an unwritten law of the Mormon guerrilla command that all officers should engage in the same duties as the enlisted men.

"One other thing, Port," said the corporal. "General Wells ordered you to recruit 20 men from Major McAllister's company and take them to drive off the Army's cattle."

"Like wheat in the old mill," said Porter, "it's as good as done."

As Porter turned to walk away, he heard Ballard groan:

"So what do you think, Port, really? Do we have a chance in Hades against twenty-five hundred trained soldiers?"

Porter thought a moment. "No, Henry. But we ain't in Hades."

Porter Rockwell and his 12 man army rode to McAllister's camp and obtained 20 more men. With his new force of recruits, he arrived at the U.S. Army's second camp, which had twice as many soldiers as the last group: 600 soldiers. His plans were to stampede the cattle. But upon arriving, he was immediately frustrated. The Army had secured the cattle in a field behind the wagons for protection. Corporal Ballard turned to him:

"'Looks like they second-guessed us."

"I don't see a problem, Henry," snapped Porter, his mind searching for a solution.

Porter suddenly broke out galloping with his torch. He lit the field directly behind the Army. His men followed, also torching the field. The spreading fire suddenly caused the cattle to stampede, and the animals knocked empty wagons to the side and charged up the canyon toward Porter's laughing men.

Army artillery shells began bursting about, as Porter's men pounded down a narrow canyon on horseback and just out of range. Finally, he halted his men and took a quick count — they had all the cattle, and all his men were unscathed.

They laughed even harder and shook hands.

Hours later, they discovered 75 Army wagons. These were civilian teamsters with no attending armed guard. Darkness shrouded Porter's force as it came upon the wagon train.

The teamster's captain, Bill Rankin, stepped forward. Rankin was tall, stoop-shouldered and gruff:

"What do you want?"

"Nothing much," said Porter. "Just for your train to turn the other way till you reach the States."

"By what authority do you issue such orders?"

Porter nodded behind him. "That's part of it. The others are back there."

Rankin did not know the number of Porter's men. He could see only a few guerrillas; the rest trailed off into the darkness behind. Rankin was left to his imagination. He feared several hundred.

Porter had 32.

Rankin grumbled but complied; he turned his train around and retreated without resistance.

Porter and his 32 disappeared into the darkness and rode south. In the moonlight they saw troops ahead, and halted. He ordered his men to cock their weapons. Suddenly the lead horseman of the opposing group came to a stop 20 yards in front of them. His troops stopped behind him. Porter could hear their weapons cock. After several long seconds of regarding each other in the vague light, Porter finally heard the lead horseman break the silence in a soft, curious voice:

"Porter?"

Porter peered more closely at the moonlit face — and recognized Lot Smith.

"Rockwell, you codger, what the devil are you doing out here? It's good to see you but you're in my way!"

"Smith, you old fool, you're in my way!"

Lot Smith told Porter of three Mormon soldiers taken prisoner by the Army, with plans to execute them in one week. Smith and Porter argued for 10 minutes then finally agreed on a strategy: They would take their separate missions immediately, then meet back at the main camp of the Army in one week at twilight for their final confrontation. At that point they would rescue the Mormon prisoners according to Porter's plan.

CHAPTER 53

Later that night, Porter and his men came upon a U.S. Army supply train. They charged down the mountain getting the drop on six Army guards. The soldiers dropped their weapons and whipped up their hands.

"Where's your captain?" said Porter.

Philip Dawson stepped forward. He was wide and over-weight, with large, liquor-induced, puffy cheeks. "I'm your man."

"I have a little business with your wagons," said Porter.

"What about our oxen?" said Dawson.

"What about them?"

"Are you going to take them?"

"It looks a little as if we will," said Porter.

Dawson looked down sheepishly. "Can I have enough to retreat back to the States?"

"How many do you need?" said Porter.

"Nineteen."

"Take 20. You and your men can have steaks tonight," said Porter. "You've been through a lot, what with us thundering down on you and what-not, so you deserve a nice meal on us."

Porter and his men rode from wagon to wagon with torches. The dry canvas lit immediately.

Dawson shouted at Porter, "What're you doing!"

"What does it look like we're doing?" said Porter. He then laid a torch to the lead wagon. His men finally took the Army's oxen — all but 20 — and disappeared.

Porter and his men next rode to Fort Bridger.

All the while, he wondered how Mary Ann was faring. He feared the direction in which her emotions might be riding. A slight twinge of uncertainty haunted him; he pushed the feelings from his heart and made up his mind to think only of the war.

Half way to the fort he scanned the valley before him. Despite his determination to think only of the tasks at hand which could save his people, he could not fight the recurring, nagging, haunting thoughts of daughter Emily. He was suddenly interrupted.

"Captain Rockwell," said Henry Ballard with more formality in front of the privates listening nearby, "the general has a message for you." He handed Porter a paper.

"You think I can read this, Corporal?" laughed Porter. "First of all, it's dark; second, I can't read!"

His men laughed.

"I took the liberty to read it," said Ballard, chuckling.

"Yeah. What does it say?"

"Squaw-killer Harney has been replaced," said the corporal.

"That's a stinking shame."

"Sir?" said Ballard, confused.

"I wanted to confront Squaw-killer Harney myself," said Porter. "He's a ruthless, witless fool and I wanted to humble the man into the dust like I'm going to this entire Army — and President James Buchanan himself." Porter was deep down frustrated over tactlessly scaring the daylights out of Judge Drummond, even in the manner in which he had done it without saying a word to the judge. He realized that he, responsible even indirectly, had brought on this maniacal onslaught by a government-gone-crazy.

"I'm sorry, sir," said Ballard.

"I'm sorry too, Corporal. A horrible evening this is turning out to be," said Porter, tongue in cheek. "I was hoping to at least challenge General Harney to a duel."

"As in slapping his face with a glove?" laughed Ballard.

Porter's men laughed again.

"More like slapping his face with a glove full of manure," said Porter.

They laughed even harder.

"Well all is not lost, sir. Johnston's a good general, I hear."

"Albert Sydney Johnston?" said Porter.

"Yes, sir — he's replacing General Harney."

"Thank goodness for that. At least there's some consolation in this war. He'll make it loads more fun to whip than even Harney. I hear he's the President's best!"

With the same 32 now-somewhat-seasoned troops under his belt, Porter felt he could take on the entire U.S. division.

Riding through a canyon, he and his men came upon the trail of a U.S. Cavalry detachment.

"I think we should get out of here," said Ballard

"I think not," said Porter, who then decided to follow it. "We'll figure out some kind of problems to give them," he mumbled.

Suddenly they came on a large force of cavalry — several hundred strong — and found themselves precariously close.

Porter halted. He and his men were now 40 yards from an armed and angry Army regiment.

CHAPTER 54

Porter peered across his men and read their faces. He saw in them what he himself felt — confidence mixed with apprehension at the sheer size of their foe. He rode forward and met U.S. Army Captain Randolph B. Marcy, who also rode forward, meeting him half way between their two forces. Marcy was stocky, 40ish, greying, and thick-limbed. He radiated well his authority and could pass for a colonel.

"I suppose you are Porter Rockwell?" said Captain Marcy, sneering, having been briefed about the long-haired fighter, the wildcat with nine lives.

"Yes, sir."

"These soldiers under my command are United States troops. What armed forces do you have?"

"They're from Utah," said Porter.

"Is that supposed to impress us?"

"I should think so. We're mountaineers — and we know how to defend our valley."

"We'll see about that," grumbled Marcy. His men behind him laughed. "So what do you want with us at this moment, Mr. Rockwell? Why're you here?"

Porter laughed. His men chortled at his audaciousness.

"You haven't answered my question," said Captain Marcy.

"I'm watching you," said Porter. "Why're you here?"

Marcy sighed, feeling the Mormon guerilla was not as clever as he thought. "I'm looking for a way into Deseret," smiled Captain Marcy. "That's why I'm here."

"Nonsense," said Porter.

"Oh?" smiled March. "What's nonsense about it?"

"Two reasons, with all due respect, sir," said Porter.

Captain Marcy glanced back at his troops. They all laughed at Porter, thinking him a fool.

"Well?" said Marcy. "Tell me what's nonsensical about my looking to get into Deseret?"

"First of all," said Porter, "you'll never make it to Deseret alive."

Marcy glanced back at his own men again and they laughed even louder.

"Second of all," said Porter, "you're headed the wrong way!" He broke out laughing and all his men howled. Porter then spoke louder, "Deseret is that way!" The Army lost their smiles, watching Porter's men hooting at them.

Within moments, however, Porter realized that, while they had been talking, a number of Marcy's troops had formed a long line to the sides and behind his men, nearly surrounding them. Despite his mistake of leading his men the wrong direction, Marcy had cleverly laid plans for an ambush.

Marcy gritted his teeth. "We'll see who has the last laugh."

Porter suddenly realized there was no way out but to escape up a steep hill to his left.

Marcy read his eyes and shouted a command. Suddenly Marcy's main force thundered down on the guerrillas and closed the circle.

Porter shouted an order to his men. Within seconds they charged up the slope, gunshots trailing after them. While galloping up the hill, Porter was surprised to discover a ravine. His men followed him and, before the U.S. Army could realize what was happening, the guerrillas had cut back down the hill right within the Army's midst, going the opposite direction down the ravine, leaving the U.S. soldiers up on the mountain. The small band had literally slithered away, and the soldiers stared at them, chagrinned, as they disappeared.

Porter yelled back, "Well see who does have the last laugh!"

Captain Marcy shook his fist, angry as a hornet.

Porter dismounted and sat on a rock. He gazed across a creek and imagined how discouraged his pursuers must have felt, and he smiled. Suddenly Henry Ballard came riding up, shouting, "The troops are on us again!"

Amazed, Porter turned and saw sixty of Marcy's most elite footsoldiers behind him, sneaking forward. They had snuck around his force again and were now loading weapons for an ambush.

Porter suddenly shouted to his men. They quickly mounted horses and took off in a gallop — right past the disconcerted footsoldiers.

About eighty shots were fired by the Army — but none took effect, although one did pass through the hat of one private. Although not hit by lead, two Mormon guerrillas did fall from their horses. The Army troops shouted exultingly — figuring they had killed them.

Until the two riders sprung from the ground, onto the back of their comrades' horses, and galloped away. The Army's cheering came to an abrupt halt. They watched in awe as Porter's men escaped them once again, going right through their fingers, as it were, like butter.

Porter and his men answered with a cheer and rode down the hill to safety unscathed, leaving the U. S. forces up on the mountain, amazed.

Porter and his men arrived at Fort Bridger. The saints had bought the fort several months previously, paying Jim Bridger with gold. This structure held strategic importance of which Porter was well aware: Johnston's Army could travel north to it and settle in like termites. Therefore, he and his men rode forward to put their torches to it. After that, they stood back and watched the fire turn the fort into a blazing tower of flames. He finally pulled away from the sight, then led his men to nearby Fort Supply.

At night when they arrived, Porter confronted a small crowd of Mormon settlers who occupied the fort:

"How many of you are willing to let the Army take over this settlement?"

John Fredericks, a tall, intense mill owner, spoke up: "Well I ain't letting them drive me out again. It took me five years to build this. But I'll put my own torch to it first!"

Porter stared at him, finding some difficulty speaking:

"How many else of you feel the same?"

Without hesitation, every man and woman in the settlement raised their hands in unison. They took torches by which to see as they removed their valuables, then immediately applied the fire to their homes and businesses. Quickly they backed away from the massive flames. The former town of Fort Supply was quickly consumed, its inhabitants watching, many tearfully.

Porter winced at the sight. He turned away from the crowd, fighting his emotions.

When Colonel Alexander of the U.S. Infantry arrived at Fort Bridger, he exploded. His 400-man detachment was astonished to discover that, while they had hoped the fort would be its final retreat for the winter, it was now merely a huge pile of ashes. The Colonel dismounted, took a few steps toward the phantom structure, grabbed his hat off his head, and hit it against his leg.

Porter meanwhile rode with his men, on to City Supply. There they burned 15 more buildings. They warmed themselves by the flames, then galloped towards the southern campaign for their final confrontation with the main force of the U.S. Army . . .

CHAPTER 55

Brigadier General Albert Sidney Johnston, recently promoted from Colonel, emerged from his tent. He was a husky, bright-eyed Virginian who spoke with a noticeable accent. His pride was the uniform and his life was the corps. He was dark complexioned and had fine, brown hair and dark eyes. He knew if he performed well in this campaign, major assignments would be his to lead in the future, and his name would go down in history with distinction. He yearned — even craved — to whip the Mormon rebels. He could taste the victory. Certain, carefully chosen officers in his force were brilliant tactitions, others were smitten with unsatiable bloodlust — to him, they were a perfect mix for the division, and all were true warriors; indeed, as President Buchanan had told him, he was taking the hand-picked flower of the American military. The elite of the elite. Johnston scanned the mountainside for enemy. He saw nothing . . . but knew they would come. Three Mormon prisoners were in his camp and would be executed on the morrow.

Captain Jesse Gove, the assistant to the ground troops' commander, rode up to Johnston and dismounted. Verbally he presented a message from his direct commander, Colonel Alexander.

Captain Gove wore thick spectacles which gave one who spoke to him the feeling they were looking into the eyes of a reptile. He spoke the memorized message slowly:

"The weather here is the worst I have ever seen,' says Colonel Alexander, "But worse than that, our own mules are now attacking us. And eating our tents. I've never seen anything like it."

General Johnston commented icily, "Is the intrepid colonel haunted by Brigham Young's ludicrous threats of divine interplay?"

"Certainly not, sir . . . " said Captain Gove. Less emphatically: "I don't think so, sir." Gove handed Johnston the written letter.

General Johnston grabbed the letter, wadded it up, and threw it into the mud.

Porter and his men arrived at Echo Canyon. They were ready for the final confrontation — this time with General Albert Sydney Johnston himself. Porter's volunteers — and all other guerrilla units — took their positions atop the mountain as General Johnston lead the Army into Echo Canyon. All was going like clockwork . . . except for the fact Lot Smith and his band had not yet arrived. Without them, Porter's rescue plan would be substantially hampered.

Through his telescope he caught sight of the three Mormon prisoners. They were tied inside an Army wagon 50 yards from Johnston's tent and were surrounded by over 2,000 sleeping soldiers.

"Now this is what I call a chance in Hades," quipped Ballard. "When do you suppose Lot Smith's group will show up?"

"As soon as he quits lolly-gagging around, and realizes we're in a war," said Porter. His respect for Smith was out-weighed only by his own impatience.

He glanced at the moon and saw its glow emerging from a mountain peak. He knew he had to stage the rescue in pitch dark, before the moon appeared . . . so he had only minutes to act. He turned to his corporal:

"Prepare the men to cover me!"

Porter jumped from behind a boulder and bounded down the hillside towards camp. Arriving inside the Army's huge camp, he ran toward the prisoners' wagon, stopping at a tree.

There, he caught sight of a guard 30 yards away. When the guard looked the other way, Porter dashed toward the prisoners' wagon. Suddenly he stepped on loose rocks.

The guard glanced back just as Porter dove into the prisoner's wagon, and . . .

CHAPTER 56

The guard saw only the heel of Porter's boot as Porter landed in the back of the vehicle. Suspicious, the guard arose to inspect closer.

Inside the wagon, the three Mormon prisoners stared at Porter in amazement. He pulled out a bowie knife. Within seconds he had their ropes cut. He allowed them to stretch a moment, then the guard appeared.

The guard's eyes widened when he saw Porter, and he yelled, "Enemy in camp!"

The guard was about to repeat the warning when Porter kicked him cold. He flew back to the ground unconscious. Porter jumped from the wagon and the prisoners followed. He led them as fast as their aching legs would carry them, back to the mountainside at the edge of camp.

As they hobbled their last 20 yards, the nearest soldiers came running from their tents. When they spotted the prisoners, they shouted and began firing. The entire Army was alerted.

Hundreds of soldiers grabbed rifles and ran toward the prisoners.

Seeing them approaching the mountain, other hundreds opened fire.

Porter ran with the prisoners to safety, diving behind boulders into a deep ravine, just as the second volley of fire began. Porter's regiment, hidden 50 yards up the mountain, now provided cover: They opened fire on the U.S. soldiers.

Several hundred soldiers who were chasing the prisoners and reloading on the run suddenly came to a halt. Little did they know that Porter's men were intending to not hit them. The marksmen among Porter's force aimed only as close to the soldiers' feet as possible and fired. Dirt danced around them. Terrified, the U.S. soldiers ran back for cover and dove behind wagons for protection amidst flying lead balls.

Meanwhile, a hundred shots whizzed over Porter's head, above the ravine.

Lot Smith and his unit finally arrived. Porter saw them and yelled up the slope:

"I see you finished your stroll to Echo Canyon!"

"We're not stupid," yelled back Smith. "Looks like you've already done the work!"

Porter looked at the three prisoners beside him and rolled his eyes.

Lot Smith then yelled a command, and his force opened a barrage of fire. This provided protection for Porter and the prisoners on their last leg of escape. They took off running again and wound their way up the side of the mountain in the ravine, as two thousand soldiers fired at them to no avail. The soldiers were prevented from following them into the ravine by Lot Smith's firepower. One platoon did jump into the ravine, but as Lot Smith's marksmen chipped pieces of stone off the ravine walls just inches from the soldiers' faces, they jumped right back out. In this manner, Porter and the prisoners made their escape to the top of the mountain, finally out of rifle range.

Porter's and Smith's men cheered. At the mountain top, Porter ambled up to Lot Smith.

Smith smiled, "I hear from Major McAllister that our officers were scared me and you couldn't get along — but we proved 'em wrong, eh, Port? You're more fun than I thought you'd be."

"Yeah, all we need's a war," said Porter, "and we get along just fine."

"Especially when I'm shootin' lead balls over your head, just inches from that bossy mouth." chuckled Smith.

"Maybe we'll be lucky and have another war soon," said Porter, turning and waving his men on to their next phase of the attack. "So it can be my turn to shoot lead just inches from your mouth. 'Course I ain't as accurate as I used to be, but that's all right."

"A war this fun only comes along once a century or so," said Lot with a smile.

Across camp, four of Porter's horsemen went charging into the main Army campground. All the camp's guards had been occupied at the west end of camp, shooting at Porter and the escaping prisoners, so at the east end the four horsemen had free reign: They galloped with torches straight for the munitions wagons.

General Johnston and his officers were stunned. When they heard the first explosion they whirled and saw a third group of horsemen — seven in number — galloping across the north side of camp, tossing torches into other munitions wagons, and cheering. Johnston saw the cacophony and shouted conflicting orders to his men. One wagon after another began exploding, sending meteoric showers into the night like gigantic fireworks.

Infantrymen ran through camp in a panic, a few hopping about with trousers half on, just waking up. Johnston then noticed huge, forking flames shooting to the canvas covers of other wagons. Not only were their munitions all disappearing into thin air, but the attack was causing another interesting problem: The Army's cattle began stampeding, forcing hundreds of soldiers to jump out of the way.

Porter and Smith watched atop the mountain, laughing until their sides ached.

General Johnston gazed up and suddenly discovered thousands of campfires. His eyes dilated. He shouted orders to his officers to prepare a new attack. His field telescope revealed gunbarrels of soldiers seated at every fire. He knew he was overwhelmed.

"What did they do?" shouted Johnston to his first assistant. "Recruit Santa Ana and the entire Mexican Army?"

"It looks that way, sir," muttered the captain.

It did not occur to them that Porter's men had built unmanned campfires — running from one end of the canyon to the other and propping sticks beside each to give the appearance of gunbarrels silhouetted against the flames — nor did Johnston have the faintest idea that the Mormon fighters were in fact outnumbered at least 10 to one.

Johnston's second aide mumbled, "I don't know how they did it. More handcart companies came out here than we calculated."

Another officer muttered, "We can't beat these odds."

If General Johnston were not convinced of that before, certainly he would be three seconds later when Porter's men then set off strategically-placed explosions atop a dozen cliffs arching over them. This caused the general to stare in awe at boulders the size of cabins cascading down the mountainside — straight towards him. His men once again scattered helplessly as the boulders bounced like giant balls, landing upon and crushing two dozen wagons, now hedging up the way for all the Army's other wagons. Their front exit was now completely blocked.

Then, another series of explosions was heard atop the cliffs. Gigantic logs from tall trees came barreling down, forcing the soldiers to jump forward — behind the newly arrived boulders — for protection, as the huge logs crashed onto still other wagons, smashing them into millions of pieces and blocking the wagons moving off the road.

Upon Porter's signal, another explosion blew out the small dam they'd constructed at the river — sending a flood down both sides of the road.

Johnston shouted, "Get the vehicles off the road — quick!"

An Army scout galloped hard and came to a sudden stop at General Johnston's feet, sending a wad of loose mud onto the general's fastidiously pressed uniform. The scout reported, "General, sir! The enemy has turned the roadside into quicksand. We cannot maneuver in it! We are stuck, sir!"

General Johnston took off his hat and whipped it onto the ground. He shouted to his men to abandon the supply wagons.

Porter observed the massive havoc he had unleashed, spying their vulnerability through his field telescope and smiling even harder as he watched the confused soldiers below running about like ants.

While his mandate from Brigham was to shed no blood, one Army officer with a weakening heart suddenly gave his last gasp and collapsed dead. Another, an enlisted man, dropped cold dead from fright. These were the only two casualties of the Utah War.

General Johnston stood gaping at the sight. He scanned the panoramic view of several dozen blazes, munitions still shooting into the air. Then the last standing wagon in camp caught fire.

In anger, his eyes searched the mountains. He then heard the fireworks and gunfire cease, and in the sudden silence, he heard a voice echoing down the canyon. All the soldiers heard it, stopped, and stared up at the direction from which it boomed. It was the voice of the madman fighter, Porter Rockwell . . . and Johnston saw him silhouetted against the moon, standing atop a precipice on the mountain side . . .

"General, you may as well head to that big pile of ashes you called Fort Bridger — and stay there — 'cause you ain't botherin' us again. Ever again. We will fly the stars and stripes proudly, while you can just figure out what the devil it all stands for."

The general and his men stood staring at Porter.

"Want me to pull the artillery around to fire at him, sir?" said an aide.

Johnston didn't respond. He just kept staring at the famed wildcat, the maniacal gunfighter about whom he had heard so much. He finally mumbled to his aide:

"Don't bother — before you could aim, he'd disappear like a phantom."

The flames of the burning wagons soared high into the midnight sky, as General Johnston bellowed angrily back at the mountain peak:

"President Buchanan will only send more armies until you surrender!"

Porter echoed back:

"Then you can tell him we'll just keep facing them until he runs out of armies to send, because . . . we cannot lose. And as God is our witness . . . we won't!" Porter saw the red flames' reflections dancing off two thousand soldiers' faces. They stood as still as statues, listening and staring up the mountainside.

General Johnston blew out a silent sigh. He began pacing and kicking the dust. His men stared in awe at his behavior, then heard Porter's men breaking out laughing all across the mountainside. And laughing harder. Then laughing still harder, with guffaws, chuckles and chortles echoing through the canyons . . .

Johnston kicked his foot accidentally into a boulder and began swearing.

Porter's men laughed even harder.

The war was basically over.

CHAPTER 57

Porter sat at a campfire. Lot Smith and several other guerrilla officers ate jerked buffalo with him, telling stories and laughing, when a messenger rode up. It was Porter's assistant, Corporal Henry Ballard, who proclaimed:

"Brethren, our commander, has a directive for you. General Wells says he wants you to stay and watch the Army a few days with your units. But Brother Rockwell, Brigham has a special message for you, sir." He looked directly at Porter.

Porter studied Ballard. "Is it about Mary Ann?" he said.

"Lot Huntington," said Ballard.

"Lot Huntington?"

"It seems the young fellow was involved in a robbery."

"What're you talking about?"

"He and some other Mormon lads stole a horse from Sam Bennion at a tithing settlement party."

"Where ?"

"Outside a West Jordan chapel. Young Bennion is heartbroken — he raised the horse since birth — and his father asked Brother Brigham to have you help. He wants you to find the boys, since you know Lot so well."

Porter felt a shiver shoot through his body. He knew that a confrontation with young Lot, now that he was steeped in bad company — and also the boy's unpredictability — could be potentially dangerous. For Lot. He blew out a sigh as he stared into the campfire.

"Is he the boy that worked for you?" said Lot Smith.

Porter nodded.

"Want me to come along? I'd like to help."

Porter glanced at him, then at the other five anxious faces at the fire. They had heard of Porter's working with the boy and his problems and saw his overwhelming frustration.

"We'll all go if you want, Port," said another guerrilla fighter.

"We'll get the boys back safely to their parents," said Smith. "That's all they need. And we'll see the Bennion boy gets his horse back."

Porter appreciated their concern, but finally looked back at only the fire.

"I've got a long history with this boy," muttered Porter. "I was at his baptism, and later his ordination when he turned 12. When he got older, I spent many a late night talking and laughing with this kid, learning about girls he likes and places he hunts. Even his favorite fishing hole that nobody on earth knows about but me. I think I know him better than his own pa. I better take care of this myself."

"You sure?" said Ballard.

Porter nodded. "Thanks, boys."

He arose, looked at their grave expressions, and winked at them. "It'll be all right," he mumbled. He felt sick inside. He then turned to two — Lot Smith and Henry Ballard. "I guess I could use just two of you if you want to help."

They nodded quickly, proud to be asked.

CHAPTER 58

Porter, Smith, and Ballard found the distraught Bennion boy at home. Sam Bennion immediately led the three to a mass of tracks outside his West Jordan church meeting house.

Porter dismounted and studied the tracks carefully. He saw where Bennion's horse, "Brown Sal," had been stolen while Bennion had attended the party inside. Porter managed to sort out her prints among dozens of other tracks, by depth and by spacing of the horseshoes.

He re-mounted and said simply, "Let's go."

Lot Smith and Henry Ballard glanced at each other and smiled, amazed.

Several minutes and a mile down the road, Porter came to a road crossing and turned southwest.

Lot Smith halted at the intersection. "There's hundreds of prints crossing here, Port. How the devil can you see anything?"

"'Cause I got eyes, fool. Keep up with me."

Ballard broke out chuckling, and Smith joined him.

The next day before sunset, they arrived at a settlement called Fort Harriman. Presently they came upon several men riding out of town for firewood. Young Bennion described to them the lost mare, when the shortest one replied, "No such animal's been this way, boys."

Lot Smith piped up, "We're on a wild goose chase, Porter. I've enjoyed riding with you, but I'm gettin' cold."

"Shush up and keep goin'," said Porter.

"Nobody's seen the horse," argued Smith.

"That only proves one thing," said Porter. "That the boys are riding at night. They are out this way. Follow me."

At dawn they continued following him, riding through Cedar Valley. Soon they found the mare's tracks. But several yards later they were covered by a herd of cattle.

"It's over," said Smith.

"No, it ain't," said Porter.

"This is useless, Port," said Henry Ballard.

"We ain't slept in two nights," added Smith. "I think we've given you long enough." Anger was now noticeable in his voice. They were all at the end of their ropes emotionally and physically.

"I think he's right, Brother Rockwell," said Sam Bennion.

"You want your horse back or not?" bellowed Porter. "Just have faith in what I'm doing. You asked for my help, and anybody who ever has was never steered wrong."

"Except Joseph," muttered Lot Smith.

Porter glared at him. "What do you mean by that?"

"Just what I said!" he snapped.

Porter seethed, glaring at him and breathing harder. "Tell me what you meant by it!"

"I meant what I said!"

Porter launched from his horse and tackled Smith off his saddle.

Both men rolled in the snow, only feet from the edge of a 100 foot cliff, but the trees lining the cliff hid the view.

Ballard and young Bennion dismounted and tried pulling them apart.

Porter pulled up Smith and shouted three inches from his nose, "Why would you say that?"

"'Cause that's what half of us think of you! You were all-fired close to him, which any of us would've given our eye teeth to be. But if we'd been in your shoes, we at least would've gone to Carthage!"

Porter felt an avalanche of buried emotions resurfacing. Without thought, he punched Lot Smith.

"Don't you think," yelled Porter, "I haven't re-lived that a thousand nights — with a thousand nightmares? "

"Then why didn't you go with him!"

"He told me not to!"

Smith stood up and stared at him, rubbing his jaw. Porter arose beside him.

"I hate you judging on me!" said Porter, crashing his fist against Smith's jaw again, sending him back into the snow. They were now precariously close to the edge of the cliff.

Porter panted and glared at him, then sighed. He walked over to him, panting. Smith wore a considerably softened countenance.

"I'm sorry, Port," said Smith. "I didn't know."

As Porter gazed off he immediately realized from where much of his anger stemmed for years — a self-anger he had subconsciously born over Joseph's death, but on which he had never let himself dwell. "I should've gone."

"Port, you were only following orders," said Smith. "Maybe Joseph knew you woulda brought down the whole state militia on our people," he chuckled.

"In my deepest dreams I've lived one thing over and over," said Porter. "If I only had gone to Carthage."

"You're still a warrior, Port," said Lot Smith.

Porter cringed inside, feeling otherwise. He then stared at him and noticed his nose bleeding. "I am sorry," my friend. He walked forward a couple steps, extended his hand to help him up, and suddenly focused over Smith's shoulder: He saw the steep cliff through the trees. And below them was a campfire. All three boys were there — only 200 yards down. He motioned for the others to come forward and look.

Lot Smith turned, wiping the blood on his coat sleeve, when he saw the campsite below. "I think we're in business, boys."

"There's my horse!" whispered Sam Bennion.

Porter and his three companions snuck down the mountain, leading their horses. They stayed out of sight, and hoped the boys would not leave, so they could surround and capture them.

Making their way through thick snow, the four men remained silent, concealed from the gang by the slope of the hill. As they wound toward the bottom, still far from the boys' camp, they caught sight through heavy brush of the three boys mounting up.

"What can we do now?" said Bennion.

"Only one thing we can," said Porter. "We gotta take a chance of them seeing us, and mount up ourselves."

"Won't that give us too high a profile?" said Henry Ballard.

"'Got no choice," said Porter.

"He's right," piped in Smith.

Porter and his group mounted their horses and hurried down the hill faster.

Apparently, they were not seen. On one occasion they spotted the boys on a distant elevation, upon which Porter's group rode into a gully and waited till the boys could not see them, then they rode out.

But the boys were gone.

Hours passed. Ballard and Smith were growing concerned. One glanced at the other as they rode behind their leader.

Ballard finally spoke:

"This is pure stone we're riding on — how can you follow their tracks?"

"I can't," said Porter dryly. "I smell 'em."

"What's your plan, Port?" said Smith. "We're not gettin' anywhere this way. They're likely gone for good."

"I know where they're at," muttered Porter.

Smith, Ballard and Bennion looked at one another.

Directly ahead, they came upon Faust Station, a stage station run by H. J. "Doc" Faust, a noted horse rider and frontiersman. Porter descried the boys' tracks near his station/ house.

"How'd you know to come here?" said young Bennion.

"It's the last decent outpost between Utah and California," said Porter. "I knew the boys would head for water and a meal, plus a decent place to sleep before they hit the long desert ride."

He and his three compadres surrounded the station's main house, with Porter silently motioning them to strategic positions — one at a haystack, another at a boulder beside the corral, and another at a shed — while he himself stood behind a pile of cedar posts near the stable.

Sundown was only an hour away, so he figured Doc Faust would be emerging from the house soon to check the horse water trough before night set in. They waited patiently. Presently, Faust emerged from the house and approached the stable. As Doc passed him, Porter made the sound of a horse whinny. Faust spotted him, and Porter motioned him over. He came to the cedar post pile where Porter was concealed.

"Is Lot Huntington with the boys in there?" said Porter softly, his revolver still in his belt.

"Yeah, why?" said Faust.

"See that brown mare in the stable?" said Porter, pointing to Brown Sal.

"Yeah?"

"It belongs to that boy there," said Porter, nodding toward Sam Bennion, who gave him a nod.

"The boys're on their way to California," said Faust. "Huntington was going to sell me that mare and buy a cheaper one from me, so they'd have cash in California."

"All right," said Porter. "You go in there and tell Lot I'm here. Tell him to come out and surrender with the others. But you stay out of the line of fire — and hide behind the house."

"He's talkin' right tough," said Faust. "He strikes me as no one to just give up."

Said Porter, "Just tell him."

Hopeful, Porter watched Faust return to the house. A minute passed. Two. Then Porter glanced at his companions.

"Should we charge the place?" said Lot Smith behind the shed. "I'm game."

"I want 'em alive," said Porter.

"I do, too," explained Smith. "I'm thinking they'll come out if we move on the place from four directions, firing a shot or two in the air."

"I don't think so," said Porter. "They must feel like cornered wolves by now."

"There he is!" whispered Smith.

Porter whipped his head around and beheld Lot Huntington stepping onto the porch, sporting his large Army Colt pistol, searching his eyes for Porter and his men. Seeing nothing, he ran toward the stable.

"Lot — halt!" yelled Porter.

CHAPTER 59

Lot Huntington laughed and kept running to the stable. "I'll see you in Hades first, Porter." He had every intention to escape.

Porter was amazed at how much he had changed — even his countenance was different.

"I'll shoot his feet!" yelled Smith to Porter.

"No, you could hit arteries and he'd bleed to death!" said Porter.

Lot disappeared inside the stable.

"You afraid to hunt me to the death, boys?" said Huntington, now exiting the stable with the mare.

"I won't do that, Lot," said Porter.

He then noticed Lot was cleverly keeping the mare between himself and the other possemen in order to protect himself from all lines of fire — all except Porter's. He meanwhile maneuvered toward the bars of the corral gate. Soon, he arrived at the gate, and lifted the boards.

"You gonna follow me on your tired roan, Porter? That thing will never catch me on this spirited mare!"

"Give me the horse back!" yelled Sam Bennion.

"Whoa!" said Huntington mockingly. "That's little Brother Bennion himself. You've brought yourself quite a posse, Porter. I'm a-tremblin' in my boots!"

"She ain't your horse, Lot." barked Bennion. "I raised her myself."

"That's a touching story," said Lot. "Real sweet. So when I see you again, you can just tell me the rest of it." He laughed as he lifted the boards. But the boards would not budge more than six inches. A wire was wrapped around them, effectively tying the wooden gate to the gate post.

When Porter saw that, he knew he had a moment to reason with him. "Lot, you'll be shot by Lot Smith and Henry Ballard here. They're Brigham's top guerrilla fighters, and they just held off twenty-five hundred crack U.S. soldiers."

"Oooh, I am impressed," Lot sang sarcastically. "But we're dealing with something different here, aren't we?"

Porter knew what he meant.

"We're looking at them matters of the heart," said Lot. "Am I right?" He was buying time as he unwired one strand of wire at a time from the corral gate in order to make his escape.

"You may be, boy," said Porter.

"Of course I am," said Lot. "You wouldn't shoot me yourself! Think of all the campfires we laughed over and sang ballads together at."

"You've been the best partner I've had," said Porter. "Along with Joseph himself."

"By the way," said Lot with self-amusement, "How come you never saved his life?"

"Don't push it, boy!" yelled Lot Smith behind the shed. "I almost got my face smashed in over that," he added with a sparkle. "Tell you what, Huntington, why don't you put that Army Colt down and just let us sit together and see if we can't chat this thing through."

There was no response from Lot, who struggled with the gate wires with his cold hands.

"Talk to us, boy!" said Smith.

"You want an answer?" Lot Huntington suddenly whipped his pistol around and fired it towards Smith, just missing him. "Who-ee!" yelled Huntington. "You just came within inches of meeting your Maker! Does that answer your question?"

"It does, boy," said Smith, hiding behind the shed. "But if we blow you to kingdom come, it'll be a little tough for us explaining to your folks how all this happened, don't you think?"

"I think Porter's the only one with a bead on me, Brother Smith. Brown Sal's keeping me concealed from you and Bennion, and even that Ballard fellow over there," said Huntington, impressing them with his keen observation. Ballard had been watching the ordeal well-hidden behind a nearby boulder, with only one eye looking through tall brush. "That means," continued Huntington, glancing back at Porter and smiling, ". . . let's face it, fellows, there ain't gonna be no shooting from his pistol, just as I ain't shooting him with mine."

"What happens when he tackles you?" said Ballard, wanting Huntington to know their options.

"Then I guess I'd be forced into using this big bad Colt after all," laughed Lot. "But none of us want to do that, now do we?"

"None of us want you or the others hurt," said Porter. "So why don't you put that Colt down like Brother Smith said, and we'll all go home and forget this little mess. That way Sam gets his horse back and you stay outa jail, Lot."

"And we can all go hunting together afterwards and have a big, happy party?" said Huntington. "No, I don't think so, Port. I'm tired of our 'hunting trips,' Port."

The comment stung Porter, as intended.

"Ballard, Smith? I'm talking to you boys now. Has he taken you hunting yet?" yelled Lot. "He taught me how to shoot decent, but he got too busy, I reckon, hunting down bad boys and making himself feel useful. Too useful for some of us common folks. Anyway, we all got new friends now, don't we? My friends do hunt with me, and the way things are, it looks like we've hunted ourselves up a pretty good horse now, don't it?"

The other two boys laughed from the doorway of the house.

Porter winced at every word, and stared down at the mud between him and Huntington.

"What about your friends, Lot?" called out Smith. "'You leaving your friends in there stranded?"

The two boys inside suddenly broke out glass from the windows and opened fire, then ran outside.

Porter and his men ducked behind cover as the two mounted horses beside the house and took off in a gallop to hide behind it. They fired revolvers at Porter's men until they were safely behind the house, then the gunshots stopped.

"Does that answer your questions?" said young Huntington. "It looks like they can fare for themselves, don't it? I ain't deserting them, but I do know something about being deserted."

Another dagger to Porter.

"We're ready when you are, Lot!" yelled one of his friends behind the house.

"Whoo—eee!" yelled the other. "Bring it on!"

Smith called to Porter:

"The little snots don't realize we coulda taken them out with two shots, between me and Ballard alone!"

"Hold your horses," said Porter to Smith. "Remember what we're doing here."

"Oh, what are we doing here?" said Huntington. "Are we out to put these boys back in Sunday School where they belong, is that it? My, am I touched."

"We're all touched!" yelled one of the other two behind the house. The other broke out laughing.

Lot continued: "Now if my Pa had talked to me in Sunday School I woulda gone once in a while — cause he sure never did at home. So maybe I *shoulda* gone to Sunday School," he laughed. "But then when I was at home, he was always off at his ward. So how do you figure I win?"

"Just hold on," said Porter. "Lot, we gotta pow-wow, son. Put down your gun! I'm coming out now!"

Lot was unwrapping the last wires one by one. His hands were colder now and he was losing patience with his numbness.

"Lot, did you hear me? I'm comin' out."

"You try that, old friend, and you'll still be a friend, but a dead one," said Lot.

"Young man . . . you remember my telling you about fishing when I was a youngster? I had a favorite place in New York, and I wanna go back there someday. Everything was pure and simple and happy — back at that fishing hole before others tried taking it away . . . But what I had there for awhile was a fishing hole all my own — and the fish were the biggest I'd ever seen and the countryside was as peaceful as heaven. I wanna go back there with you, Lot. To heaven itself."

Lot looked over his way, with the child in him caressing the invitation of his words, his eyes momentarily wide with wonder.

"What's the matter, Lot!" yelled one of the boys behind the house. "Is he inviting you to heaven with him?"

Both boys laughed harder than ever.

The second yelled out, "Is that sorta like being invited to church?"

Lot shook out of his reverie. He flashed a shrewd smile back at his friends, then glanced over his shoulder at the long-haired lawman:

"Good try, Porter." He then lifted the last wire and swung open the gate. "Catch me if you can, old man."

Porter felt an intolerable anger consuming him. "Don't bait me, boy!"

"Oh, we're getting mad, now, are we. Do they get mad in heaven?"

Porter whipped up his Colt Navy to shoot Lot's weapon, but Lot swung up his own Colt Army and shot Porter's weapon out of his hand. Porter remembered Lot getting better and better when they had target-practiced together.

Just then, the end of the gate bar rebounded and struck the mare in the flank. This caused the horse to plunge away from him. Lot was left without the cover of the horse, and he was wide open.

Porter dove for his pistol, picked it up, and in one motion fired at Lot. The ball struck him in the left arm.

Angrily, Lot turned on Porter with his pistol and aimed, but the hammer was not yet cocked.

"I only wounded you, Lot. Drop the weapon while you're still alive!"

CHAPTER 60

Lot held his Colt Army aimed on Porter.

"No, Lot, don't! We've got a life to see together, son."

Lot paused and studied his eyes.

"I will do these things with you that I have promised," said Porter.

Lot's eyes again widened, and Porter could see the fear and hope of a young child once again.

Henry Ballard yelled out, "Should I cut him down at the legs?"

Lot Smith also shouted, "I've got a sight on him — just give me the word, Porter — before he cocks it!"

Porter glanced to the others, "He won't!" Porter was stretched out on the ground aiming up at Lot 30 feet away. "Drop it, Lot. We have everything in front of us — you and me. You mean everything . . ."

"To who! To what? What have I got? You tell me what I've got! Nobody's helped me with nothin' — So-called family ain't got time! Neighbors treat me like dirt. Only the friends back there are real friends!"

"It'll change!" said Porter. "Let me help it change."

Lot's eyes welled with tears. "It can't. I'm sorry." He lowered the Colt Army, but at the same moment cocked the hammer.

Porter yelled, "No!"

Lot moved the pistol toward Porter's face, and aimed . . .

And Porter fired.

Lot swirled back, but aimed again at Porter.

Porter fired again — and the boy fell backwards across the slanting bars of the corral gate, his body stuck in the gate with one leg outside the corral. He bled profusely from the abdomen.

His two friends behind the house suddenly bolted in a panic: They turned their horses from the house, ready to gallop — when Doc Faust appeared to their side with a shotgun aimed at them:

"This thing's got two barrels — and I'm good with both."

The boys raised their hands, dropping their pistols.

As the two dismounted with hands raised, Porter ran to Lot's side. He was barely conscious. He stared at Porter filled with boyish fear.

"Don't let me go, Port."

Porter held a cloth to the young man's wounds. "You'll be O.K., Lot."

Lot clenched his eyes in pain, then his body tightened.

Porter stared at his face. He slowly shook his head. "No, please. No." He pulled Lot close to him, hugging him. "You've meant more than any brother or even son I've had. Oh, Lot, please . . . don't." Porter stared off in shock . . . in horror . . . feeling his body go limp in his arms.

Lot Smith, Henry Ballard, and Sam Bennion stepped up beside them, gazing down. Smith finally began walking into the house, and nodded to the others to join him. They left Porter alone with Lot.

Night came, and Smith stared out the window, studying Porter holding Lot's body outside in the twilight.

Faust built a fire in the fireplace.

The two prisoners had their hands tied behind their backs, seated in chairs. Meanwhile Ballard and Smith stared at the burning logs.

Hours passed.

At midnight the door finally creaked open and Porter wandered in. He stopped and stared at the others, finally conscious of them.

He studied the two young prisoners. Both were 18.

"I reckon I'll be seeing their folks when we get back," said Porter to Smith, Ballard, and Bennion. "But can you take them to the jail?"

Smith nodded.

"I reckon I'll be seeing Lot's folks first," added Porter, thinking aloud in a daze. "I'll have to figure out what to say. I guess I didn't do things too awful right by him."

"You can't blame yourself," offered Smith.

"I can blame his folks and some of his leaders. Maybe some of his friends. And maybe himself some. But definitely me. We're all to blame. And since I'm looking after me in this life, I'm definitely to blame most."

He walked to the fire, sat, and stared into it, warming his hands. What he felt was not only the death of the boy, but the failed relationships he had with others in his life. Certainly, circumstances had created a rift between him and his first wife — their backgrounds and levels of commitment to the faith were on different levels — but he always wondered if he could not have done more — especially to communicate better, to work harder through their differences, and perhaps to have turned down an assignment or two with Joseph just to be with her when she needed him most. The result, no matter whose fault it was — although with time he tended to blame himself for everything — was the severing of his children from not only him but from the Kingdom, leaving a never-ending question burning in his soul — which, if any, would ever return to him and — even more significantly — to the fold? As he studied the burning embers, he realized he had rarely felt so devastated. Everything young Lot was to him represented his children and how he had spiritually let them down. His depression knew no bounds. And what would happen with Emily? Could their once-close bond be repaired and could she forgive his stubbornness and conflicts with her? Would he even see her again? Another awakening hit him: Whatever anger he had felt — or any satisfaction that had recently entered his soul from ridding the earth of outlaws — had now completely evaporated from him. The metamorphosis was complete.

Faust offered him bread and warm milk, but Porter shook his head.

No one said another word the remainder of the night.

CHAPTER 61

Leaving Lot Huntington's parents, Porter realized he had just performed the most difficult task of his life. Riding slowly away on his horse, he could still hear Lot's mother sobbing through the wax-papered window.

He realized he had not felt so numb, drained, and spent since Joseph's death, except perhaps the day he found Alpheas Cutler in his cabin with Luana when he returned from Independence Jail; as well as the day he rode West, leaving little Emily in Iowa to cry and run after him as he galloped away; and of course the day Emily announced she had married her kidnapper.

Porter felt he had no more feeling left . . . until he thought again of Emily . . . and of Mary Ann. Both of whom were now likely gone from his life forever.

Lot Smith and Henry Ballard had escorted young Sam Bennion to his home in West Jordan. On the way, the two prisoners had tried to escape, and Smith had yelled for them to stop, but they would not. So he and Ballard shot them. Before they could apply bandages, the boys were dead.

Smith and Ballard returned immediately to the guerrilla units stationed at Echo Canyon. They were guarding the Army which was still stalemated in the canyon.

One night, Smith and Ballard sat at a campfire atop the same mountain as before the Huntington expedition, with the same officers. They still felt depressed over the two boys they had shot. Ballard glanced up and saw Porter arriving at their campfire.

As Porter dismounted, he said nothing. Then sat with them to warm his hands. One of the officers broke the heavy silence: "Smith, here, told us what you went through. I'm sorry."

Another muttered, "We're all sorry, Porter. We know what that kid meant to you."

After a long pause, Ballard tried to cheer them:

"Life with our families begins tomorrow. We got orders from Brigham to pull in. There's a celebration waiting for us like never the valley has seen."

Porter just stared into the flames.

Lot Smith glanced at the others, and they all looked back at the fire in silence.

CHAPTER 62

Porter rode with most of his men toward Salt Lake Valley, helping to herd 624 steer and 104 mules they'd acquired from the U.S. Army for their troubles.

He and his men were confident that Johnston's force would remain stalemated outside the Valley until Brigham could negotiate with Buchanan's peace commission, which was on its way that moment to the territory. The commission had been sent because a non-Mormon ally, Thomas Kane, had interceded in the Mormons' behalf and convinced President James Buchanan that former Judge William Drummond's accusations were false, and that the Mormons were not in a state of rebellion and lawlessness, as Drummond had asserted to the press. A few Mormon scouts meanwhile would take turns spying the Army's camp.

At the entrance to Emigration Canyon Porter stopped his horse and gazed at the distant, silver-colored Great Salt Lake. Since it was late afternoon, the sun shot colored, filtered fingers through cirrus clouds, bouncing crystal-like beams off the shimmering lake's surface. His feelings were torn between despair and hope. Mary Ann and Emily were his chiefest worries. His men halted behind him as he stared at the lake. Momentarily, he ordered his men to ride onward. For another hour he sat atop his horse and studied the lake, thinking and alone, realizing the consequences of his life's choices. With the Utah War over, he had nothing planned now but to face his problems with Mary Ann head-on. He prayed silently, asking for help in handling the problems of his heart, with which he was now feeling overwhelmed. Looking up at the view again, an idea occurred.

He had lived as a free man long enough. While he had somewhat realized this before, he now far more fully comprehended how his independent, willful spirit had practically destroyed their ties, and he realized essentially for the first time that deep down he had somehow resented her not accepting about him what he thought should only be natural in a man — to come and go at will. There was an order of things to life and nature to which he had not complied, so it was time for a change. He had agreed with her complaints logically, but in the deepest recesses of his heart he still had questioned them and therefore was not ready to truly commit — until now. If indeed he could keep the commitment — which was another matter. But for the first time ever, he felt he was *actually* willing to try.

He spurred his animal and rode downhill into Great Salt Lake Valley. He would deal with another concern after solving problems with Mary Ann — he wished with all his heart to have another chance with Emily.

Porter caught up to his men and rode with them through celebrating thousands on city streets. Hundreds were dancing on the road, throwing their hats into the air, as bands played stirring music. When Porter and his men dismounted and turned a corner, additional celebrators saw Porter and broke into a cheer. Children by the dozen ran to him, hugging his legs and touching him, then mobbing the rest of the guerrilla force, who picked up children and hugged them.

Turning the corner of South Temple Street onto Main, Porter discovered Mary Ann leaning against a building, gazing at the thousands of celebrating citizens. She still had not decided what to do, but was leaning toward leaving him. Yet when her eyes rested on his countenance, seeing him coming down the parade route, she discerned in him a countenance different than what she had ever before observed. The next thing she noticed was his smile. He ambled up to her and stopped.

Then, as he stood in front of her, she stared into his blue eyes as if they were open windows . . .

CHAPTER 63

Porter, standing before Mary Ann, was slapped on the shoulder from behind. He turned and beheld Henry Ballard:

"Brother Brigham wants to see you in his office right away."

Mary Ann added quickly, "I've got to get back to the children. Mama's had them all day. Will you come to their place tonight? We have a lot to discuss," she said soberly.

Porter nodded, fearful she had only been relieved to find him safe, but that she might be leaving him after all.

In his office, Brigham gravely held up a letter and said, "Porter, let me read you this. It's from a friend of Emily's."

In her cabin near the now-nearly-depleted gold fields outside Sacramento, California, Emily was leading a peaceful life emersed in simplicity. She enjoyed the companionship of a hard-working and faithful husband, young David Tyrrell, who had retired from gold-panning as had many when the creeks were panned dry, and he had taken up farming.

Their pride prevented them from moving to Salt Lake Valley where they'd have to start over and seek help from her father; additionally, she had issues with her pa that at this point she was not certain could be resolved very painlessly. One sacrifice of his she did appreciate was the gift of his sending Ugly. She found him a delightful companion, and he adored her. But she sensed he missed Porter, and every time she saw that pensive look on his face — usually at night when Ugly lay down by the fireplace — she fought her own yearnings.

As she baked oatmeal cookies laced with local, sun-dried raisins, she talked with her next door neighbor, Linda Carol Whitmore from a quarter-mile away, a young woman of 22, pregnant but otherwise bored with life. There was a lull in the conversation when David Tyrrell strode in and kissed Emily.

"What's the matter?" said Tyrrell.

"Nothing," said Emily. "'Just thinking."

"About your pa again?"

"'Wish I could get him out of my life."

"He is out of your life."

"He could walk through that door any minute," she said. "And I still feel imprisoned to him. Though I think I understand him better."

"Sounds like you don't want him out of your life," said her husband. "I best get back to old Joshua and dig out the plow."

"Did he leave the plow stuck in the mud again?" said Emily, exasperated.

"Yeah, I wish we could afford to get rid of him," said Tyrrell.

"Then why don't you just trade him away?" said Linda Carol, piping in. "My husband would trade for her."

"Well," said Tyrrell, scratching his head, "I can't. He's the only animal I've had that felt to me like family, and I guess I just plain love the old codger, and know he loves me. That's the best part," he winked. "As much as I'd like to shoot him."

Emily stared out the window at the mule. Her husband and girlfriend caught the expression of realization in her eyes.

Tyrrell smiled, pulled his hat over his head and strode out towards the mule for another tussle. Ugly began barking ferociously. When he licked Emily's hand, she laughed and pushed him away.

After another minute of pondering out the window, Emily pulled the final batch of oatmeal raisin cookies from the cast-iron oven and glanced at her girlfriend.

"Wait till I get back from the field, Linda Carol, and we'll eat some of these ourselves. David likes these best when they're warm." Emily burst out the doorway, proud as punch of her batch of sensuous, lightly browned, piping hot oatmeal cookies. Ugly followed her outside, licking her hand again. She pulled it away. "You'll get some in a minute, Ugly."

But he kept licking her. "Look, I'm not my father and you're not going to get me to shoot outlaws," she laughed. "Now get away." As she looked up to find her husband, she caught sight of him running the opposite direction, with three horseback Indians 50 yards behind and chasing him.

He changed directions, trying to lose his pursuers in the rows of corn, but the stalks were too low to completely conceal him.

He attempted to lead them in the direction opposite the cabin, away from the two women.

Emily stopped at the edge of the porch, paralyzed with fear as the three braves narrowed the gap, bearing down on him. She watched helplessly as one caught up to Tyrrell and tomahawked him. Another lanced him with a spear in the back. As he crumpled to the earth, he turned and caught sight of Emily, his eyes filled with concern, horror, and love for her — even more, if possible, than with anguish for himself.

Emily walked slowly forward in shock. The three braves began riding away, when one glanced back and noticed her across the cornfield.

Emily caught the brave's eyes, and she gasped, then froze.

Linda Carol came to the doorway, grasped the scene, and whispered harshly, "Emily, quick — out the back way with me! Emily!"

Ugly began barking at Emily, but she merely stood there, frozen.

Linda Carol panicked as she saw the three warriors turn their horses toward the cabin.

"Emily, come on!"

But Emily did not. Linda Carol's fear filled her bloodstream with icewater.

"Emily!" Linda Carol choked from the futility of trying to rescue her friend, and finally rushed out the back door, directly into the thick forest.

Through the woods she ran and sobbed.

Sitting across the desk, Porter listened to Brigham reading Linda Carol's letter. Sorrow pushed Porter's soul deep into anguish.

His face slumped down, listening to the final paragraph:

"I tried doing all I could. Since then, no one has seen her body. We were very close. Like you, I loved her very much. Your daughter was a special lady.

"Sincerely, Linda Carol Whitmore."

Brigham slowly moved his eyes from the letter and beheld Porter's anguish. He was too grieved to even cry.

Brigham, finding no words, looked back down at the letter on his desk.

Both men sat for a minute in solid silence.

CHAPTER 64

Walking outside into the still-celebrating city's "victory party," Porter felt removed from all life — and even from time itself — as he half-consciously strolled through a tidal wave of pedestrians, hundreds of whom were passing him, anxious to get to the fireworks about to be set off from South Temple Street. Twilight quickly faded and the explosions began. Colors reflected off thousands of faces. Porter walked alone down the wide sidewalk of Main Street.

Down the first block he walked, then another. Smoke was filling the entire merchant section as fireworks exploded in the air behind him. Through the fog-like smoke he caught sight of someone who faintly reminded him of Emily. He could not tell who it was, but from wisps of partial clearings in the fireworks fog — and with dozens of children whizzing excitedly past in front of him — he caught enough of the woman's identity to realize it was someone he knew.

She also spotted him, and walked quickly towards him, dodging the increasing numbers of late-comers passing between her and him on their way to the fireworks.

The woman finally arrived before him and stopped. She and Porter stared at each other.

"Porter?" said the woman.

Porter continued gazing at her.

"Do you remember me? I'm Luana's cousin, Julia."

Porter was astonished at how much she resembled both Luana and Emily. At that moment he realized how closely Emily mirrored her mother's image when Luana was in her 20's. He had almost forgotten what Luana looked like, so complete had been his erasure of bittersweet memories.

As the woman spoke, Porter saw her lips moving but did not hear a word. Then the fireworks momentarily paused.

"So would you?" she said as the only sentence Porter heard.

"I'm sorry," said Porter. "What did you say?"

"I said, I'm just passing through here on my way to California, where I'll be living with one of my daughters."

"Have you seen her?" said Porter.

"Who?" said the woman. "What're you talking about?"

"Luana."

"Not since Iowa. You know she moved to Minnesota."

Porter was disappointed the woman had no more news of Luana.

"Anyway, I want to know if you'll take on my second cousin. She's a delightful young woman to raise."

"What?" said Porter.

"Can you take one of my second cousins? She's still but a child in many ways, but is growing up fast."

Shaking his head slowly, still stunned over the news of Emily and now with his senses dulled by the smoke and pounding fireworks resuming in the sky, he mumbled, "I don't know. This might be kinda' hard since I've remarried. I've got a new family, Julia."

At that moment, a young lady emerged from the crowd and Porter stared at her, astonished.

The woman who had been talking with Porter finally beamed with a big smile and proclaimed:

"Meet my second cousin. Porter, you've got to bone up on family trees. We're talking about your daughter . . . Emily!"

CHAPTER 65

Porter walked forward towards Emily a few steps, too overwhelmed to believe what he was seeing.

Music suddenly struck up by a band two blocks away, as torches were lit across the city in unison.

Thousands of people arose from the wide city sidewalks and poured onto the streets, dancing to wild fiddle and harmonica music. Porter continued walking forward towards his daughter, then saw her burst into tears and raise her arms toward her father.

He saw her mouth the words, "Papa," but did not hear a sound from her because of the cheering and dancing, whooping, hollering and music filling the air.

At that moment he slowed his walk towards Emily, stopped before her . . . and hugged her.

She cried in his arms like a little girl. Then he heard a dog barking, and looked down. There stood Ugly, old grey Ugly, beside Emily.

Emily's cousin laughed through her tears at the scene, hoping the small ruse she had played — about her second cousins — had not teased Porter too terribly. She had not known — nor did Emily — of the report that Emily was no doubt dead.

Porter said, "Brigham just read me a letter from Linda Carol."

Emily gasped. "Everyone must think I'm dead."

Porter nodded, and with a faint smile said, "Can I pinch you — just to see you're not a ghost?"

"As long as it's not too hard."

Julia now spoke:

"Emily was taken by Indian braves who killed her husband, and they traded her — and the dog that she wouldn't let go — to white scouts up on the Humboldt River. One of 'em was my cousin, and he brought her to my wagon train. Life indeed has interesting twists and turns."

Tears streamed down her face as she saw Porter and Emily hugging each other harder amidst the celebrating and dancing.

Ugly jumped up and barked, and Porter laughed. When he had sent Ugly to California he was certain he'd never see him again.

As Julia walked downstreet alone, she looked back through the dancing crowds and spotted Porter and Emily still hugging, then together they hugged the big, black dog.

The thought crossed her mind that it was a moment neither would soon forget . . .

The crowds had mostly drifted home, leaving just several hundred people milling about in the moonlight. Porter and Emily walked together to a small fountain near the street and sat on a bench. Porter held Ugly with one arm and with the other waved at a couple friends, then turned to his daughter with a smile:

"So with three husbands behind you," said Porter, "are you finally going to pack that marrying stuff in?"

"I believe so," said Emily, smiling. "In any case, I don't think I'll be leaving town again. Is that cabin built for me yet?"

"It is, but I hope you'll sell it and move closer to Mary Ann and me. I've even dug a little creek off the main stream, and put your favorite chair beside it — just like the way you have it in the painting — right beside the rushing waters."

Emily's eyes filled with tears.

"I couldn't take it, seeing David killed — 'cause I loved him the most. I really loved him." Her eyes glistened in the light. "But I have a comfort I haven't known before: I know we'll be together again — if I live worthy of him, and I get us sealed in the Temple. He was a worthy and faithful man."

Porter felt tears of compassion welling up, as well as a strong gratitude that she had deepened her appreciation for the Plan of Salvation.

Emily continued, "You probably don't know this, but Mary Ann and I have been writing, and we've gotten a good friendship going. We also got you figured out a little bit, I think."

"I like all that going on behind my back," he said dryly. "But I ain't sure I wanna know." Ugly jumped on the bench beside him, and seemed mesmerized by the lights reflecting off the fountain water streaming in the air.

"Ugly don't seem to be in a hurry to go nowhere, so I reckon I'll be hearing it after all," he smiled.

"It's not all bad," she smiled. "I've put pieces together — and so has she. We may be wrong, but we figure a lot of what you are comes from Joseph. I've heard you talk in your sleep about him. And it's no secret about you blaming yourself for his death and wanting to somehow help out the Saints even harder after he was killed. But what is new to me — what we have figured out about you — goes deeper than that. And some of it goes back to your own pa. He was a sweet man, and always gave you everything you needed, even in your younger years — except attention. I've heard you say that much."

Porter studied her in the light reflected from the lanterns beside the fountains. Additional light was filled in by the moon and stars.

Emily continued, "As a kid you wanted to be with him. But he was always taking off to explore and hunt, leaving your ma and his kids. Just as his pa had before him. But later he did settle down as he grew older. I've heard all that from your other family members back in Nauvoo. I suppose you felt hurt he left you like that. I reckon it hurt a lot your whole life, because you adored him so much. And I think you've felt alone deep down ever since — and hurt. But at the same time it wrote a map inside you that you probably can't even remember being written. I can imagine you probably always wanted to go hunting and fishing with him more than anything in the world. But he pushed you aside as he'd head out the house for one trip after another. But when I was young, you'd at least take me. So you got rid of some of that map that had been written. But you still left the other kids — and Ma — time and time again. so I believe this is what's made you restless your whole life."

Porter looked away, not wanting to hear this.

Emily continued, "Mary Ann says she thinks you also felt abandoned by Luana in the ways of feelings. The reason she left you in her heart was because you were gone so much. I figure you already know that."

Porter looked at her and nodded slowly, rather surprised at her perceptions, and intrigued.

"Then after I got married each time and left you alone, you felt left again, by another person you loved. Once I figured this out, I still wanted to forget about you, but I just couldn't. I saw my last husband couldn't give up on his old mule, and it made me realize the missing piece of this whole puzzle. That happened just before he was killed."

"I'm sorry he died, Emily," said Porter. "I really am."

Through tears, she took her father's arm and held it as they continued sitting there facing the fountain.

"So the real puzzle to figure out," she said, "was not you, but me. No matter what you're like, or what I don't like about you, I am part of you, as you are of me, and I am cut out to love you no matter what stubborn streak I see that drives me crazy. Just like with that stupid mule."

"I appreciate the comparison," said Porter sarcastically.

"And I'm probably too much like you for my own good,"
she continued. "That's the hardest part of all this for me. But
one thing I can tell you. I will never lose my love for you. I have
tried — believe me, I have — but I can not and never will, just
as Mama never will, though she claimed otherwise."

"Claimed? What're you talking about?" said Porter, eyes
wide.

"I could see through Mama's claims, even as young as I
was."

"What do you mean?"

"It's obvious she's never lost her love for you. Only she
feared the future with you — and also not knowing about being
left alone in the future. She was no different than many women.
Mama will never love her new husband — just as she didn't
love Alpheas. But they gave her what she needed for the moment. A steady feeling of knowing they'd be there every night."

Porter fought old feelings rearing up inside. "I didn't know
she's had such a rough go of things since," said Porter, not
knowing what else to say.

"Well I know a lot more about you now — and so does
Mary Ann. I just saw her a few blocks south, heading home.
I told her what I had decided and she cried a little and said
she'd stick by your side no matter what. She has said that
before, but this time she means it. A lot of what we have
figured about you goes back to Joseph's teachings. I believe
he said there are two kinds of sins — those by disobedience
— and we've all disobeyed some way or another and we know
what that's all about. But the other sin he talked about comes
from tradition. Tradition I believe comes from that map that

was written inside you by your folks and their folks and so on. But I think you're trying to settle down and re-write those maps. All in all you've been as faithful to the Lord's kingdom as any man I could imagine, because you've always at least tried, and gone the extra mile for others, no matter what weaknesses and traditions were pulling at you. I think Mary Ann and I both see the rock you are, deep deep down, below the traditions. And I believe it's your faith that put you there. I also think Joseph saw it. I know Brigham does. And I know I do, too, Papa." Her eyes glistened as she then looked down. "I guess I just can't get away from the fact you're my hero. I can't."

Porter felt a ton of boulders lifted from his shoulders.

"Most importantly for me," said Emily, "is that I know I'm home."

Porter looked at her, then down for a moment, thinking. He knew that "from the mouth of babes" he had his answers. His own daughter had resolved the mystery that for years had so haunted him of why he had always felt driven to desert his loved ones. Furthermore, despite her overall, optimistic assessment of him, he saw his own imperfections glaring him in the face, and knew he had to do something about it. He knew he had to devote his life — the time left in his life — to Emily, to Mary Ann, to his other children, and to every friend and soul in need with whom he'd come in contact who needed his time. He had lost Luana. He had lost Lot Huntington. He had a second chance, and he wasn't about to let that float away. Not for anything in the world. He kissed Emily on the forehead and gazed upward.

As Porter sat by the fountain, the night's celebration faded before the tranquility of the moon, a sight so peaceful and consistent with the feelings of his heart that the light which it shed on them defined a new, sweet victory, overshadowing all the anguish and agony — including the gunfights and wars — which had once consumed him but which now paled before the simple, clear light of a nightly heavenly body that would, like the spiritual forces influencing their lives, always be there for him when he simply looked skyward.

EPILOGUE

Porter Rockwell resumed marshaling and built a ranching empire. He and Mary Ann would have three more children, and he would spend all the time with them that they needed as a father and husband.

Brigham Young negotiated a peace treaty with President James Buchanan, and the Army was forced to settle 30 miles south of Salt Lake City. General Albert Sydney Johnston soon joined the Confederate Army and was killed in battle April 6, the most significant date of the year in Latter-day Saint lore (including the anniversary of the founding of the church), in the year 1862.

Judge William W. Drummond hoped his letter to the Eastern press would crush the Mormon empire, but he never succeeded, nor were his aspirations ever fulfilled in replacing Brigham Young as governor. His life quickly spiraled downhill. His mistress left him and his wife divorced him. He was later convicted on two counts of fraud and stealing postage stamps, and eventually became a sewing machine salesman in St. Louis. He died as a vagrant in a Chicago asylum.

Perhaps the greatest of ironies is the apparent fulfillment of a rumored prophecy uttered by Joseph Smith regarding Governor Lilburn Boggs — that he would wind up forever in the shadows of the kingdom. Today his grave is in sight of a California Mormon chapel where the head of his casket literally faces the building.

Porter Rockwell Limited Edition Prints and Commissioned Paintings

Porter's Ranch at Point of the Mountain
by Clark Kelley Price

L imited-edition art prints of the oil painting featured on the dust jacket for this volume are available at $75 each plus $1 shipping and handling. (See order form on last page.) The edition consists of 880 11" × 14" prints on canvas, signed and numbered by the artist.

Mr. Price's work, found in private collections worldwide, sells in exclusive art galleries and has often been featured on covers of *The Ensign* magazine. A longtime friend of the author, Mr. Price was among the first to inspire Richard Lloyd Dewey about the life of Porter Rockwell. He did the illustrations and back cover painting for Dewey's *Porter Rockwell: A Biography*.

Mr. Price is willing to paint, by commission, additional scenes from Rockwell's life (or any subject that appeals to him) at a minimum size of 24" × 36" (or any dimension of at least 864 square inches) for interested patrons. Commissioned oil paintings are priced at $10 per square inch ($8640 for 24" × 36"). Contact the artist at (307) 883-2322, or P.O. Box 211, Thayne, Wyoming 83127.

The artist requests a lead time of one year. A down payment of 33% is required on the commission. Paintings come on canvas, unframed, and patron pays for shipping.

Porter Rockwell: A Biography
by Richard Lloyd Dewey

Hardcover, $24.95   ISBN: 0-9616024-0-6

The epic biography that traces Porter Rockwell from turbulent
Eastern beginnings to battles with Midwestern mobs to extra-
ordinary gunfights on the American frontier. Quotes hundreds of
journals, letters, and court records. Illustrated by western artist, Clark
Kelley Price.

See order form on last page.

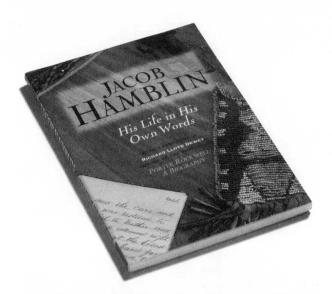

Jacob Hamblin: His Life in His Own Words
Foreword by Richard Lloyd Dewey

Softcover, $10.95   ISBN: 0-9616024-5-7

Far from the gun-toting reputation of super-lawman Porter Rockwell, Jacob Hamblin was known in early Western history as the supreme peacemaker.

No less exciting than Porter's account, Jacob's adventures encountered apparent Divine intervention at every turn, a reward seemingly bestowed to certain souls given to absolute faith. And in his faith, like Porter, Jacob Hamblin was one of those incredibly rare warriors who are *absolutely fearless*.

His migrations from Ohio to Utah with life-and-death adventures at every turn keep the reader spellbound in this unabridged, autobiographical account of the Old West's most unusual adventurer among Native Americans.

In his own words, Jacob Hamblin bares his soul with no pretense, unveiling an eye-witness journal of pioneer attempts to co-exist peacefully with Native brothers, among whom he traveled unarmed, showing his faith in God that he would not be harmed.

Easily considered the most successful — and bravest — diplomat to venture into hostile territory single-handedly, Hamblin takes the reader into hearts of darkness and hearts of light.

See order form on last page.

Nauvoo, Illinois, mid-1840s
by Dan Thornton

Art prints of *Nauvoo, Illinois, mid-1840s*, depicted on the dust jacket of Volume 2 of *The Porter Rockwell Chronicles*, are available from the publisher.

- **Limited Edition**
  signed and numbered, large size (28.5"w × 19"h)
  $135.00 each, plus $15.00 shipping & handling (add $1.00 shipping & handling for each additional print sent to same address)

- **Artist's Proof**
  (same size)
  $200.00 each, plus $15.00 shipping & handling (add $1.00 shipping & handling for each additional print sent to same address)

- **Greeting Card Packs**
  unsigned, 10 cards and envelopes
  $25.00 per pack, plus $3.00 shipping & handling (add $1.00 for each additional pack sent to same address)

As the 860 Limited Edition art prints sell out, the collectors' value may substantially increase.

Send check or money order to:
Stratford Books, P.O. Box 1371, Provo, Utah 84603-1371

Utah residents, add 6.25% sales tax .

Heber C. Kimball Home, Nauvoo
by Al Rounds

Full-color, 25" × 15" signed-and-numbered, limited-edition art prints of *Heber C. Kimball Home, Nauvoo*, depicted on the dust jacket of Volume 3 of *The Porter Rockwell Chronicles*, are available from the publisher at the price of $150.00 each plus shipping and handling.

Shipping and handling charges are $15.00 for the first print, plus $1.00 additional shipping and handling for each additional print ordered at the same time and shipped to the same address.

As the 700 limited-edition art prints sell out, the collectors' value may substantially increase.

Send check or money order to:
Stratford Books, P.O. Box 1371, Provo, Utah 84603-1371
Utah residents, add 6.25% sales tax .

Porter Rockwell Returns
by Clark Kelley Price

36"w × 24"h, $30.00   ISBN: 0-929753-0-6

This classic color print of the painting by renowned western artist Clark Kelley Price depicts Porter Rockwell coming home at night in a lightning storm through downtown Lehi, Utah.

In this vivid scene, Rockwell is returning from a hard day's work, with an outlaw draped over the horse he has in tow.

See order form on facing page.

ORDERING INFORMATION

☛All books ordered by mail are autographed.

The Porter Rockwell Chronicles, Vol. 1   (Reg. $27.50) **$23.88**
by Richard Lloyd Dewey. Hardcover, 490 pp. ISBN: 0-9616024-6-5

The Porter Rockwell Chronicles, Vol. 2   (Reg. $27.50) **$23.88**
by Richard Lloyd Dewey. Hardcover, 452 pp. ISBN: 0-9616024-7-3

The Porter Rockwell Chronicles, Vol. 3   (Reg. $27.95) **$23.88**
by Richard Lloyd Dewey. Hardcover, 527 pp. ISBN: 0-9616024-8-1

The Porter Rockwell Chronicles, Vol. 4   (Reg. $27.95) **$24.88**
by Richard Lloyd Dewey. Hardcover, 568 pp. ISBN: 0-9616024-9-X

Porter Rockwell: A Biography   **$24.95**
by Richard Lloyd Dewey. Hardcover, 612 pp. ISBN: 0-9616024-0-6

Jacob Hamblin: His Life in His Own Words   **$10.95**
Foreword by Richard Lloyd Dewey. Softcover, 128 pp.
ISBN: 0-9616024-5-7

Porter's Ranch at Point of the Mountain Art Print   **$75.00**
by Clark Kelley Price. 14"w × 11"h, signed and numbered
limited-edition print on canvas. ISBN: 0-929753-11-9

Porter Rockwell Returns Art Print   **$30.00**
by Clark Kelley Price. 36"w × 24"h, unsigned. ISBN: 0-929753-0-6

Utah residents, add 6.25% sales tax to price of items
(before shipping & handling).

SHIPPING & HANDLING:

For books and Clark Kelley Price art prints, add $1.00 each.

Send check or money order to:
Stratford Books
P.O. Box 1371, Provo, Utah 84603-1371

Prices subject to change.